Secrets

Enid Blyton

The Secret Island
The Secret of Spiggy Holes

MULBERRY EDITIONS

This edition published exclusively for Mulberry Editions
by HarperCollins Children's Books 1992

A division of HarperCollins Publishers Ltd,
77–85 Fulham Palace Road, Hammersmith,
London W6 8JB

All rights reserved

Printed in England by Clays Ltd, St Ives plc

Contents

The Secret Island

First published in a single volume in hardback in 1938 by Basil
Blackwell Ltd.
First published in paperback in 1964 in Armada

The Beginning Of The Adventures

Mike, Peggy and Nora were sitting in the fields, talking together. They were very unhappy. Nora was crying, and would not stop. As they sat there, they heard a low call. "Coo-ee!"

"There's Jack," said Mike. "Dry your eyes, Nora. Jack will cheer you up!"

A boy came running by the hedge and sat down by them. He had a face as brown as a berry and bright blue eyes that shone with mischief.

"Hallo!" he said. "What's up, Nora? Crying again?"

"Yes," said Nora, wiping her eyes. "Aunt Harriet slapped me six times this morning because I didn't wash the curtains well enough. Look!"

She showed him her arm, red with slaps.

"It's a shame!" said Jack.

"If only our father and mother were here they wouldn't let us live like this," said Mike. "But somehow I don't believe they'll ever come back now."

"How long is it since they've been gone?" asked Jack.

"It's over two years now," said Mike. "Dad built a fine new aeroplane, you know, and he set off to fly to Australia. Mother went with him, because she loves flying, too. They got nearly there—and then nothing more was heard of them!"

"And I know Aunt Harriet and Uncle Henry think they will never come back again," said Nora, beginning to cry once more, "or they would never treat us as they do."

"Don't cry any more, Nora," said Peggy. "Your eyes

9

will get so red and horrid. I'll do the washing instead of you next time."

Jack put his arm round Nora. He liked her best of them all. She was the smallest, although she was Mike's twin. She had a little face, and a head of black curls. Mike was exactly like her, but bigger. Peggy had yellow hair and was a year older. Nobody knew how old Jack was. He didn't know himself. He lived with his grandfather on a tumble-down farm, and worked as hard as a man, although he wasn't much bigger than Mike.

He had made friends with the children as they wandered through the fields. He knew how to catch rabbits. He knew how to catch fish in the river. He knew where the best nuts and blackberries were to be found. In fact, he knew everything, the children thought, even the names of all the birds that flew about the hedges, and the difference between a grass snake and an adder, and things like that.

Jack was always dressed in raggedy things, but the children didn't mind. His feet were bare, and his legs were scratched with brambles. He never grumbled; he never whined. He made a joke of everything, and he had been a good friend to the three miserable children.

"Ever since Aunt Harriet made up her mind that Mummy and Daddy wouldn't come back, she has been perfectly horrid," said Nora.

"And so has Uncle Henry," said Mike. "We none of us go to school now, and I have to help Uncle in the fields from morning to night. I don't mind that, but I do wish Aunt Harriet wouldn't treat the two girls so badly. They are not very old, and she makes them do all the work of the house for her."

"I do every bit of the washing now," said Nora. "I wouldn't mind the little things, but the sheets are so big and heavy."

"And I do all the cooking," said Peggy. "Yesterday I burnt a cake because the oven got too hot, and Aunt Harriet sent me to bed for the rest of the day without anything to eat at all."

"I climbed through the window and gave her some bread and cheese," said Mike. "And Uncle caught me and shook me so hard that I couldn't stand up afterwards. I had to go without my supper, and my breakfast this morning was only a small piece of bread."

"We haven't had any new clothes for months," said Peggy. "My shoes are dreadful. And I don't know what we shall do when the winter comes, because none of our coats will fit us."

"You are much worse off than I am," said Jack. "I have never had anything nice, so I don't miss it. But you have had everything you wanted, and now it is all taken away from you—you haven't even a father and mother you can go to for help."

"Do you remember *your* father and mother, Jack?" asked Mike. "Did you always live with your old grandfather?"

"I never remember anyone except him," said Jack. "He's talking of going to live with an aunt of mine. If he does I shall be left all alone, for she won't have me, too."

"Oh, Jack! Whatever will you do?" asked Nora.

"I shall be all right!" said Jack. "The thing is what are *you* three going to do? I hate to see you all unhappy. If only we could all run away together!"

"We should be found at once and brought back," said Mike gloomily. "I know that. I've read in the papers about boys and girls running away, and they are always found by the police and brought back. If I knew some place where we would never be found, I *would* run away—and take the two girls with me too. I hate to see them slappd and worked hard by Aunt Harriet."

11

"Now listen to me," said Jack suddenly, in such an earnest voice that all three children turned to him at once. "If I tell you a very great secret will you promise never to say a word about it to anyone?"

"Oh, yes, Jack, we promise," said all three.

"You can trust us, Jack," said Mike.

"I know I can," he said. "Well, listen. I know a place where nobody could find us—if we ran away!"

"Where is it, Jack?" they all cried in great excitement.

"I'll show you this evening," said Jack, getting up. "Be by the lakeside at eight o'clock, when all your work is done, and I'll meet you there. I must go now, or Grandpa will be angry with me, and perhaps lock me into my room so that I can't get out again to-day."

"Good-bye, Jack," said Nora, who was feeling much better now. "We'll see you this evening."

Jack ran off, and the three children made their way slowly back to Uncle Henry's farm. They had taken their dinner out into the fields to eat—now they had to go back to work. Nora had a great deal of ironing to do, and Peggy had to clean the kitchen. It was a big stone kitchen, and Peggy knew it would take her until supper-time—and, oh dear, how tired she would be then! Aunt Harriet would scold her all the time, she knew.

"I've got to go and clean out the barn," said Mike to the girls, "but I'll be in at supper-time, and afterwards we'll see about this great secret of Jack's."

They each began their work, but all the time they were thinking excitedly of the evening. What was Jack's secret? Where was the place he knew of? Could they really and truly run away?

They all got into trouble because they were thinking so hard of the evening that they did not do their work to Aunt Harriet's liking nor to Uncle Henry's either. Nora got a few more slaps, and Peggy was scolded so hard that she cried bitterly into her overall. She was made to scrub the kitchen floor all over again, and this made her late for supper.

Mike was shouted at by Uncle Henry for spilling some corn in the barn. The little boy said nothing, but he made up his mind that if it was possible to run away in safety he would do so, and take the girls with him, too.

"Nora and Peggy ought to be going to school and wearing nice clothes that fit them, and having friends to tea," said Mike to himself. "This is no life for them. They are just very hard-worked servants for Aunt Harriet, and she pays them nothing."

The children ate their supper of bread and cheese in silence. They were afraid of speaking in case their aunt and uncle shouted at them. When they had finished Mike spoke to his aunt.

"Please may we go for a walk in the fields before we go to bed?" he asked.

"No, you can't," said Aunt Harriet in her sharp voice. "You'll just go to bed, all of you. There's a lot of work to do tomorrow, and I want you up early."

The children looked at one another in dismay. But they had to do as they were told. They went upstairs to the big bedroom they all shared. Mike had a small bed in the corner behind a screen, and the two girls had a bigger bed between them.

"I believe Aunt Harriet and Uncle Henry are going out tonight, and that's why they want us to go to bed early," said Mike. "Well, if they do go out, we'll slip down and meet Jack by the river."

"We won't get undressed then," said Nora. 'We'll just slip under the sheets, dressed—and then it won't take us long to run down to the lake."

The three children listened hard. They heard the front door close. Mike popped out of bed and ran to the front

13

room. From there he could see the path to the gate. He saw his uncle and aunt walk down it, dressed to go out.

He ran back to the others. "We'll wait for five minutes," he said, "then we'll go."

They waited quietly. Then they all slipped downstairs and out of the back door. They ran down to the lake as fast as they could. Jack was there waiting for them.

"Hallo, Jack," said Mike. "Here we are at last. They sent us to bed, but when they went out we slipped down here to meet you."

"What's your great secret, Jack?" asked Nora; "we are longing to know."

"Well, listen," said Jack. "You know what a big lake this is, don't you, perfectly wild all round, except at the two ends where there are a few farmhouses and cottages. Now I know a little island, a good way up the south side of the lake, that I'm sure nobody knows at all. I don't think anyone but me has ever been there. It's a fine island, and would make the best hiding-place in the world!"

The three children listened, their eyes wide with astonishment. An island on the big lake! Oh, if only they could really go there and hide—and live by themselves— with no unkind aunt and uncle to slap them and scold them and make them work hard all day long!

"Are you too tired to walk down the lakeside to a place where you can see the island?" asked Jack. "I only found it quite by chance one day. The woods come right down to the lakeside opposite the island, and they are so thick that I don't think anyone has ever been through them, and so no one can have seen my island!"

"Jack! Jack! Take us to see your secret island!" begged Nora. "Oh, we must go. We're all tired—but we must, *must* see the secret island."

"Come on, then," said Jack, pleased to see how excited the others were. "Follow me. It's a good way."

The bare-footed boy took the three children across the fields to a wood. He threaded his way through the trees as if he were a rabbit. The wood thinned out and changed to a common, which, in turn, gave way to another wood, but this time the trees were so thick that it seemed as if there was no way through them at all.

But Jack kept on. He knew the way. He led the children without stopping, and at last they caught sight of the gleam of water. They had come back to the lakeside again. The evening was dim. The sun had sunk long since, and the children could hardly see.

Jack pushed his way through the trees that grew down to the waterside. He stood there and pointed silently to something. The children crowded round him.

"My secret island!" said Jack.

And so it was. The little island seemed to float on the dark lake-waters. Trees grew on it, and a little hill rose in the middle of it. It was a mysterious island, lonely and beautiful. All the children stood and gazed at it, loving it and longing to go to it. It looked so secret—almost magic.

"Well," said Jack at last. "What do you think? Shall we run away, and live on the secret island?"

"Yes!" whispered all the children. "Let's!"

An Exciting Day

The three children thought of nothing else but Jack's secret island all the next day. Could they possibly run away and hide there? Could they live there? How could they get food? What would happen if people came to look for them? Would they be found? How busy their minds were, thinking, thinking, planning, planning! Oh, the excitement of that secret island! It seemed so mysterious and lovely. If only, only they were all there, safe from slappings and scoldings!

The first time the children had a little time together to talk, they spoke about the island.

"Mike, we *must* go!" said Nora.

"Mike, let's tell Jack we'll go," said Peggy.

Mike scratched his curly black head. He felt old and worried. He wanted to go very badly—but would the three of them really be able to stand a wild life like that? No proper beds to sleep in—perhaps no proper food to eat—and suppose one of them was ill? Well, they would have to chance all that. They could always come back if things went too wrong.

"We'll go," said Mike. "We'll plan it all with Jack. He knows better than we do."

So that night, when they met Jack, the four of them laid their plans. Their faces were red with excitement, their eyes were shining. An adventure! A real proper adventure, almost like Robinson Crusoe—for they were going to live all by themselves on a lonely island.

"We must be careful in our plans," said Jack. "We

16

mustn't forget a single thing, for we ought not to go back to get anything, you know, or we might be caught."

"Could we go over to the island and just see what it's like before we go to live there?" asked Nora. "I would so love to see it."

"Yes," said Jack. "We'll go on Sunday."

"How can we go?" asked Mike. "Do we have to swim?"

"No," said Jack. "I have an old boat. It was one that had been left to fall to pieces, and I found it and patched it up. It still gets water in, but we can bale that out. I'll take you over in that."

The children could hardly wait for Sunday to come. They had to do a certain amount of work on Sundays, but usually they were allowed to take their dinner out and have a picnic afterwards.

It was June. The days were long and sunny. The farm garden was full of peas, broad beans, gooseberries, and ripening cherries. The children stole into it and picked as many pea-pods as they could find, and pulled up two big lettuces. Aunt Harriet gave them so little to eat that they always had to take something else as well. Mike said it wasn't stealing, because if Aunt Harriet had given them the food they earned by the hard work they did, they would have twice as much. They were only taking what they had earned. They had a loaf of bread between them, some butter, and some slices of ham, as well as the peas and lettuces. Mike pulled up some carrots, too. He said they would taste most delicious with the ham.

They hurried off to meet Jack. He was by the lakeside, carrying a bag on his back. He had his dinner in it. He showed them some fine red cherries, and a round cake.

"Mrs. Lane gave me those for hoeing her garden yesterday," he said. "We'll have a fine dinner between us."

"Where's the boat, Jack?" said Nora.

"You wait and see!" said Jack. "I don't leave my secret things out for everyone to see! No one else but you three knows about my boat!"

He set off in the hot June sunshine, and the three children followed him. He kept close to the lakeside and although the children kept a sharp look-out for the boat they did not see it until Jack stopped and showed it to them.

"See that great alder bush hanging over the lake just there?" he said. "Well, my boat's underneath it! It's well hidden, isn't it?"

Mike's eyes shone. He loved boats. He did hope Jack would let him help to row. The children pulled out the boat from under the thick tree. It was quite a big one, but very, very old. It had a good deal of water in, and Jack set everyone to work baling it out. There was an old pair of oars in the boat, and Jack put them in place.

"Now get in," he said. "I've a good way to row. Would you like to take an oar, Mike?"

Of course Mike would! The two boys rowed over the water. The sun shone down hotly, but there was a little breeze that blew every now and again. Soon the children saw the secret island in the distance. They knew it because of the little hill it had in the middle.

The secret island had looked mysterious enough on the night they had seen it before—but now, swimming in the hot June haze, it seemed more enchanting than ever. As they drew near to it, and saw the willow trees that bent over the water-edge and heard the sharp call of moorhens that scuttled off, the children gazed in delight. Nothing but trees and birds and little wild animals. Oh, what a secret island, all for their very own, to live on and play on.

"Here's the landing-place," said Jack, and he guided the boat to a sloping sandy beach. He pulled it up on the sand, and the children jumped out and looked round. The

18

They rowed across to the secret island

landing-place was a natural little cove—a lovely spot for a picnic—but picnickers never came here! Only a lonely otter lay on the sand now and again, and moorhens scuttled across it. No fire had ever been made on this little beach to boil a kettle. No bits of old orange peel lay about, or rusty tins. It was quite unspoilt.

"Let's leave our things here and explore a bit," said Mike, who was simply longing to see what the island was like. It seemed very big now they were on it.

"All right," said Jack, and he put his bag down.

"Come on," said Mike to the girls. "This is the beginning of a big adventure."

They left the little cove and went up through the thick trees. There were willows, alders, hazels, and elderberries at first, and then as they went up the hill that lay behind the cove there were silver birches and oaks. The hill was quite steep, and from the top the children could see a very long way—up the lake and down the lake.

"I say! If we come here to live, this hill will make an awfully good place to watch for enemies from!" said Mike excitedly. "We can see everything from here, all around!"

"Yes," said Jack. "Nobody would be able to take us by surprise."

"We *must* come here, we must, we must!" said Nora. "Oh, look at those rabbits, Peggy—they are as tame as can be, and that chaffinch nearly came on to my hand! Why are they so tame, Mike?"

"I suppose because they are not used to people," said Mike. "What's the other side of the hill, Jack? Shall we go down it?"

"There are caves on the other side of the hill," said Jack. "I haven't explored those. They would make good hiding-places if anyone ever came to look for us here."

They went down the hill on the other side. Gorse grew there and heather and bracken. Jack pointed out a big cave in the hillside. It looked dark and gloomy in the hot sunshine.

"We haven't time to go there now," said Jack. "But a cave would be an awfully good place to store anything in, wouldn't it? It would keep things nice and dry."

A little way down the hill the children heard a bubbling noise.

"What's that?" asked Peggy, stopping.

"Look! It's a little spring!" cried Mike. "Oh, Jack! This shall be our water-supply! It's as cold as can be, and as clear as crystal!"

"It tastes fine, too," said Jack. "I had a drink last time I was here. Lower down, another spring joins this one, and there is a tiny brook."

At the bottom of the hill was a thick wood. In clear patches great bushes of brambles grew. Jack pointed them out.

"There will be thousands of blackberries in the autumn," he said. "And as for hazel nuts, you should see them! And in another place I know here, on a warm slope, you can find wild raspberries by the score!"

"Oh, do show us!" begged Mike. But Jack said there was not time. Besides, the raspberries wouldn't be ripe yet.

"The island is too big to explore all over to-day," said Jack. "You've seen most of it—this big hill with its caves, the springs, the thick wood, and beyond the wood is a grassy field and then the water again. Oh, it is a glorious place!"

"Jack, where shall we live on this island?" said Peggy, who always liked to have everything well settled in her mind.

"We shall build a house of wood," said Jack. "I know how to. That will do finely for the summer, and for the winter we will have to find a cave, I think."

21

The children gazed at one another in glee. A house of wood, built by themselves—and a cave! How lucky they were to have a friend like Jack, who had a boat and a secret island!

They went back to the little landing-place, hungry and happy. They sat down and ate their bread and ham, carrots and peas, cherries and lettuces, and cake. It was the loveliest meal they had ever had in their lives, they thought. A little moorhen walked up to them and seemed surprised to see so many people in its home. But it did not run away. It ran round, pecking at the lettuce leaves, saying, "Fulluck, fulluck!" in its loud voice.

"If I could live here on this secret island always and always and always, and never grow up at all, I would be quite happy," said Nora.

"Well, we'll have a shot at living here for a good while at least!" said Jack. "Now, when shall we come?"

"And what shall we bring?" said Mike.

"Well, we don't really need a great deal at present," said Jack. "We can make soft beds of heather and bracken to lie on at night. What would be useful would be things like enamel mugs and plates and knives. I'll bring an axe and a very sharp woodman's knife. We'll need those when we build our house. Oh—and matches would be *most* useful for lighting fires. We shall have to cook our meals. I'll bring my fishing-line along, too."

The more the children talked about their plan, the more excited they got. At last they had arranged what to bring. They were gradually to hide things in a hollow tree by the lakeside, and then, when the time came, they could carry them to the boat and row off to the secret island, ready to set up house there.

"A frying-pan would be useful," said Nora.

"And a saucepan or two," said Peggy, "and a kettle. Oh! What fun it will be. I don't care how much we are slapped or scolded now—I shall think of this exciting plan all day long!"

"We had better fix a day for starting off," said Jack. "What about a week from now? Sunday would be a good day for running away, because no one will come to look for us until night-time, when we don't go home!"

"Yes! A week to-day!" cried everyone. "Oooh! How happy we shall be!"

"Now we must go home," said Jack, setting off to the boat. "You can row if you like, Mike, and I'll bale out the water as we go. Get in, you girls."

"Ay, ay, Captain!" they sang out, full of joy to think they had such a fine leader as Jack! Off they all went, floating across the water in the evening light. What would they be doing next Sunday?

The Escape

All that week the three children carried out their plans. Aunt Harriet and Uncle Henry could not understand what was different about the children—they did not seem to mind being scolded at all. Even Nora took a slapping without tears. She was so happy when she thought of the secret island that she couldn't shed a tear!

The children took all the clothes they possessed down to the hollow tree by the lakeside. Mike took four enamel cups, some enamel plates, and two enamel dishes. Nora smuggled down an old kettle that Aunt Harriet had put away in a cupboard. She did not dare to take one of those on the stove. Peggy took a frying-pan and a saucepan to the hollow tree, and had to put up with a dreadful scolding when her aunt could not find them.

Jack took a saucepan too, and an axe and a fine sharp knife. He also took some small knives and forks and spoons, for the other children did not dare to take these. There were only just enough put out for them and their aunt and uncle to use. So they were glad when Jack found some and brought them along.

"Can you get some empty tins to store things in?" asked Jack. "I am trying to get sugar and things like that, because we must have those, you know. Grandad gave me some money the other day, and I'm buying a few things to store."

"Yes, I'll get some empty tins," said Mike. "Uncle has plenty in the shed. I can wash them out and dry them. And could you get matches, Jack? Aunt only leaves one box out, and that won't go far."

"Well, I've got a small magnifying glass," said Jack, and he showed it to the others. "Look, if I focus the rays of the sun on to that bit of paper over there, see what happens. It burns it, and, hey presto, there's a fire ready-made!"

"Oh, good!" said Mike. "We'll use that on a sunny day, Jack, and save our matches!"

"I'm bringing my work-basket in case we need to sew anything," said Peggy.

"And I've got a box of mixed nails and an old hammer," said Mike. "I found them in the shed."

"We're getting on!" said Jack, grinning, "I say—what a time we're going to have!"

"I wish Sunday would come!" sighed Nora.

"I shall bring our snap cards and our game of ludo and our dominoes," said Peggy. "We shall want to play games sometimes. And what about some books?"

"Good for you!" cried Mike. "Yes—books and papers we'll have, too—we shall love to read quietly sometimes."

The old hollow tree by the lakeside was soon full of the queerest collection of things. Not a day went by without something being added to it. One day it was a plank of wood. Another day it was half a sack of potatoes. Another day it was an old and ragged rug. Really, it was a marvel that the tree held everything!

At last Sunday came. The children were up long before their uncle and aunt. They crept into the kitchen garden and picked a basket of peas, pulled up six lettuces, added as many ripe broad beans as they could find, a bunch of young carrots, some radishes, and, putting their hands into the nest-boxes of the hens, they found six new-laid eggs!

Nora crept indoors and went to the larder. What could she take that Aunt Harriet would not notice that morning? Some tea? Yes! A tin of cocoa from the top shelf. A packet of currants and a tin of rice from the store shelf, too. A big loaf, a few cakes from the cake-tin! The little girl stuffed them all into her basket and raced out to join the others. Long before Aunt Harriet was up all these things were safely in the hollow tree.

Peggy didn't quite like taking anything from the larder, but Mike said that as Aunt and Uncle wouldn't have to keep them after that day, they could quite well spare a few odds and ends for them.

"Anyway, if they paid us properly for our work, we would have enough to buy all these things and more," he said, as he stuffed them into the tree.

They went back to the farm for the last time, to breakfast. Peggy cooked the breakfast, and hoped Aunt would not notice that her long iron cooking spoon was gone. She also hoped that Aunt would not want to get another candle from the packet in the larder, for Peggy knew Mike had taken the rest of them, and had taken an old lantern of Uncle's, too!

The children ate their breakfast in silence.

Aunt Harriet looked at them. "I suppose you think you are going off for a picnic today!" she said. "Well, you are not! You can stay and weed the kitchen garden, Peggy and Nora. And I've no doubt Uncle Henry can set Mike something to do. *Someone* has been taking cakes out of my tin, and so you'll all stay in today!"

The hearts of the three children sank. Today of all days! As soon as the girls were washing up alone in the scullery, Mike looked in at the window.

"You girls slip off down to the lake as soon as you get a chance," he said. "Wait there for me. I won't be long!"

Peggy and Nora felt happier. They were to escape after all, then! They washed up a few more things and then saw their aunt going upstairs.

"She has gone to look out Uncle's Sunday suit and shirt," whispered Nora. "Quick! Now's our chance. We can slip out of the back door."

Peggy ran to the cupboard under the dresser and took out a long bar of soap. "We forgot all about soap!" she said. "We shall want some! I just remembered in time!"

Nora looked round for something to take, too. She saw a great slab of margarine on the dresser, and she caught it up.

"This will help us in our frying!" she said. "Come on, Peggy—we've no time to lose."

They raced out of the back door, down the path, and out into the fields. In five minutes' time they were by the hollow tree, well out of sight. Jack was not yet there. They did not know how long Mike would be. He would not find it so easy to get away!

But Mike had laid his plans. He waited for the moment when his aunt discovered that the girls had gone, and then walked into the kitchen.

"What's the matter, Aunt Harriet?" he asked, pretending to be very much surprised at her angry face and voice.

"Where have those two girls gone?" cried his aunt.

"I expect they have only gone to get in the clothes or something," said Mike. "Shall I go and find them for you?"

"Yes, and tell them they'll get well slapped for running off like this without finishing their work," said his aunt in a rage.

Mike ran off, calling to his uncle that he was on an errand for his aunt. So Uncle Henry said nothing, but let him go. Mike tore across the fields to the lakeside and met the two girls there. They hugged one another in joy.

"Now, where's Jack?" said Mike. "He said he would meet us as soon as he could."

"There he is!" said Nora; and sure enough, there was Jack coming across the field, waving to them. He carried a heavy bag into which he had crammed all sorts of things at the very last moment—rope, an old mackintosh, two books, some newspapers, and other things. His face was shining with excitement.

"Good! You're here!" he said.

"Yes, but we nearly couldn't come," said Nora, and she told Jack what had happened.

"I say! I hope this won't mean that your uncle and aunt will start to look for you too soon," said Jack.

"Oh, no!" said Mike. "It only means that they will make up their minds to whip us well when we get back this evening, but we shan't go back! They'll think we've gone off on our usual Sunday picnic."

"Now we've got a lot to do," said Jack seriously. "This is all fun and excitement to us—but it's work, too—and we've got to get on with it. First, all these things must be carried from the hollow tree to the boat. Mike, you get out some of them and give them to the girls. Then we'll take the heavier things. I expect we shall have to come back to the tree three or four times before it's emptied."

The four of them set off happily, carrying as much as they could. The sun was hot, and they puffed and panted, but who cared? They were off to the secret island at last!

It was a good walk to the boat, and they had to make four journeys altogether, carrying things carefully. At last there was nothing left in the hollow tree. They need not come back again.

"I'm jolly glad," said Mike. "Every time I get back to that hollow tree I expect to find Aunt or Uncle hidden inside it, ready to pop out at us!"

"Don't say such horrid things," said Nora. "We're leaving Aunt and Uncle behind for ever!"

They were at the boat, and were stowing things there as well as they could. It was a good thing the boat was fairly big or it would never have taken everything. The children had had to bale out a good deal of water before they could

28

put anything in the bottom. It leaked badly, but as long as someone could bale out with a tin it was all right.

"Now then," said Jack, looking round at the shore to see that nothing was left behind, "are we ready?"

"Ay, ay, Captain!" roared the other three. "Push off!"

The boat was pushed off. Mike and Jack took an oar each, for the boat was heavy and needed two people to pull it. It floated easily out on to the deeper water.

"We're off at last!" said Nora, in a little happy voice that sounded almost as if she were going to cry.

Nobody said anything more. The boat floated on and on, as Mike and Jack rowed strongly. Peggy baled out the water that came in through the leaks. She wondered what it would be like not to sleep in a proper bed. She wondered what it would be like to wake up under the blue sky—to have no one to make her do this, that and the other. How happy she felt!

It was a long way to the island. The sun rose higher and higher. The adventurers felt hotter and hotter. At last Nora pointed excitedly in front.

"The secret island!" she cried. "The secret island."

Mike and Jack stopped rowing for a moment and the boat floated on slowly by itself whilst the four gazed at the lonely little island, hidden so well on the heart of the lake. Their own island! It had no name. It was just the Secret Island!

Mike and Jack rowed on again. They came to the little sandy cove beneath the willow trees. Jack jumped out and pulled the boat in. The others jumped out too and gazed round.

"We're really here, we're really here, we're really here!" squealed Nora, jumping up and down and round and round in delight. "We've escaped. We've come to live on this dear little hidden island."

"Come on, Nora, give a hand," ordered Jack. "We've a lot to do before night, you know!"

Nora ran to help. The boat had to be unloaded, and that

29

was quite a job. All the things were put on the beach under the willow trees for the time being. By the time that was finished the children were hotter than ever and very hungry and thirsty.

"Oh, for a drink!" groaned Mike.

"Peggy, do you remember the way to the spring?" asked Jack. "You do? Well, just go and fill this kettle with water, will you? We'll all have a drink and something to eat!"

Peggy ran off up the hill and down the other side to the spring. She filled the kettle and went back. The others had put out enamel mugs ready to drink from. Mike was busy looking out something to eat, too. He had put out a loaf of bread, some young carrots, which they all loved to nibble, a piece of cheese each, and a cake.

What a meal that was! How they laughed and giggled and chattered! Then they lay back in the sun and shut their eyes. They were tired with all their hard work. One by one they fell asleep.

Jack awoke first. He sat up. "Hey!" he said. "This won't do! We've got to get our beds for the night and arrange a good sleeping-place! We've dozens of things to do! Come on, everyone, to work, to work!"

But who minded work when it was in such a pleasant place? Peggy and Nora washed up the mugs and dishes in the lake water and set them in the sun to dry. The boys put all the stores in a good place and covered them with the old mackintosh in case it should rain. To-morrow they would start to build their house.

"Now to get a sleeping-place and bedding," said Jack. "Won't it be fun to sleep for the first time on the Secret Island!"

The First Night On The Island

"Where do you think would be the best place to sleep?" said Peggy, looking round the little cove.

"Well," said Jack, "I think it would be best to sleep under some thick trees somewhere, then, if it rains tonight, we shall not get too wet. But I don't think it will rain; the weather is quite settled."

"There are two nice, big, thick oak trees just beyond the cove," said Mike, pointing. "Shall we find a place there?"

"Yes," said Jack. "Find a bramble bush or gorse bush near them to keep any wind off. Let's go and see what we think."

They all went to the two big oak trees. Their branches swung almost down to the ground in places. Below grew clumps of soft heather, springy as a mattress. To the north was a great growth of gorse, thick and prickly.

"This looks a fine place to sleep," said Jack. "Look. Do you see this little place here, almost surrounded by gorse, and carpeted with heather? The girls could sleep here, and we could sleep just outside their cosy spot, to protect them. The oak trees would shelter us nicely overhead."

"Oh, I do think this is fine; I do, I do!" cried Nora, thinking that their green, heathery bedroom was the nicest in the world. She lay down on the heather. "It is as soft as can be!" she said; "and oh! there is something making a most delicious smell. What is it?"

"It is a patch of wild thyme," said Jack. "Look, there

is a bit in the middle of the heather. You will smell it when you go to sleep, Nora!"

"All the same, Jack, the heather won't feel quite so soft when we have lain on it a few hours," said Mike. "We'd better get some armfuls of bracken too, hadn't we?"

"Yes," said Jack. "Come on up the hill. There is plenty of bracken there, and heaps of heather too. We will pick the bracken there, and put it in the sun to dry. The heather doesn't need drying. Pick plenty, for the softer we lie the better we'll sleep! Heyho for a starry night and a heathery bed!"

The four children gathered armfuls of bracken and put it out in the sun to wither and dry. The heather they carried back to their green bedroom under the oak tree. They spread it thickly there. It looked most deliciously soft! The thick gorse bushes kept off the breeze, and the oaks above waved their branches and whispered. What fun it all was!

"Well, there are our bedrooms ready," said Jack. "Now, we'd better find a place to put our stores in. We won't be too far from the water, because it's so useful for washing ourselves and our dishes in."

The children were hungry again. They got out the rest of the cakes, and finished up the bread, eating some peas with it, which they shelled as they ate.

"Are we going to have any supper?" asked Mike.

"We might have a cup of cocoa each and a piece of my cake," said Jack. "We must be careful not to eat everything at once that we've brought, or we'll go short! I'll do some fishing to-morrow."

"Shall we begin to build the house to-morrow?" asked Mike, who was longing to see how Jack meant to make their house.

"Yes," said Jack. "Now you two girls wash up the

mugs again, and Mike and I will find a good place for the stores."

The girls went to the water and washed the things. The boys wandered up the beach—and, at the back of the sandy cove, they found just the very place they wanted!

There was a sandy bank there, with a few old willows growing on top of it, their branches drooping down. Rain had worn away the sandy soil from their roots, and underneath there was a sort of shallow cave, with roots running across it here and there.

"Look at that!" said Jack in delight. "Just the place we want for our stores! Nora, Peggy, come and look here!"

The girls came running. "Oh," said Peggy, pleased, "we can use those big roots as shelves, and stand our tins and cups and dishes on them! Oh, it's a proper little larder!"

"Well, if you girls get the stores from the cove and arrange them neatly here," said Jack. "Mike and I will go and fill the kettle from the spring, and we'll see if there isn't a nearer spring, because it's a long way up the hill and down the other side."

"Can't we come with you?" asked Peggy.

"No, you arrange everything," said Jack. "It had better all be done as quickly as possible, because you never know when it's going to turn wet. We don't want our stores spoilt."

Leaving Peggy and Nora to arrange the tins, baskets, and odds and ends neatly in the root-larder, the two boys went up the hill behind the cove. They separated to look for a spring, and Mike found one! It was a very tiny one, gushing out from under a small rock, and it ran down the hill like a little waterfall, getting lost in the heather and grass here and there. Its way could be seen by the rushes that sprang up beside its course.

"I expect it runs down into the lake," said Mike. "It's a very small spring, but we can use it to fill our kettle, and it won't take us quite so long as going to the other spring. If we have to live in the caves during the winter, the other spring will be more useful then, for it will be quite near the cave."

They filled the kettle. It was lovely up there on the hillside in the June sun. Bees hummed and butterflies flew all round. Birds sang, and two or three moorhens cried "Fulluck, fulluck!" from the water below.

"Let's go to the top of the hill and see if we can spy anyone coming up or down the lake," said Jack. So they went right up to the top, but not a sign of anyone could they see. The waters of the lake were calm and clear and blue. Not a boat was on it. The children might have been quite alone in the world.

They went down to the girls with the full kettle. Nora and Peggy proudly showed the boys how they had arranged the stores. They had used the big roots for shelves, and the bottom of the little cave they had used for odds and ends, such as Jack's axe and knife, the hammer and nails, and so on.

"It's a nice dry place," said Peggy. "It's just right for a larder, and it's so nice and near the cove. Jack, where are we going to build our house?"

Jack took the girls and Mike to the west end of the cove, where there was a thicket of willows. He forced his way through them and showed the others a fine clear place right in the very middle of the trees.

"Here's the very place," he said. "No one would ever guess there was a house just here, if we built one! The willows grow so thickly that I don't suppose anyone but ourselves would ever know they could be got through."

They talked about their house until they were tired out. They made their way back to the little beach and Jack said they would each have a cup of cocoa, a piece of cake, and go to bed!

He and Mike soon made a fire. There were plenty of dry twigs about, and bigger bits of wood. It did look cheerful to see the flames dancing. Jack could not use his little magnifying glass to set light to the paper or twigs because the sun was not bright enough then. It was sinking down in the west. He used a match. He set the kettle on the fire to boil.

"It would be better tomorrow to swing the kettle over the flames on a tripod of sticks," he said. "It will boil more quickly then."

But nobody minded how slowly the kettle boiled. They lay on their backs in the sand, looking up at the evening sky, listening to the crackle of the wood, and smelling a mixture of wood-smoke and honeysuckle. At last the kettle sent out a spurt of steam, and began to hiss. It was boiling.

Nora made the cocoa, and handed it round in mugs. "There's no milk," she said. "But there is some sugar."

They munched their cake and drank their cocoa. Though it had no milk in it, it was the nicest they had ever tasted.

"I do like seeing the fire," said Nora. "Oh, Jack, why are you stamping it out?"

"Well," said Jack, "people may be looking for us to-night, you know, and a spire of smoke from this island would give our hiding-place away nicely! Come on, now, everyone to bed! We've hard work to do tomorrow!"

Peggy hurriedly rinsed out the mugs. Then all of them went to their green, heathery bedroom. The sun was gone. Twilight was stealing over the secret island.

"Our first night here!" said Mike, standing up and looking down on the quiet waters of the lake. "We are all alone, the four of us, without a roof over our heads even, but I'm so happy!"

"So am I!" said everyone. The girls went to their hidden

green room in the gorse and lay down in their clothes. It seemed silly to undress when they were sleeping out of doors. Mike threw them the old ragged rug.

"Throw that over yourselves," he said. "It may be cold tonight, sleeping out for the first time. You won't be frightened, will you?"

"No," said Peggy. "You two boys will be near, and, anyway, what is there to be frightened of?"

They lay down on the soft heather, and pulled the old rug over them. The springy heather was softer than the old hard bed the two girls had been used to at home. The little girls put their arms round one another and shut their eyes. They were fast asleep almost at once.

But the boys did not sleep so quickly. They lay on their heathery beds and listened to all the sounds of the night. They heard the little grunt of a hedgehog going by. They saw the flicker of bats overhead. They smelt the drifting scent of honeysuckle, and the delicious smell of wild thyme crushed under their bodies. A reed-warbler sang a beautiful little song in the reeds below, and then another answered.

"Is that a blackbird?" asked Mike.

"No, a reed-warbler," said Jack. "They sing as beautifully as any bird that sings in the daytime! Listen, do you hear that owl?"

"Oooo-ooo-ooo-oooo!" came a long, quivering sound; "ooo-ooo-ooo-ooo!"

"He's hunting for rats and voles," said Jack. "I say, look at the stars, Mike?"

"Don't they seem far away?" said Mike, looking up into the purple night sky, which was set with thousands of bright stars. "I say, Jack, it's awfully nice of you to come away with us like this and share your secret island."

"It isn't nice of me at all," said Jack. "I wanted to. I'm doing just exactly what I most want to do. I only hope we shan't be found and taken back, but I'll take jolly good care no one finds us! I'm laying my plans already!"

But Mike was not listening. His eyes shut, he forgot the owls and the stars; he fell asleep and dreamt of building a house with Jack, a lovely house.

Jack fell asleep, too. And soon the rabbits that lived under their gorse-bush came slyly out and peeped at the sleeping children in surprise. Who were they?

But, as the children did not move, the rabbits grew bold and went out to play just as usual. Even when one ran over Mike by mistake, the little boy did not know it. He was *much* too fast asleep!

The Building Of The House

What fun it was to wake up that first morning on the island! Jack awoke first. He heard a thrush singing so loudly on a tree near by that he woke up with a jump.

"Mind how you do it," said the thrush, "mind how you do it!"

Jack grinned. "I'll mind how I do it all right!" he said to the singing thrush. "Hi, Mike! Wake up! The sun is quite high!"

Mike woke and sat up. At first he didn't remember where he was. Then a broad smile came over his face. Of course—they were all on the secret island! How perfectly glorious!

"Peggy, Nora! Get up!" he cried. The girls awoke and sat up in a hurry. Wherever were they? What was this green bedroom—oh, of course, it was their heathery bedroom on the secret island!

Soon all four children were up and about. Jack made them take off their things and have a dip in the lake. It was simply lovely, but the water felt cold at first. When they had dried themselves on an old sack—for they had no towels—the children felt terribly hungry. But Jack had been busy. He had set his fishing-line, and, even as they bathed, he had seen the float jerk up and down. It was not long before Jack proudly laid four fine trout on the sand of the cove, and set about to make a fire to cook them.

Mike went to fill the kettle to make some tea. Peggy got some big potatoes out of the sack and put them almost in the fire to cook in their skins. Jack found the frying-pan in their storeroom and put a piece of margarine in to fry the fish, which he knew exactly how to clean.

"I don't know what we should do without you," said Mike, as he watched Jack. "Goodness! How I shall enjoy my breakfast!"

They all did. The tea did not taste very nice without milk. "It's a pity we can't get milk," said Jack. "We shall miss that, I'm afraid. Now let's all wash up, and put everything away—and then we'll start on our house!"

In great excitement everything was washed up and put away. Then Jack led the way through the thick willow trees, and they came to the little clear place in the centre of them.

"Now, this is how I mean to build the house," he said. "Do you see these little willow trees here—one there —one there—two there—and two there. Well, I think you will find that if we climb up and bend down the top branches, they will meet each other nicely in the centre, and we can weave them into one another. That will make the beginning of a roof. With my axe I shall chop down some other young willow trees, and use the trunk and thicker branches for walls. We can drive the trunks and branches into the ground between the six willow trees we are using, and fill up any cracks with smaller branches woven across. Then if we stuff every corner and crevice with bracken and heather, we shall have a fine big house, with a splendid roof, wind-proof and rain-proof. What do you think of that?"

The other children listened in the greatest excitement. It sounded too good to be true. Could it be as easy as all that?

"Jack, can we really do it?" said Mike. "It sounds all right—and those willow trees are just the right distance from one another to make a good big house—and their top branches will certainly overlap well."

"Oh, let's begin, let's begin!" cried Nora, impatient as usual, dancing up and down.

"I'll climb up this first willow tree and swing the branches over with my weight," said Jack. "All you others must catch hold of them and hold them till I slip down. Then I'll climb another tree and bend those branches over too. We'll tie them together, and then I'll climb up the other trees. Once we've got all the top branches bending down touching one another, and overlapping nicely, we can cut long willow-sticks and lace our roof together. I'll show you how to."

Jack swung himself up into one of the little willow trees. It was only a young one, with a small trunk—but it had a head of long, fine branches, easy to bend. Jack swung them down, and the girls and Mike caught them easily. They held on to them whilst Jack slid down the tree and climbed another. He did the same thing there, bending down the supple branches until they reached and rested on top of those bent down from the other tree.

"Tie them together, Mike!" shouted Jack. "Peggy, go and find the rope I brought."

Peggy darted off. She soon came back with the rope. Mike twisted it round the branches of the two trees, and tied them firmly together.

"It's beginning to look like a roof already!" shouted Nora, in excitement. "Oh, I want to sit underneath it!"

She sat down under the roof of willow boughs, but Jack called to her.

"Get up, Nora! You've got to help! I'm up the third tree now—look, here come the top branches bending over with my weight—catch them and hold them!"

Nora and Peggy caught them and held on tightly. The branches reached the others and overlapped them. Mike was soon busy tying them down, too.

The whole morning was spent in this way. By

40

dinnertime all the six trees had been carefully bent over. Jack showed Mike and the girls how to weave the branches together, so that they held one another and made a fine close roof. "You see, if we use the trees like this, their leaves will still grow and will make a fine thick roof," said Jack. "Now, although our house has no walls as yet, we at least have a fine roof to shelter under if it rains!"

"I want something to eat," said Nora. "I'm so hungry that I feel I could eat snails!"

"Well, get out four eggs, and we'll have some with potatoes," said Jack. "We'll boil the eggs in our saucepan. There's plenty of potatoes, too. After the eggs are boiled we'll boil some potatoes and mash them up. That will be nice for a change. We'll nibble a few carrots, too, and have some of those cherries."

"We do have funny meals," said Peggy, going to get the saucepan and the eggs, "but I do like them! Come on, Nora, help me get the potatoes and peel them whilst the eggs are boiling. And Mike, get some water, will you? We haven't enough."

Soon the fire was burning merrily and the eggs were boiling in the saucepan. The girls peeled the potatoes, and Jack washed the carrots. He went to get some water to drink, too, for everyone was very thirsty.

"You'd better catch some more fish for tonight, Jack," said Peggy. "I hope our stores are going to last out a bit! We do seem to eat a lot!"

"I've been thinking about that," said Jack, watching the potatoes boiling. "I think I'll have to row to land occasionally and get more food. I can get it from Granddad's farm. There are plenty of potatoes there, and I can always get the eggs from the hen-house. Some of the hens are mine—and there's a cow that's really mine too, for Granddad gave her to me when she was a calf!"

41

"I wish we had hens and a cow here!" said Peggy. "We should have lots of milk then and plenty of eggs!"

"How would we get hens and a cow here?" said Mike, laughing. "I think Jack's idea of rowing across to land sometimes is a good one. He can go at night. He knows the way, and could get back before day breaks."

"It's dangerous, though," said Peggy. "Suppose he were caught? We couldn't do without Jack!"

The children ate their dinner hungrily. They thought that eggs and potatoes had never tasted so nice before. The sun shone down hotly. It was simply perfect weather. Nora lay down when she had finished her meal and closed her eyes. She felt lazy and sleepy.

Jack poked her with his foot. "You're not to go to sleep, Nora," he said. "We must get on with our house, now we've started. We've got to clear up as usual, and then we must get back to the house. We'll start on the walls this afternoon."

"But I'm sleepy," said Nora. She was rather a lazy little girl, and she thought it would be lovely to have a nap whilst the others got on with the work. But Jack was not the one to let anyone slack. He jerked Nora to her feet and gave her a push.

"Go on, lazy-bones," he said. "I'm captain here. Do as you're told."

"I didn't know you were captain," said Nora, rather sulkily.

"Well, you know now," said Jack. "What do the others say about it?"

"Yes, you're captain, Jack," said Mike and Peggy together. "Ay, ay, sir!"

Nobody said any more. They washed up in the lake and cleared the things away neatly. They put some more wood on the fire to keep it burning, because Jack said it was silly to keep on lighting it. Then they all ran off to the willow thicket.

Jack made himself busy. He chopped down some willow

42

saplings—young willow trees—with his axe, and cut off the longer branches.

"We'll use these to drive into the ground for walls," said Jack. "Where's that old spade, Mike? Did you bring it as I said?"

"Yes, here it is," said Mike. "Shall I dig holes to drive the sapling trunks into?"

"Yes," said Jack. "Dig them fairly deep."

So Mike dug hard in the hot sun, making holes for Jack to ram the willow wood into. The girls stripped the leaves off the chopped-down trees, and with Jack's knife cut off the smaller twigs. They trimmed up the bigger branches nicely.

Everyone worked hard until the sun began to go down. The house was not yet built—it would take some days to do that—but at any rate there was a fine roof, and part of the wall was up. The children could quite well see how the house would look when it was done—and certainly it would be big, and very strong. They felt proud of themselves.

"We'll do no more today," said Jack. "We are all tired. I'll go and see if there are any fish on my line."

But, alas! there were no fish that night!

"There's some bread left and a packet of currants," said Peggy. "And some lettuces and margarine. Shall we have those?"

"This food question is going to be a difficult one," said Jack thoughtfully. "We've plenty of water—we shall soon have a house—but we must have food or we shall starve. I shall catch rabbits, I think."

"Oh, no, Jack, don't do that," said Nora. "I do like rabbits so much."

"So do I, Nora," said Jack. "But if rabbits were not caught, the land would soon be overrun with them, you know. You have often had rabbit-pie, haven't you? And I guess you liked it, too!"

"Yes, I did," said Nora. "Well, if you are sure you can

43

catch them so that they are not hurt or in pain, Jack, I suppose you'll have to."

"You leave it to me," said Jack. "I don't like hurting things any more than you do. But I know quite well how to skin rabbits. If it makes you feel squeamish, you two girls can leave it to Mike and me. So long as you can cook the rabbits for dinner, that's all you need worry about. And ever since Peggy said she wished we had a cow and some hens, I've been thinking about it. I believe we could manage to get them over here on to the island—then we *would* be all right!"

Mike, Peggy, and Nora stared at Jack in amazement. What a surprising boy he was! However could they get a cow and hens?

"Let's hurry up and get the supper," said Jack, smiling at their surprised faces. "I'm hungry. We'll think about things tomorrow. We'll have our meal now and a quiet read afterwards, then to bed early. Tomorrow we'll go on with the house."

Soon they were munching bread and margarine, and eating lettuce. They saved the currants for another time. Then they got out books and papers and sprawled on the soft heather, reading whilst the daylight lasted. Then they had a dip in the lake, threw on their clothes again, and settled down for the night in their heathery beds.

"Good-night, everyone," said Mike. But nobody answered—they were all asleep!

Willow House Is Finished

The next day, after a meal of fish and lettuce, the children were ready to go on with the building of their house in the willow thicket. It was lucky that Jack had caught more fish on his line that morning, for stores were getting low. There were still plenty of potatoes, but not much else. Jack made up his mind that he would have to take the boat and see what he could bring back in it that night. There was no doubt but that food was going to be their great difficulty.

All morning the four children worked hard at the house. Jack cut down enough young willows to make the walls. Mike dug the holes to drive in the willow stakes. He and Jack drove them deeply in, and the girls jumped for joy to see what fine straight walls of willow the boys were making.

The willow stakes were set a little way apart, and Jack showed the girls how to take thin, supple willow branches and weave them in and out of the stakes to hold the walls in place, and to fill up the gaps. It was quite easy to do this when they knew how, but they got very hot.

Mike went up and down to the spring a dozen times that morning to fetch water! They all drank pints of it, and were glad of its coldness. The sun was really very hot, though it was nice and shady in the green willow thicket.

"It begins to look like a house now," said Jack, pleased. "Look, this front gap here is where we shall have the door. We can make that later of long stakes interwoven with willow strips, and swing it on some sort of a hinge so that it opens and shuts. But we don't need a door at present."

That day all the walls were finished, and the girls had gone a good way towards weaving the stakes together so that the walls stood firmly and looked nice and thick.

"In the olden days people used to fill up the gaps with clay and let it dry hard," said Jack. "But I don't think there's any clay on this island, so we must stuff up the cracks with dried bracken and heather. That will do nicely. And the willow stakes we have rammed into the ground will grow, and throw out leaves later on, making the wall thicker still."

"How do you mean—the stakes we have cut will grow?" asked Mike in surprise. "Sticks don't grow, surely!"

Jack grinned. "Willow sticks do!" he said. "You can cut a willow branch off the tree—strip it of all buds and leaves, and stick it in the ground, and you'll find that, although it has no roots, and no shoots—it will put out both and grow into a willow tree by itself! Willows are full of life, and you can't stamp it out of them!"

"Well—our house will be growing all the year round, then!" cried Nora. "How funny!"

"I think it's lovely!" said Peggy. "I like things to be as alive as that. I shall love to live in a house that's growing over me—putting out roots and shoots and buds and leaves! What shall we call our house, Jack?"

"Willow House!" said Jack. "That's the best name for it!"

"It's a good name," said Peggy. "I like it. I like everything here. It's glorious. Just us four—and our secret island. It's the loveliest adventure that ever was!"

"If only we had more to eat!" said Mike, who seemed to feel hungry every hour of the day. "That's the only thing I don't like about this adventure!"

"Yes," said Jack. "We'll have to put that right! Don't worry. We shall get over it somehow!"

That night there was nothing much to eat but potatoes. Jack said he would go off in the boat as soon as it was dark, to see what he could find at his old farm.

So he set off. He took with him a candle, set in the lantern, but he did not light it in case he should be seen.

"Wait up for me," he said to the others, "and keep a small fire going—not big, in case the glow could be seen."

The other three waited patiently for Jack to come back. He seemed a long, long time. Nora stretched herself out on the old rug and fell asleep. But Mike and Peggy kept awake. They saw the moon come up and light everything. The secret island seemed mysterious again in the moonlight. Dark shadows stretched beneath the trees. The water lapped against the sand, black as night, close by them, but silvered where the moon caught it beyond. It was a warm night, and the children were hot, even though they had no covering.

It seemed hours before they heard the splash of oars. Mike ran down to the edge of the water and waited. He saw the boat coming softly over the water in the moonlight. He called Jack.

"Hallo, there, Jack! Are you all right?"

"Yes," said Jack's voice. "I've got plenty of news too!"

The boat scraped on the sand and stones. Mike pulled it up the beach, and Jack jumped out.

"I've got something here for us!" said Jack, and they saw his white teeth in the moonlight as he grinned at them. "Put your hands down there in the boat, Nora."

Nora did—and squealed!

"There's something soft and warm and feathery there!" she said. "What is it?"

"Six of my hens!" said Jack. "I found them roosting in the hedges! I caught them and trussed them up so that

47

they couldn't move! My word, they were heavy to carry! But we shall have plenty of eggs now! They can't escape from the island!"

"Hurrah!" cried Peggy. "We can have eggs for breakfast, dinner, and tea!"

"What else have you brought?" asked Mike.

"Corn for the hens," said Jack. "And packets of seeds of all kinds from the shed. And some tins of milk. And a loaf of bread, rather stale. And lots more vegetables!"

"And here are some cherries," said Nora, pulling out handfuls of red cherries from the boat. "Did you pick these, Jack?"

"Yes," said Jack. "They are from the tree in our garden. It's full of them now."

"Did you see your grandfather?" asked Mike.

"Yes," grinned Jack, "but he didn't see me! He's going away—to live with my aunt. The farm is to be shut up, and someone is to feed the animals until it's sold. So I think I shall try and get my own cow somehow, and make her swim across the lake to the island!"

"Don't be silly, Jack," said Peggy. "You could never do that!"

"You don't know what I can do!" said Jack. "Well, listen—I heard my Granddad talking to two friends of his, and everyone is wondering where we've all gone! They've searched everywhere for us—in all the nearby towns and villages, and in all the country round about!"

"Oooh!" said the three children, feeling rather frightened. "Do you suppose they'll come here?"

"Well, they may," said Jack. "You never know. I've always been a bit afraid that the smoke from our fire will give the game away to someone. But don't let's worry about that till it happens."

"Are the police looking for us, too?" asked Peggy.

"Oh yes," said Jack. "Everyone is, as far as I can make

Mike shone the lantern onto the hens

49

out. I heard Granddad tell how they've searched barns and stacks and ditches, and gone to every town for twenty miles round, thinking we might have run away on a lorry. They don't guess how near we are!"

"Is Aunt Harriet very upset?" asked Peggy.

"Very!" grinned Jack. "She's got no one to wash and scrub and cook for her now! But that's all she cares, I expect! Well, it's good news about my Granddad going to live with my aunt. I can slip to and fro and not be seen by him now. My word, I wished you were with me when I got these hens. They did peck and scratch and flap about. I was afraid someone would hear them."

"Where shall we put them?" said Mike, helping Jack to carry them up the beach.

"I vote we put them into Willow House till the morning," said Jack. "We can stop up the doorway with something."

So they bundled the squawking hens into Willow House, and stopped up the doorway with sticks and bracken. The hens fled to a corner and squatted there, terrified. They made no more noise.

"I'm jolly tired," said Jack. "Let's have a few cherries and go to bed."

They munched the ripe cherries, and then went to their green bedroom. The bracken which they had picked and put on the hillside to dry had been quite brown and withered by that afternoon, so the girls had added it to their bed and the boys', and tonight their beds seemed even softer and sweeter-smelling than usual. They were all tired. Mike and Jack talked for a little while, but the girls went to sleep quickly.

They slept late the next morning. Peggy woke first, and sat up, wondering what the unusual noise was that she heard. It was a loud cackling.

"Of course! The hens!" she thought. She slipped off her

bracken-and-heather bed, jumped lightly over the two sleeping boys and ran to Willow House. She pulled aside the doorway and squeezed inside. The hens fled to a corner when they saw her, but Peggy saw a welcome sight!

Four of the hens had laid eggs! Goody! Now they could have a fine breakfast! The little girl gathered them up quickly, then, stopping up the doorway again, she ran out. She soon had a fire going, and, when the others sat up, rubbing their eyes, Peggy called them.

"Come on! Breakfast! The hens have laid us an egg each!"

They ran to breakfast. "We'll have a dip afterwards," said Mike. "I feel so hungry."

"We must finish Willow House properly today," said Jack. "And we must decide what to do with the hens, too. They can't run loose till they know us and their new home. We must put up some sort of enclosure for them."

After breakfast the four of them set to work to make a tiny yard for the hens. They used willow stakes again and quickly built a fine little fence, too high for the hens to jump over. Jack made them nesting-places of bracken, and hoped they would lay their eggs there. He scattered some seed for them, and they pecked at it eagerly. Peggy gave them a dish of water.

"They will soon know this is their home and lay their eggs here," said Jack. "Now, come on, let's get on with Willow House! You two girls stuff up the cracks with heather and bracken, and Mike and I will make the door."

Everyone worked hard. The girls found it rather a nice job to stuff the soft heather and bracken into the cracks and make the house rain- and wind-proof. They were so happy in their job that they did not notice what a fine door Jack and Mike had made of woven willow twigs. The boys called the girls, and proudly showed them what they had done.

The door had even been fixed on some sort of a hinge, so that it swung open and shut! It looked fine! It did not quite fit at the top, but nobody minded that. It was a door—and could be shut or opened, just as they pleased. Willow House was very dark inside when the door was shut—but that made it all the more exciting!

"I'm so hungry and thirsty now that I believe I could eat all the food we've got!" said Mike at last.

"Yes, we really must have something to eat," said Jack. "We've got plenty of bread and potatoes and vegetables. Let's cook some broad beans. They are jolly good. Go and look at my fishing-line, Mike, and see if there are any fish on it."

There was a fine trout, and Mike brought it back to cook. Soon the smell of frying rose on the air, and the children sniffed hungrily. Fish, potatoes, bread, beans, cherries, and cocoa with milk from one of Jack's tins. What a meal!

"I'll think about getting Daisy the cow across next," said Jack, drinking his cocoa. "We simply must have milk."

"And, Jack, we could store some of our things in Willow House now, couldn't we?" said Peggy. "The ants get into some of the things in the cave-larder. It's a good place for things like hammers and nails, but it would be better to keep our food in Willow House. Are we going to live in Willow House, Jack?"

"Well, we'll live in the open air mostly, I expect," said Jack, "but it will be a good place to sleep in when the nights are cold and rainy, and a fine shelter on bad days. It's our sort of home."

"It's a lovely home," said Nora; "the nicest there ever was! What fun it is to live like this!"

The Cow Comes To The Island

A day or two went by. The children were busy, for there seemed lots of things to do. The door of Willow House came off and had to be put on again more carefully. One of the hens escaped, and the four children spent nearly the whole morning looking for it. Jack found it at last under a gorse bush, where it had laid a big brown egg.

They made the fence of the hen-yard a bit higher, thinking that the hen had been able to jump over. But Mike found a hole in the fence through which he was sure the hen had squeezed, and very soon it was blocked up with fronds of bracken. The hens squawked and clucked, but they seemed to be settling down, and always ran eagerly to Nora when she fed them twice a day.

Mike thought it would be a good idea to make two rooms inside Willow House, instead of one big room. The front part could be a sort of living-room, with the larder in a corner, and the back part could be a bedroom, piled with heather and bracken to make soft lying. So they worked at a partition made of willow, and put it up to make two rooms. They left a doorway between, but did not make a door. It was nice to have a two-roomed house!

One evening Jack brought something unusual to the camp-fire on the little beach. Mike stared at what he was carrying.

"You've caught some rabbits!" he said, "and you've skinned them, too, and got them ready for cooking!"

"Oh, Jack!" said Nora. "Must you catch those dear

little rabbits? I do love them so much, and it is such fun to watch them playing about round us in the evenings."

"I know," said Jack, "but we must have meat to eat sometimes. Now, don't worry, Nora—they did not suffer any pain and you know you have often eaten rabbit-pie at home."

All the same, none of the children enjoyed cooking the rabbits, though they couldn't help being glad of a change of food. They were getting a little tired of fish. Nora said she felt as if she couldn't look a rabbit in the face that evening!

"In Australia, rabbits are as much of a pest as rats are here," said Jack, who seemed to know all sorts of things. "If we were in Australia we would think we had done a good deed to get rid of a few pests."

"But we're not in Australia," said Peggy. Nobody said any more, and the meal was finished in silence. The girls washed up as usual, and the boys went to get some water from the spring ready to boil in the morning. Then they all had a dip in the lake.

"I think I'll have a shot at getting my cow along tonight," said Jack, as they dressed themselves again.

"You can't, Jack!" cried Nora. "You'd never get a cow here!"

"I'll come with you, Jack," said Mike. "You'll want someone to help you."

"Right!" said Jack. "We'll start off as soon as it's dark."

"Oh, Jack!" said the girls, excited to think of a cow coming. "Where shall we keep it?"

"It had better live on the other side of the island," said Jack. "There is some nice grass there. It won't like to eat heather."

"How will you bring it, Jack?" asked Mike. "It will be difficult to get it into the boat, won't it?"

"We shan't get it into the boat, silly!" said Jack, laughing. "We shall make it swim *behind* the boat!"

The other three stared at Jack in surprise. Then they began to laugh. It was funny to think of a cow swimming behind the boat to their secret island!

When it was dark, the two boys set off. The girls called good-bye, and then went to Willow House, for the evening was not quite so warm as usual. They lighted a candle and talked. It was fun to be on the secret island alone.

The boys rowed down the lake and came to the place where Jack usually landed—a well-hidden spot by the lake-side, where trees came right down to the water. They dragged the boat in and then made their way through the wood. After some time they came to the fields that lay round the house of Jack's grandfather. Jack looked at the old cottage. There was no light in it. No one was there. His grandfather had gone away. In the field nearby some cows and horses stood, and the boys could hear one of the horses saying, "Hrrrumph! Hrrrrumph!"

"Do you see that shed over there, Mike?" said Jack, in a low voice. "Well, there are some lengths of rope there. Go and get them whilst I try to find which is my own cow. The rope is in the corner, just by the door."

Mike stumbled off over the dark field to the tumble-down shed in the corner. Jack went among the cows, making a curious chirrupy noise. A big brown and white cow left the others and went lumbering towards Jack.

Jack cautiously struck a match and looked at it. It was Daisy, the cow he had brought up from a calf. He rubbed its soft nose, and called to Mike:

"Hurry up with that rope! I've got the cow."

Mike had been feeling about in the shed for rope and had found a great coil of it. He stumbled over the field to Jack.

"Good," said Jack, making a halter for the patient

animal. "Now, before we go, I'd like to pop into the old cottage and see if I can find anything we'd be glad of."

"Could you find some towels, do you think?" asked Mike. "I do hate having to dry myself with old sacks."

"Yes, I'll see if there are any left," said Jack, and he set off quietly towards the old cottage. He found the door locked, but easily got in at a window. He struck a match and looked round. There were only two rooms in the cottage, a living-room and a bedroom. All the furniture had gone. Jack looked behind the kitchen door, and found what he had hoped to see—a big roller-towel still hanging there. It was very dirty, but could easily be washed. He looked behind the bedroom door—yes, there was a roller-towel there, too! Good! His grandfather hadn't thought of looking behind the doors and taking those when he went. Jack wondered if the old carpet left on the floor was worth taking, too, but he thought not. Good clean heather made a better carpet!

Jack wandered out to the little shed at the back of the cottage—and there he did indeed make a find! There was an old wooden box there, and in it had been put all the clothes he possessed! His grandfather had not thought it worth while to take those with him. There they were, rather ragged, it is true, but still, they were clothes! There were three shirts, a few vests, an odd pair of trousers, an overcoat, a pair of old shoes, and a ragged blanket!

Jack grinned. He would take all these back with him. They might be useful when the cold weather came. He thought the best way to take them back would be to wear them all—so the boy put on all the vests, the shirts, the trousers, the shoes, and the overcoat over his own clothes, and wrapped the blanket round him, too! What a queer sight he looked!

Then he went out to the garden and filled his many pockets with beans and peas and new potatoes. After that he thought it was time to go back to Mike and the cow. Mike would be tired of holding the animal by now!

So, carrying the two dirty towels, Jack made his way slowly over the field to Mike.

"I thought you were never coming!" said Mike, half-cross. "Whatever happened to you? This cow is getting tired of standing here with me."

"I found a lot of my clothes," said Jack, "and an old blanket and two towels. The cow will soon get some exercise! Come on! You carry the towels and this blanket, and I'll take Daisy."

They went back over the fields and through the thick wood to the boat. The cow did not like it when they came to the wood. She could not see where they were going and she disliked being pulled through the close-set trees. She began to moo.

"Oh, don't do that!" said Jack, scared. "You will give us away, Daisy."

"Moo-oo-oo!" said Daisy sorrowfully, trying her hardest to stand still. But Jack and Mike pulled her on.

It was hard work getting her down to the boat. It took the boys at least two hours before they were by the lake, panting and hot. Daisy had mooed dozens of times, each time more loudly than before, and Jack was beginning to think that his idea of taking her across to the island was not such a good one after all. Suppose her mooing gave them away, and people came after them? Suppose she mooed a great deal on the island? Whatever would they do?

Still, they had at last got her to the boat. Jack persuaded the poor, frightened cow to step into the water. She gave such a moo that she startled even the two boys. But at last she was in the water. The boys got into the boat, and pushed off. Jack had tied the cow's rope to the stern of the boat. The boys bent to their oars, and poor Daisy found that she was being pulled off her feet into deeper water!

It was a dreadful adventure for a cow who had never been out of her field before, except to be milked in a nearby shed! She waggled her long legs about, and began to swim in a queer sort of way, holding her big head high out of the water. She was too frightened to moo.

Jack lighted the lantern and fixed it to the front of the boat. It was very dark and he wanted to see where he was going. Then off they rowed up the lake towards the secret island, and Daisy the cow came after them, not able to help herself.

"Well, my idea is working," said Jack after a bit.

"Yes," said Mike, "but I'm jolly glad it's only *one* cow we're taking, not a whole herd!"

They said no more till they came in sight of the island, which loomed up near by, black and solid. The girls had heard the splashing of the oars, and had come down to the beach with the candle.

"Have you got the cow, Jack?" they called.

"Yes," shouted back the boys. "She's come along behind beautifully. But she doesn't like it, poor creature!"

They pulled the boat up the beach and then dragged out the shivering, frightened cow. Jack spoke to her kindly and she pressed against him in wonder and fear. He was the one thing she knew, and she wanted to be close to him. Jack told Mike to get a sack and help him to rub the cow down, for she was cold and wet.

"Where shall we put her for tonight?" asked Mike.

"In the hen-yard," said Jack. "She's used to hens and hens are used to her. There is a lot of bracken and heather there and we can put some more armfuls in for her to lie on. She will soon be warm and comfortable. She will like to hear the clucking of the hens, too."

So Daisy was pushed into the hen-yard, and there she

lay down on the warm heather, comforted by the sound of the disturbed hens.

The girls were so excited at seeing the cow. They asked the boys over and over again all about their adventure till Mike and Jack were tired of telling it.

"Jack! You do look awfully fat tonight!" said Nora suddenly, swinging the lantern so that its light fell on Jack. The others looked at him in surprise. Yes, he did look enormous!

"Have you swollen up, or something?" asked Peggy anxiously. Jack laughed loudly.

"No!" he said, "I found some clothes of mine in a box and brought them along. As the easiest way to carry them was to wear them, I put them on. That's why I look so fat!"

It took him a long time to take all the clothes off, because they were all laughing so much. Peggy looked at the holes in them and was glad she had brought her work-basket along. She could mend them nicely! The blanket, too, would be useful on a cold night.

"What's that funny light in the sky over there?" said Nora, suddenly, pointing towards the east. "Look!"

"You silly! It's the dawn coming" said Jack. "It must be nearly daylight! Come on, we really must go to sleep. What a night we've had!"

"Moo-oo-oo!" said Daisy, from the hen-yard, and the children laughed.

"Daisy thinks so, too!" cried Peggy.

A Lazy Day—With A Horrid Ending

The next morning the children slept very late indeed. The sun was high in the sky before anyone stirred, and even then they might not have awakened if Daisy the cow hadn't decided that it was more than time for her to be milked. She stood in the hen-yard and bellowed for all she was worth.

Jack sat up, his heart thumping loudly. Whatever was that awful noise? Of course—it was Daisy! She wanted to be milked!

"Hi, you others!" he shouted. "Wake up! It must be about nine o'clock! Look at the sun, it's very high! And Daisy wants to be milked!"

Mike grunted and opened his eyes. He felt very sleepy after his late night. The girls sat up and rubbed their eyes. Daisy bellowed again, and the hens clucked in fright.

"Our farmyard wants its breakfast," grinned Jack. "Come on, lazy-bones, come and help. We'll have to see to them before we get our own meal."

They scrambled up. They were so very sleepy that they simply had to run down to the lake and dip their heads into the water before they could do anything!

Then they all went to gloat over their cow. How pretty she was in her brown and white coat! How soft and brown her eyes were! A cow of their own! How lovely!

"And what a voice she has!" said Jack, as the cow mooed again. "I must milk her."

"But I say—we haven't a pail!" said Mike.

The children stared at one another in dismay. It was true—they had no pail.

"Well, we must use the saucepans," said Jack firmly. "And we can all do with a cup or two of milk to start the day. I'll use the biggest saucepan, and when it's full I'll have to pour it into the bowls and jugs we've got—and the kettle, too. We must certainly get a pail. What a pity I didn't think of it last night!"

There was more than enough milk to fill every bowl and jug and saucepan. The children drank cupful after cupful. It was lovely to have milk after drinking nothing but tea and cocoa made with water. They could not have enough of it!

"I say! Daisy has trodden on a hen's egg and smashed it," said Nora, looking into the hen-yard. "What a pity!"

"Never mind," said Jack. "We won't keep her here after to-day. She shall go and live on that nice grassy piece, the other side of the island. Nora, feed the hens. They are clucking as if they'd never stop. They are hungry."

Nora fed them. Then they all sat down to their breakfast of boiled eggs and creamy milk. Daisy the cow looked at them as they ate, and mooed softly. She was hungry, too.

Jack and Mike took her to the other side of the island after they had finished their meal. She was delighted to see the juicy green grass there and set to work at once, pulling mouthfuls of it as she wandered over the field.

"She can't get off the island, so we don't need to fence her in," said Jack. "We must milk her twice a day, Mike. We must certainly get a pail from somewhere."

"There's an old milking-pail in the barn at Aunt Harriet's farm," said Peggy. "I've seen it hanging there often."

"Has it got a hole in it?" asked Jack. "If it has it's no use to us. We'll have to stand our milk in it all day and we don't want it to leak away."

61

"No, it doesn't leak," said Peggy. "I filled it with water one day to take to the hens. It's only just a very old one and not used now."

"I'll go and get it tonight," said Mike.

"No, I'll go," said Jack. "You might be caught."

"Well, so might you," said Mike. "We'll go together."

"Can't we come, too?" asked the girls.

"Certainly not," said Jack, at once. "There's no use the whole lot of us running into danger."

"How shall we keep the milk cool?" wondered Peggy. "It's jolly hot on this island."

"I'll make a little round place to fit the milk-pail into, just by one of the springs," said Jack, at once. "Then, with the cool spring water running round the milk-pail all day, the milk will keep beautifully fresh and cool."

"How clever you are, Jack!" said Nora.

"No, I'm not," said Jack. "It's just common sense, that's all. Anyone can think of things like that."

"I do feel tired and stiff today," said Mike, stretching out his arms. "It was pretty hard work pulling old Daisy along last night!"

"We'd better have a restful day," said Jack, who was also feeling tired. "For once in a while we won't do anything. We'll just lie about and read and talk."

The children had a lovely day. They bathed three times, for it was very hot. Nora washed the two big roller towels in the lake, and made them clean. They soon dried in the hot sun, and then the two boys took one for themselves and the two girls had the other. How nice it was to dry themselves on towels instead of on rough sacks!

"Fish for dinner," said Jack, going down to look at his lines.

"And custard!" said Nora, who had been doing some cooking with eggs and milk.

"Well, I feel just as hungry as if I'd been hard at work building all morning!" said Mike.

The afternoon passed by lazily. The boys slept. Nora read a book. Peggy got out her work-basket and began on the long, long task of mending up the old clothes Jack had brought back the night before. She thought they would be very useful indeed when the cold weather came. She wished she and Nora and Mike could get some of their clothes, too.

The hens clucked in the hen-yard. Daisy the cow mooed once or twice, feeling rather strange and lonely—but she seemed to be settling down very well.

"I hope she won't moo too much," thought Peggy, her needle flying in and out busily. "She might give us away with her mooing if anyone came up the lake in a boat. But thank goodness no one ever does!"

Everyone felt very fresh after their rest. They decided to have a walk round the island. Nora fed the hens and then they set off.

It was a fine little island. Trees grew thickly down to the water-side all round. The steep hill that rose in the middle was a warm, sunny place, covered with rabbit runs and burrows. The grassy piece beyond the hill was full of little wild flowers, and birds sang in the bushes around. The children peeped into the dark caves that ran into the hillside, but did not feel like exploring them just then, for they had no candles with them.

"I'll take you to the place where wild raspberries grow," said Jack. He led them round the hill to the west side, and there, in the blazing sun, the children saw scores of raspberry canes, tangled and thick.

"Jack! There are some getting ripe already!" cried Nora, in delight. She pointed to where spots of bright red dotted the canes. The children squeezed their way through and began to pick the raspberries. How sweet and juicy they were!

"We'll have some of these with cream each day," said

"Look," cried Jack alarmingly, "some people in a boat."

Peggy. "I can skim the cream off the cow's milk, and we will have raspberries and cream for supper. Oooh!"

"Oooh!" said everyone, eating as fast as they could.

"Are there any wild strawberries on the island, too?" asked Nora.

"Yes," said Jack, "but they don't come till later. "We'll look for those in August and September."

"I do think this is a lovely island," said Peggy happily. "We've a spendid house of our own—hens—a cow, wild fruit growing—fresh water each day!"

"It's all right now it's warm weather," said Jack. "It won't be quite so glorious when the cold winds begin to blow! But winter is a long way off yet."

They climbed up the west side of the hill, which was very rocky. They came to a big rock right on the very top, and sat there. The rock was so warm that it almost burnt them. From far down below the blue spire of smoke rose up from the fire.

"Let's play a game," said Jack. "Let's play . . ."

But what game Jack wanted the others never knew—for Jack suddenly stopped, sat up very straight, and stared fixedly down the blue, sparkling lake. The others sat up and stared, too. And what they saw gave them a dreadful shock!

"Some people in a boat!" said Jack. "Do you see them? Away down there!"

"Yes," said Mike, going pale. "Are they after us, do you think?"

"No," said Jack, after a while. "I think I can hear a radio playing—and if it was anyone after us they surely wouldn't bring that! They are probably just trippers, from the village at the other end of the lake."

"Do you think they'll come to the island?" asked Peggy.

"I don't know," said Jack. "They may—but anyway it would only be for a little while. If we can hide all traces of our being here they won't know a thing about us."

"Come on, then," said Mike, slipping off the rock. "We'd better hurry. It won't be long before they're here."

The children hurried down to the beach. Jack and Mike stamped out the fire, and carried the charred wood to the bushes. They scattered clean sand over the place where they had the fire. They picked up all their belongings and hid them.

"I don't think anyone would find Willow House," said Jack. "The trees really are too thick all round it for any tripper to bother to squeeze through."

"What about the hens?" said Peggy.

"We'll catch them and pop them into a sack just for now," said Jack. "The hen-yard will have to stay. I don't think anyone will find it—it's well hidden. But we certainly couldn't have the hens clucking away there!"

"And Daisy the cow?" said Peggy, looking worried.

"We'll watch and see which side of the island the trippers come," said Jack. "As far as I know, there is only one landing-place, and that is our beach. As Daisy is right on the other side of the island, they are not likely to see her unless they go exploring. And let's hope they don't do that!"

"Where shall *we* hide?" said Nora.

"We'll keep a look-out from the hill, hidden in the bracken," said Jack. "If the trippers begin to wander about, we must just creep about in the bracken and trust to luck they won't see us. There's one thing—they won't be *looking* for us, if they are trippers. They won't guess there is anyone else here at all!"

"Will they find the things in the cave-larder?" asked Nora, helping to catch the squawking hens.

"Peggy, get some heather and bracken and stuff up the opening to the cave-larder," said Jack. Peggy ran off at once. Jack put the hens gently into the sack one by one and ran up the hill with them. He went to the other side of

66

the hill and came to one of the caves he knew. He called to Nora, who was just behind him.

"Nora! Sit at the little opening here and see that the hens don't get out! I'm going to empty them out of the sack into the cave!"

With much squawking and scuffling and clucking the scared hens hopped out of the sack and ran into the little cave. Nora sat down at the entrance, hidden by the bracken that grew there. No hen could get out whilst she was there.

"The boat is going round the island," whispered Jack as he parted the bracken at the top of the hill and looked down to the lake below. "They can't find a place to land. They're going round to our little beach! Well—Daisy the cow is safe, if they don't go exploring! Hope she doesn't moo!"

The Trippers Come To The Island

Nora sat crouched against the entrance of the little cave. She could hear the six hens inside, clucking softly as they scratched about. Jack knelt near her, peering through the bracken, trying to see what the boat was doing.

"Mike has rowed our own boat to where the brambles fall over the water, and has pushed it under them," said Jack, in a low voice. "I don't know where he is now. I can't see him."

"Where's Peggy?" whispered Nora.

"Here I am," said a low voice, and Peggy's head popped up above the bracken a little way down the hill. "I say — isn't this horrid? I do wish those people would go away."

The sound of voices came up the hillside from the lake below.

"Here's a fine landing-place!" said one voice.

"They've found our beach," whispered Jack.

"Pull the boat in," said a woman's voice. "We'll have our supper here. It's lovely!"

There was the sound of a boat being pulled a little way up the beach. Then the trippers got out.

"I'll bring the radio," said someone. "You bring the supper things, Eddie."

"Do you suppose anyone has ever been on this little island before?" said a man's voice.

"No!" said someone else. "The countryside round about is quite deserted—no one ever comes here, I should think."

The three children crouched down in the bracken and

listened. The trippers were setting out their supper. One of the hens in the cave began to cluck loudly. Nora thought it must have laid an egg.

"Do you hear that noise?" said one of the trippers. "Sounds like a hen to me!"

"Don't be silly, Eddie," said a woman's voice scornfully. "How could a hen be on an island like this! That must have been a blackbird or something."

Jack giggled. It seemed very funny to him that a hen's cluck should be thought like a blackbird's clear song.

"Pass the salt," said someone. "Thanks. I say! Isn't this a fine little island! Sort of secret and mysterious. What about exploring it after supper?"

"That's a good idea," said Eddie's voice. "We will!"

The children looked at one another in dismay. Just the one thing they had hoped the trippers wouldn't do!

"Where's Mike, do you suppose?" said Peggy, in a low voice. "Do you think he's hiding in our boat?"

"I expect so," whispered Jack. "Don't worry about him. He can look after himself all right."

"Oh, my goodness! There's Daisy beginning to moo!" groaned Peggy, as a dismal moo reached her ears. "She knows it is time she was milked."

"And just wouldn't I like a cup of milk!" said Jack, who was feeling very thirsty.

"Can you hear that cow mooing somewhere?" said one of the trippers, in surprise.

"I expect it's a cow in a field on the mainland," said another lazily. "You don't suppose there is a cow wandering loose on this tiny island, do you, Eddie?"

"Well, I don't know," said Eddie, in a puzzled voice. "Look over there. Doesn't that look like a footprint in the sand to you?"

The children held their breath. Could it be true that they had left a footprint on the sand?

"And see here," went on the tripper, holding up something. "Here's a piece of string I found on the beach. String doesn't grow, you know."

"You are making a great mystery about nothing," said one of the women crossly. "Other trippers have been here, that's all."

"Perhaps you are right," said Eddie. "But all the same, I'm going to explore the island after supper!"

"Oh, put on the radio, Eddie," said someone. "I'm tired of hearing you talk so much."

Soon loud music blared through the air, and the children were glad, for they knew it would drown any sound of Daisy's mooing or the hens' clucking. They sat in the bracken, looking scared and miserable. They did not like anyone else sharing their secret island. And what would happen if the trippers did explore the island and found the children?

Nora began to cry softly. Tears ran down her cheeks and fell on her hands. Jack looked at her and then crept silently up. He slipped his arm round her.

"Don't cry, Nora," he said. "Perhaps they won't have time to explore. It is getting a bit dark now. Do you see that big black cloud coming up? It will make the night come quickly, and perhaps the trippers will think there's a storm coming and row off."

Nora dried her eyes and looked up. There certainly was a big black cloud.

"It looks like a thunderstorm," said Peggy, creeping up to join them.

"Oooh!" said Nora suddenly, almost squealing out loud. "Look! Someone's coming up the hill! I can see the bracken moving! It must be one of the trippers creeping up to find us!"

The children went pale. They looked to where Nora pointed—and sure enough they could see first one frond of bracken moving, and then another and another. Someone was certainly creeping up the hill hidden under the fronds.

Nora clutched hold of Jack. "Don't make a sound," he whispered. "No one can possibly know we're here. Keep quiet, Nora. We'll slip inside the cave if he comes much nearer."

They sat silently watching the swaying of the tall bracken as the newcomer crept through it. It was a horrid moment. Was someone going to spring out on them?

"Get inside the cave, you two girls," whispered Jack. "I think you'll be safe there. I'm going to slip round the hill and come up behind this person, whoever he is."

The girls crept just inside the cave and parted the bracken that grew around it to see what Jack was going to do. He was just slipping away when the person creeping up the hillside stopped his crawling. The bracken kept still. This was worse than seeing it move! Oh dear!

Then a head popped out of the bracken, and Nora gave a loud squeal.

"Mike!" she said. "Mike!"

"Sh, you silly chump!" hissed Peggy, shaking her. "You'll be heard by the trippers!"

Fortunately the radio was going loudly, so Nora's squeal was not heard. The three children stared in delight at Mike. It was he who had been creeping up through the bracken after all! What a relief! He grinned at them and put his head down again. Once more the bracken fronds began to move slightly as Mike made his way through them up to the cave.

"Oh, Mike," said Nora, when he came up to them. "You did give us such a fright. We thought you were a tripper coming after us!"

71

"I got a good view of them," said Mike, sitting down beside the others. "There are three men and two women. They are tucking into an enormous supper."

"Do you think they'll explore the island as they said?" asked Peggy anxiously.

"Perhaps this thunderstorm will put them off," said Mike, looking up at the black sky. "My word, it's brought the bats out early! Look at them!"

Certainly the little black bats were out in their hundreds. The hot, thundery evening had brought out thousands of insects, and the bats were having a great feast, catching the flies and beetles that flew through the air.

It was the bats that sent the trippers away. One of the women caught sight of two or three bats darting round under the trees, and she gave a shriek.

"Ooh! Bats! Ooh! I can't bear bats! I'm frightened of them. Let's pack up and go quickly!"

"I can't bear bats either!" squealed the other woman. "Horrid little creatures!"

"They won't hurt you," said a man's voice. "Don't be silly."

"I can't help it; I'm frightened of them," said a woman. "I'm going!"

"But I wanted to explore the island," said Eddie.

"Well, you'll have to explore it another day," said the woman. "Just look at the sky, too—there's going to be a dreadful storm."

"All right, all right," said Eddie, in a sulky voice. "We'll go. Fancy being frightened of a few bats!"

The children on the hillside stared at one another in delight. The trippers were really going. And no one had discovered them. Goody, goody!

"Good old bats!" whispered Jack. "Would you think anyone would be scared of those little flitter-mice, Nora?"

"Aunt Harriet was," said Nora. "I don't know why. I think they are dear little creatures, with their funny black wings. Anyway, I shall always feel friendly towards them now. They have saved us from being found!"

Daisy the cow mooed loudly. Jack frowned. "If only we had milked Daisy before the trippers came!" he said.

"Did you hear that?" said one of the trippers. "That was thunder in the distance!"

The four children giggled. Nora rolled over and stuffed her hands into her mouth to stop laughing loudly.

"Good old Daisy!" whispered Mike. "She's pretending to be a thunderstorm now, to frighten them away!"

Nora gave a squeal of laughter, and Jack punched her. "Be quiet," he said. "Do you want us to be discovered just when everything is going so nicely?"

The trippers were getting into their boat. They pushed off. The children heard the sound of oars, and peeped out. They could see the boat, far down below, being rowed out on to the lake. A big wind sprang up and ruffled the water. The boat rocked to and fro.

"Hurry!" cried a woman's voice. "We shall get caught in the storm. Oh! Oh! There's one of those horrid bats again! I'll never come to this nasty island any more!"

"I jolly well hope you won't!" said Jack, pretending to wave good-bye.

The children watched the boat being rowed down the lake. The voices of the people came more and more faintly on the breeze. The last they heard was the radio being played once again. Then they saw and heard no more. The trippers were gone.

"Come on," said Jack, standing up and stretching himself. "We've had a very narrow escape—but thank goodness, no one saw us or our belongings."

"Except that footprint and a bit of string," said Mike.

"Yes," said Jack, thoughtfully. "I hope that man called

73

Eddie doesn't read anywhere about four runaway children and think we might be here because of what he heard and found. We must be prepared for that, you know. We must make some plans to prevent being found if anyone comes again to look for us."

A distant rumble of thunder was heard. Jack turned to the others. "Not Daisy mooing this time!" he grinned. "Come on, there's a storm coming. We've plenty to do. I'll go and get Daisy, to milk her. Nora and Mike, you catch the hens and take them back to the hen-yard—and Mike, make some sort of shelter for them with a couple of sacks over sticks, or something, so that they can hide there if they are frightened. Peggy, see if you can light the fire before the rain comes."

"Ay, ay, Captain!" shouted the children joyfully, full of delight to think they had their island to themselves once more!

A Stormy Night In Willow House

There was certainly a thunderstorm coming. The sky was very black indeed, and it was getting dark. Nora and Mike caught the six hens in the little cave, bundled them gently into the sack, and raced off to the hen-yard with them. Mike stuck two or three willow sticks into the ground at one end of the hen-yard and draped the sack over them.

"There you are, henny-pennies!" said Nora. "There is a nice little shelter for you!"

Plop! Plop! Plop! enormous drops of rain fell down and the hens gave a frightened squawk. They did not like the rain. They scuttled under the sack at once and lay there quietly, giving each other little pecks now and again.

"Well, that settles the hens," said Mike. "I wonder how Peggy is getting on with the fire."

Peggy was not getting on at all well. The rain was now coming down fast, and she could not get the fire going. Jack arrived with Daisy the cow and shouted to Peggy:

"Never mind about the fire! Now that the rain's coming down so fast you won't be able to light it. Get into Willow House, all of you, before you get too wet."

"The girls can go," said Mike, running to help Jack. "I'll get the things to help you milk. My goodness—we haven't drunk all the milk yet that Daisy gave us this morning!"

"Put it into a dish and pop it in the hen-yard," said Jack. "Maybe the hens will like it!"

In the pouring rain Jack milked Daisy the cow. Soon all the saucepans and the kettle and bowls were full! Really, thought Jack, he simply *must* get that old milking-pail that

75

the girls had told him of at their Aunt's farm. It was such a tiring business milking a cow like this.

When the milking was finished, Jack took Daisy back to her grassy field on the other side of the island. Mike went to Willow House where the two girls were. It was dark there, and the sound of rain drip-drip-dripping from the trees all around sounded rather miserable.

Mike and the two girls sat in the front part of Willow House and waited for Jack. Mike was very wet, and he shivered.

"Poor old Jack will be wet through, too," he said. "Feel this milk, girls. It's as warm as can be. Let's drink some and it will warm us up. We can't boil any, for we haven't a fire."

Jack came to Willow House dripping wet. But he was grinning away as usual. Nothing ever seemed to upset Jack.

"Hallo, hallo!" he said. "I'm as wet as a fish! Peggy, where did we put those clothes of mine that I brought to the island last night?"

"Oh yes!" cried Peggy, in delight. "Of course! You and Mike can change into those."

"Well, I don't know about that," said Mike. "Jack only brought three old vests, a shirt or two, and an overcoat."

"Well, we can wear a vest each, and a shirt, and I'll wear the overcoat, and you can wrap the old blanket I brought all round you!" said Jack.

The boys took off their wet clothes and changed into the dry ones. "I'll hang your wet ones out to dry as soon as the rain stops," said Peggy, squeezing the rain out of them.

"I can't see a thing here," said Mike, buttoning up his shirt all wrong.

"Well, light the lantern, silly," said Jack. "What do you suppose the candles are for? Nora, find the lantern and light it. It may want a new candle inside. You know where

76

you put the candles, don't you? Over in that corner somewhere."

Nora found the lantern. It did want a new candle inside. She found a box of matches and lighted the candle. Mike hung the lantern up on a nail he had put in the roof. It swung there, giving a dim but cheerful light to the little party huddled inside Willow House.

"This really feels like a house now," said Nora, pleased. "I do like it. It's very cosy. Not a drop of rain is coming through our roof or the walls."

"And not a scrap of wind!" said Jack. "That shows how well we packed the walls with heather and bracken. Listen to the wind howling outside! We shouldn't like to be out in that! What a good thing we've got Willow House to live in! Our outdoor bedroom wouldn't be at all comfortable tonight!"

The thunderstorm broke overhead. The thunder crashed around as if someone were moving heavy furniture up in the sky.

"Hallo! Someone's dropped a wardrobe, I should think!" said Jack, when an extra heavy crash came!

"And there goes a grand piano tumbling down the stairs!" said Mike, at another heavy rumble. Everyone laughed. Really, the thunderstorm *did* sound exactly like furniture being thrown about.

The lightning flashed brightly, lighting up the inside of Willow House. Nora was not sure that she liked it. She cuddled up to Mike. "I feel a bit frightened," she said.

"Don't be silly!" said Mike. "You're as bad as those women trippers over the bats! There's nothing to be frightened of. A storm is a grand thing. We're perfectly safe here."

"A storm is just a bit of weather being noisy!" laughed Jack. "Cheer up, Nora. We're all right. You can think you're lucky you're not Daisy the cow. After all, we do know that a storm is only a storm, but she doesn't."

77

Crash! Rumble! Crash! The thunder roared away, and the children made a joke of it, inventing all kinds of furniture rumbling about the sky, as each crash came. The lightning flashed, and each time Jack said. "Thanks very much! The sky keeps striking matches, and the wind keeps blowing them out!"

Even Nora laughed, and soon she forgot to be frightened. The rain pelted down hard, and the only thing that worried Jack was whether or not a rivulet of rain might find its way into Willow House and run along the floor on which they were sitting. But all was well. No rain came in at all.

Gradually the storm died away, and only the pitter-patter of raindrops falling from the trees could be heard, a singing, liquid sound. The thunder went farther and farther away. The lightning flashed for the last time. The storm was over.

"Now we'll have something to eat and a cup of milk to drink, and off to bed we'll go," said Jack. "We've had quite enough excitement for today! And Mike and I were so late last night that I'm sure he's dropping with sleep. I know I am."

Peggy got a small meal for them all, and they drank Daisy's creamy milk. Then the girls went into the back room of Willow House and snuggled down on the warm heather there, and the boys lay down in the front room. In half a minute everyone was asleep!

Again Daisy the cow awoke them with her mooing. It was strange to wake up in Willow House instead of in their outdoor sleeping-place among the gorse, with the sky above them. The children blinked up at their green roof, for leaves were growing from the willow branches that were interlaced for a ceiling. It was dim inside Willow House. The door was shut, and there were no windows. Jack had thought it would be too difficult to make

78

windows, and they might let in the wind and the rain too much. So Willow House was rather dark and a bit stuffy when the door was shut—but nobody minded that! It really made it all the more exciting!

The children ran out of Willow House and looked around—all except Nora. She lay lazily on her back, looking up at the green ceiling, thinking how soft the heather was and how nice Willow House smelt. She was always the last out of bed!

"Nora, you won't have time for a dip before breakfast if you don't come now," shouted Peggy. So Nora ran out, too. What a lovely morning it was! The thunderstorm had cleared away and left the world looking clean and newly washed. Even the pure blue sky seemed washed, too.

The lake was as blue as the sky. The trees still dripped a little with the heavy rain of the night before, and the grass and heather were damp to the foot.

"The world looks quite new," said Mike. "Just as if it had been made this very morning! Come on—let's have our dip!"

Splash! Into the lake they went. Mike and Jack could both swim. Jack swam like a fish. Peggy could swim a little way, and Nora hardly at all. Jack was teaching her, but she was a bit of a baby and would not get her feet off the sandy bed of the lake.

Peggy was first out of the water and went to get the breakfast—but when she looked round their little beach, she stood still in disgust!

"Look here, boys!" she cried. "Look, Nora! How those trippers have spoilt our beach!"

They all ran out of the cold water, and, rubbing themselves down with their two towels, they stared round at their little beach, which was always such a beautiful place, clean and shining with its silvery sand.

But now, what a difference! Orange-peel lay everywhere. Banana skins, brown, slippery, and soaked with rain, lay where they had been thrown. A tin that had once had canned pears in, and two cardboard cartons that had been full of cream, rolled about on the sand, empty. A newspaper, pulled into many pieces by the wind, blew here and there. An empty cigarette packet joined the mess.

The children felt really angry. The little beach was theirs and they loved it. They had been careful to keep it clean, tidy, and lovely, and had always put everything away after a meal. Now some horrid trippers had come there just for one meal and had left it looking like a rubbish-heap!

"And they were grown-up people, too!" said Jack, in disgust. "They ought to have known better. Why couldn't they take their rubbish away with them?"

"People that leave rubbish about in beautiful places like this are just rubbishy people themselves!" cried Peggy fiercely, almost in tears. "Nice people never do it. I'd like to put those people into a big dustbin with all their horrid rubbish on top of them—and wouldn't I bang on the lid, too!"

The other laughed. It sounded so funny. But they were all angry about their beach being spoilt.

"I'll clear up the mess and burn it," said Mike.

"Wait a minute!" said Jack. "We might find some of the things useful."

"What! Old banana skins and orange-peel!" cried Mike. "You're not thinking of making a pudding or something of them, Jack!"

"No," said Jack, with a grin, "But if we keep the tin and a carton and the empty cigarette packet in our cave-cupboard, we might put them out on the beach if anyone else ever comes—and then, if they happen to find the remains of our fire, or a bit of string or anything like that—why, they won't think of looking for us—they'll just think trippers have been here!"

"Good idea, Jack!" cried everyone.

"You really are good at thinking out clever things," said Peggy, busy getting the fire going. Its crackling sounded very cheerful, for they were all hungry. Peggy put some milk on to boil. She meant to make cocoa for them all to drink.

Mike picked up the cigarette packet, the tin, and one of the cardboard cartons. He washed the carton and the tin in the lake, and then went to put the three things away in their little cave-cupboard. They might certainly come in useful some day!

Nora brought in five eggs for breakfast. Peggy fried them with two trout that Jack had caught on his useful lines. The smell was delicious!

"I say! Poor old Daisy *must* be milked!" said Jack, gobbling down his breakfast and drinking his hot cocoa.

Suddenly Nora gave a squeal and pointed behind him. Jack turned—and to his great astonishment he saw the cow walking towards him!

"You wouldn't go to milk her in time so she has come to you!" laughed Peggy. "Good old Daisy! Fancy her knowing the way!"

Nora Gets Into Trouble

There seemed quite a lot of jobs always waiting to be done each day on the island. Daisy had to be milked. The hens had to be seen to. The fishing-lines had to be baited and looked at two or three times a day. The fire had to be kept going. Meals had to be prepared and dishes washed up. Willow House had to be tidied up each day, for it was surprising how untidy it got when the four children were in it even for an hour.

"I'll milk Daisy each morning and Mike can milk her in the evenings," said Jack, as they sat eating their breakfast that morning. "Nora, you can look after the hens. It won't only be your job to feed them and give them water and collect the eggs, but you'll have to watch the fence round the hen-yard carefully to see that the hens don't peck out the heather we've stuffed into the fence to stop up the holes. We don't want to lose our hens!"

"What is Peggy going to do?" asked Nora.

"Peggy had better do the odd jobs," said Jack. "She can look after the fire, think of meals and tidy up. I'll see to my fishing-lines. And every now and again one or other of us had better go to the top of the hill to see if any more trippers are coming. Our plans worked quite well last time—but we were lucky enough to spot the boat coming. If we hadn't seen it when we did, we would have been properly caught!"

"I'd better go and get the boat out from where I hid it under the overhanging bushes, hadn't I?" said Mike, finishing his cocoa.

"No," said Jack. "It would be a good thing to keep it always hidden there except when we need it. Now I'm off to milk Daisy!"

He went off, and the children heard the welcome sound of the creamy milk splashing into a saucepan, for they still had no milking-pail. Mike and Jack were determined to get one that night! It was so awkward to keep milking a cow into saucepans and kettles!

Peggy began to clear away and wash up the dishes. Nora wanted to help her, but Peggy said she had better go and feed the hens. So off she went, making the little clucking noise that the hens knew. They came rushing to her as she climbed over the fence of their little yard.

Nora scattered the seed for them, and they gobbled it up, scratching hard with their strong clawed feet to find any they had missed. Nora gave them some water, too. Then she took a look round the fence to see that it was all right.

It seemed all right. The little girl didn't bother to look very hard, because she wanted to go off to the raspberry patch up on the hillside and see if there were any more wild raspberries ripe. If she had looked carefully, as she should have done, she would have noticed quite a big hole in the fence, where one of the hens had been pecking out the bracken and heather. But she didn't notice. She picked up a basket Peggy had made of thin twigs, and set off.

"Are you going to find raspberries, Nora?" called Peggy.

"Yes!" shouted Nora.

"Well, bring back as many as you can, and we'll have them for pudding at dinner-time with cream!" shouted Peggy. "Don't eat them all yourself!"

"Come with me and help me!" cried Nora, not too pleased at the thought of having to pick raspberries for everyone.

"I've got to get some water from the spring," called back Peggy; "and I want to do some mending."

So Nora went alone. She found a patch of raspberries she hadn't seen yesterday, and there were a great many ripe. The little girl ate dozens and then began to fill her basket with the sweet juicy fruit. She heard Jack taking Daisy the cow back to her grassy field on the other side of the island. She heard Mike whistling as he cut some willow stakes down in the thicket, ready for use if they were wanted. Everyone was busy and happy.

Nora sat down in the sun and leaned against a warm rock that jutted out from the hillside. She felt very happy indeed. The lake was as blue as a forget-me-not down below her. Nora lazed there in the sun until she heard Mike calling:

"Nora! Nora! Wherever are you! You've been hours!"

"Coming!" cried Nora, and she made her way through the raspberry canes, round the side of the hill, through the heather and bracken, and down to the beach, where all the others were. Peggy had got the fire going well, and was cooking a rabbit that Jack had produced.

"Where are the raspberries?" asked Jack. "Oh, you've got a basketful! Good! Go and skim the cream off the milk in that bowl over there, Nora. Put it into a jug and bring it back. There will be plenty for all of us."

Soon they were eating their dinner. Peggy was certainly a good little cook. But nicest of all were the sweet juicy raspberries with thick yellow cream poured all over them! How the children did enjoy them!

"The hens are very quiet today," said Jack, finishing up the last of his cream. "I haven't heard a single cluck since we've been having dinner!"

"I suppose they're all right?" said Peggy.

"I'll go and have a look," said Mike. He put down his plate and went to the hen-yard. He looked here—and he looked there—he lifted up the sack that was stretched over one corner of the yard for shelter—but no hens were there!

"Are they all right?" called Jack.

Mike turned in dismay. "No!" he said. "They're not here! They've gone!"

"Gone!" cried Jack, springing up in astonishment. "They can't have gone! They must be there!"

"Well, they're not," said Mike. "They've completely vanished! Not even a cluck left!"

All the children ran to the hen-yard and gazed in amazement and fright at the empty space.

"Do you suppose someone has been here and taken them?" asked Peggy.

"No," said Jack sternly, "look here! This explains their disappearance!"

He pointed to a hole in the fence of the hen-yard. "See that hole! They've all escaped through there—and now goodness knows where they are!"

"Well, I never heard them go," said Peggy. "I was the only one left here. They must have gone when I went to get water from the spring!"

"Then the hole must have been there when Nora fed the hens this morning," said Jack. "Nora, what do you mean by doing your job as badly as that? Didn't I tell you this morning that you were to look carefully round the fence each time the hens were fed to make sure it was safe? And now, the very first time, you let the hens escape! I'm ashamed of you!"

"Our precious hens!" said Peggy, in dismay.

"You might do your bit, Nora," said Mike. "It's too bad of you."

Nora began to cry, but the others had no sympathy for her. It was too big a disappointment to lose their hens. They began to hunt round to see if by chance the hens were hidden anywhere near.

Nora cried more and more loudly, till Jack got really angry with her. "Stop that silly baby noise!" he said. "Can't you help to look for the hens, too?"

85

"You're not to talk to me like that!" wept Nora.

"I shall talk to you how I like," said Jack. "I'm the captain here, and you've got to do as you're told. If one of us is careless we all suffer, and I won't have that! Stop crying, I tell you, and help to look for the hens."

Nora started to hunt, but she didn't stop crying. She felt so unhappy and ashamed and sad, and it was really dreadful to have all the others angry with her, and not speaking a word to her. Nora could hardly see to hunt for the hens.

"Well, they are nowhere about here!" said Jack, at last. "We'd better spread out and see if we can find them on the island somewhere. They may have wandered right to the other side. We'll all separate and hunt in different places. Peggy, you go that way, and I'll go over to Daisy's part."

The children separated and went different ways, calling to the hens loudly. Nora went where Jack had pointed. She called to the hens, too, but none came in answer. Wherever could they be?

What a hunt there was that afternoon for those vanished hens! It was really astonishing that not one could be found. Jack couldn't understand it! They were nowhere on the hill. They were not even in the little cave where Jack had hidden them the day before, because he looked. They were not among the raspberry canes. They were not in Daisy's field. They were not under the hedges. They were not anywhere at all, it seemed!

Nora grew more and more unhappy as the day passed. She felt that she really couldn't face the others if the hens were not found. She made a hidey-hole in the tall bracken and crouched there, watching the others returning to the camp for supper. They had had no tea and were hungry and thirsty. So was Nora—but nothing would make her go and join the others! No—she would rather stay where she was, all alone, than sit down with Mike, Jack and Peggy while they were still so cross and upset.

"Well, the hens are gone!" said Mike, as he joined Jack going down the hill to the beach.

"It's strange," said Jack. "They can't have flown off the island, surely!"

"It's dreadful, I think," said Peggy; "we did find their eggs so useful to eat."

Nora sat alone in the bracken. She meant to sleep there for the night. She thought she would never, never be happy again.

The others sat down by the fire, whilst Peggy made some cocoa, and doled out a rice pudding she had made. They wondered where Nora was.

"She'll be along soon, I expect," said Peggy.

They ate their meal in silence—and then—then oh, what a lovely sound came to their ears! Yes, it was "cluck, cluck, cluck!" And walking sedately down to the beach came all six hens! The children stared and stared and stared!

"Where *have* you been, you scamps?" cried Jack. "We've looked for you everywhere!"

"Cluckluck, cluckluck!" said the hens.

"You knew it was your meal-time, so you've come for it!" said Jack. "I say, you others! I wonder if we could let the hens go loose each day—oh no—we couldn't—they'd lay their eggs away and we'd never be able to find them!"

"I'll feed them," said Peggy. She threw them some corn and they pecked it up eagerly. Then they let Mike and Jack lift them into their mended yard and they settled down happily, roosting on the perch made for them at one end.

"We'd better tell Nora," said Jack. So they went up the hillside calling Nora. "Nora! Nora! Where are you?"

But Nora didn't answer! She crouched lower in the

bracken and hoped no one would find her. But Jack came upon her suddenly and shouted cheerfully. "Oh, there you are! The hens have all come back, Nora! They knew it was their meal-time, you see! Come and have your supper. We kept some for you."

Nora went with him to the beach. Peggy kissed her and said, "Now don't worry any more. It's all right. We've got all the hens safely again."

"Had I better see to the hens each day, do you think, instead of Nora?" Mike asked Jack. But Jack shook his head.

"No," he said. "That's Nora's job—and you'll see, she'll do it splendidly now, won't you, Nora?"

"Yes, I will, Jack," said Nora, eating her rice pudding, and feeling much happier. "I do promise I will! I'm so sorry I was careless."

"That's all right," said the other three together—and it *was* all right, for they were all kind-hearted and fond of one another.

"But what *I'd* like to know," said Peggy, as she and Nora washed the dirty things, "is *where* did those hens manage to hide themselves so cleverly?"

The children soon knew—for when, in a little while, Mike went to fetch something from Willow House he saw three shining eggs in the heather there! He picked them up and ran back to the others.

"Those cunning hens walked into Willow House and hid there!" he cried, holding up the eggs.

"Well, well, well!" said Jack, in surprise. "And to think how we hunted all over the island—and those rascally hens were near by all the time!"

The Caves In The Hillside

The days slipped past, and the children grew used to their happy, carefree life on the island. Jack and Mike went off in the boat one night and fetched the old milking-pail from Aunt Harriet's farm, and a load of vegetables from the garden. The plums were ripening, too, and the boys brought back as many as would fill the milking-pail! How pleased the girls were to see them!

Now it was easy to milk Daisy, for they had a proper pail. Peggy cleaned it well before they used it, for it was dusty and dirty. When Jack or Mike had milked Daisy they stood the pail of milk in the middle of the little spring that gushed out from the hillside and ran down to the lake below. The icy-cold water kept the milk cool, and it did not turn sour, even on the hottest day.

Jack got out the packets of seeds he had brought from his grandfather's farm, and showed them to the others. "Look," he said, "here are lettuce seeds, and radish seeds, and mustard and cress, and runner beans! It's late to plant the beans, but in the good soil on this island I daresay they will grow quickly and we shall be able to have a crop later in the year."

"The mustard and cress and radish will grow very quickly!" said Peggy. "What fun! The lettuces won't be very long, either, this hot weather, if we keep them well watered."

"Where shall we plant them?" asked Mike.

"Well, we'd better plant them in little patches in different corners of the island," said Jack. "If we dig out a big patch and have a sort of vegetable garden, and anyone comes here to look for us, they will see our garden and know someone is here! But if we just plant out tiny patches, we can easily throw heather over them if we see anyone coming."

"Jack's always full of good ideas," said Nora. "I'll help to dig and plant, Jack."

"We'll all do it," said Jack. So together they hunted for good places, and dug up the ground there, and planted their precious seeds. It was Peggy's job to water them each day and see that no weeds choked the seeds when they grew.

"We're getting on!" said Nora happily. "Milk and cream each day, eggs each day, wild raspberries when we want them, and lettuces, mustard and cress, and radishes soon ready to be pulled!"

Jack planted the beans in the little bare places at the foot of a brambly hedge. He said they would be able to grow up the brambles, and probably wouldn't be noticed if anyone came. The bean seedlings were carefully watched and nursed until they were strong and tall, and had begun to twist themselves round any stem near. Then Peggy left them to themselves, only watering them when they needed it.

It was sometimes difficult to remember which day it was. Jack had kept a count as best he could, and sometimes on Sundays the children could hear a church bell ringing if the wind was in the right direction.

"We ought to try and keep Sunday a day of rest and peace," said Mike. "We can't go to church, but we could make the day a *good* sort of day, if you know what I mean."

So they kept Sunday quietly, and the little island always seemed an extra peaceful day then. They hardly ever knew what the other days were—whether it was Tuesday or Thursday or Wednesday! But Jack always told them when it was Sunday, and it was the one day they really knew. Nora said it had a different feel, and certainly the island seemed to know it was Sunday, and was a dreamier, quieter place then.

One day Jack said they must explore the caves in the hillside.

"If anyone does come here to look for us, and it's quite likely," he said, "we must really have all our plans made as to what to do, and know exactly where to hide. People who are really looking for us won't just sit about on that beach as the trippers did, you know—they will hunt all over the island."

"Well, let's go and explore the cave today," said Mike. "I'll get the lantern."

So, with the lantern swinging in his hand, and a box of matches ready in his pocket to light it, Jack led the way to the caves. The children had found three openings into the hillside—one where the hens had been put, another larger one, and a third very tiny one through which they could hardly crawl.

"We'll go in through the biggest entrance," said Jack. He lighted the lantern, and went into the dark cave. It seemed strange to leave the hot July sunshine. Nora shivered. She thought the caves were rather queer. But she didn't say anything, only kept very close to Mike.

Jack swung the lantern round and lit up all the corners. It was a large cave—but not of much use for hiding in, for every corner could be easily seen. Big cobwebs hung here and there, and there was a musty smell of bats.

Mike went all round the walls, peeping and prying—and right at the very back of the cave he discovered a curious thing. The wall was split from about six feet downwards, and a big crack, about two feet across, yawned there. At first it seemed as if the crack simply showed rock behind

In great excitement they explored the cave

it—but it didn't. There was a narrow, winding passage there, half hidden by a jutting-out piece of rock.

"Look here!" cried Mike, in excitement. "Here's a passage right in the very rock of the hillside itself. Come on, Jack, bring your lantern here. I wonder if it goes very far back."

Jack lifted up his lantern and the others saw the curious half-hidden passage, the entrance to which was by the crack in the wall. Jack went through the crack and walked a little way down the passage.

"Come on!" he cried. "It's all right! The air smells fresh here, and the passage seems to lead to somewhere."

The children crowded after him in excitement. What an adventure this was!

The passage wound here and there, and sometimes the children had to step over rocks and piles of fallen earth. Tree-roots stretched over their heads now and again. The passage was sometimes very narrow, but quite passable. And at last it ended—and Jack found that it led to an even larger cave right in the very middle of the hill itself! He lifted his lantern and looked round. The air smelt fresh and sweet. Why was that?

"Look!" cried Nora, pointing upwards. "I can see daylight!"

Sure enough, a long way up, a spot of bright daylight came through into the dark cave. Jack was puzzled. "I think some rabbits must have burrowed into the hill, and come out unexpectedly into this cave," he said. "And their hole is where we can see that spot of daylight. Well—the fresh air comes in, anyhow!"

From the big cave a low passage led to another cave on the right. This passage was so low that the children had to crawl through it—and to their surprise they found that this second cave led out to the hillside itself, and was no other than the cave into which it was so hard to crawl because of the small entrance.

"Well, we are getting on," said Jack. "We have discovered that the big cave we knew leads by a passage to an even bigger one—and from that big one we can get into this smaller one, which has an opening on to the hillside —and that opening is too small for any grown-up to get into!"

"What about the cave we put the hens into?" asked Nora.

"That must be just a little separate cave by itself," said Jack. "We'll go and see."

So they squeezed themselves out of the tiny entrance of the last cave, and went to the hen-cave. But this was quite ordinary—just a little low, rounded cave smelling strongly of bats.

They came out and sat on the hillside in the bright sunshine. It was lovely to sit there in the warmth after the cold, dark caves.

"Now listen," said Jack thoughtfully. "Those caves are going to be jolly useful to us this summer if anyone comes to get us. We could get Daisy into that big inner cave quite well, for one thing."

"Oh, Jack! She'd never squeeze through that narow, winding passage," said Peggy.

"Oh yes, she would," said Jack. "She'd come with me all right—and what's more, Daisy is going to practise going in and out there, so that if the time comes when she has really got to hide for a few hours, she won't mind. It wouldn't be any good putting her into that cave, and then having her moo fit to lift off the top of the hill!"

Everyone laughed. Mike nodded his head. "Quite right," he said. "Daisy will have to practise! I suppose the hens can go there quite well, too?"

"Easily," said Jack. "And so can we!"

"The only things we can't take into the cave are our boat and our house," said Mike.

"The boat would never be found under those brambles by the water," said Jack. "And I doubt if anyone would ever find Willow House either, for we have built it in the very middle of that thicket, and it is all *we* can do to squeeze through to it! Grown-ups could never get through. Why, we shall soon have to climb a tree and drop down to Willow House if the bushes and trees round it grow any more thickly!"

"I almost wish someone *would* come!" said Peggy. "It would be so exciting to hide away!"

"A bit *too* exciting!" said Jack. "Remember, there's a lot to be done as soon as we see anyone coming!"

"Hadn't we better plan it all out now?" said Mike. "Then we shall each know what to do."

"Yes," said Jack. "Well, I'll manage Daisy the cow, and go straight off to fetch her. Mike, you manage the hens and get them into a sack, and take them straight up to the cave. Peggy, you stamp out the fire and scatter the hot sticks. Also you must put out the empty cigarette packet, the tin, and the cardboard carton that the trippers left, so that it will look as if trippers have been here, and nobody will think it's funny to find the remains of a fire, or any other odd thing."

"And what shall I do?" asked Nora.

"You must go to the spring and take the pail of milk from there to the cave," said Jack. "Before you do that scatter heather over our patches of growing seeds. And Peggy, you might make certain the cave-cupboard is hidden by a curtain of bracken or something."

"Ay, ay, Captain!" said Peggy. "Now we've all got our duties to do—but you've got the hardest, Jack! I wouldn't like to hide Daisy away down that narrow passage! What will you do if she gets stuck?"

"She won't get stuck," said Jack. "She's not as fat as all that! By the way, we'd better put a cup or two in the cave, and some heather, in case we have to hide up for a good many hours. We can drink milk then, and have somewhere soft to lie on."

"We'd better keep a candle or two in the entrance," said Peggy. "I don't feel like sitting in the dark there."

"I'll tell you what we'll do," said Jack thoughtfully. "We won't go in and out of that big inner cave by the narrow passage leading from the outer cave. We'll go in and out by that tiny cave we can hardly squeeze in by. It leads to the inner cave, as we found out. If we keep using the other cave and the passage to go in, we are sure to leave marks, and give ourselves away. I'll have to take Daisy that way, but that can't be helped."

"Those caves will be cosy to live in in the winter-time," said Peggy. "We could live in the outer one, and store our things in the inner one. We should be quite protected from bad weather."

"How lucky we are!" said Nora. "A nice house made of trees for the summer—and a cosy cave-home for the winter!"

"Winter's a long way off yet," said Jack. "I say!—I'm hungry! What about frying some eggs, Peggy, and sending Mike to get some raspberries?"

"Come on!" shouted Peggy, and raced off down the hillside, glad to leave behind the dark, gloomy caves.

The Summer Goes By

No one came to interfere with the children. They lived together on the island, playing, working, eating, drinking, bathing—doing just as they liked, and yet having to do certain duties in order to keep their farmyard going properly.

Sometimes Jack and Mike went off in the boat at night to get something they needed from either Jack's farm or Aunt Harriet's. Mike managed to get into his aunt's house one night and get some of his and the girls' clothes—two or three dresses for the girls, and a coat and shorts for himself. Clothes were rather a difficulty, for they got dirty and ragged on the island, and as the girls had none to change into, it was difficult to keep their dresses clean and mended.

Jack got a good deal of fruit and a regular amount of potatoes and turnips from his grandfather's farm, which still had not been sold. There was always enough to eat, for there were eggs, rabbits, and fish, and Daisy gave them more than enough milk to drink.

Their seeds grew quickly. It was a proud day when Peggy was able to cut the first batch of mustard and cress and the first lettuce and mix it up into a salad to eat with hard-boiled eggs! The radishes, too, tasted very good, and were so hot that even Jack's eyes watered when he ate them! Things grew amazingly well and quickly on the island.

The runner beans were now well up to the top of the bramble bushes, and Jack nipped the tips off, so that they would flower well below.

"We don't want to have to make a ladder to climb up and pick the beans," he said. "My word, there are going to be plenty—look at all the scarlet flowers!"

"They smell nice!" said Nora, sniffing them.

"The beans will taste nicer!" said Jack.

The weather was hot and fine, for it was a wonderful summer. The children all slept out of doors in their "green bedroom," as they called it, tucked in the shelter of the big gorse bushes. They had to renew their beds of heather and bracken every week, for they became flattened with the weight of their bodies and were uncomfortable. But these jobs were very pleasant, and the children loved them.

"How brown we are!" said Mike one day, as they sat round the fire on the beach, eating radishes, and potatoes cooked in their jackets. They all looked at one another.

"We're as brown as berries," said Nora.

"What berries?" said Mike. "I don't know any brown berries. Most of them are red!"

"Well, we're as brown as oak-apples!" said Nora. They certainly were. Legs, arms, faces, necks, knees—just as dark as could be! The children were fat, too, for although their food was a queer mixture, they had a great deal of creamy milk.

Although life was peaceful on the island, it had its excitements. Each week Jack solemnly led poor Daisy to the cave and made her squeeze through the narrow passage into the cave beyond. The first time she made a terrible fuss. She mooed and bellowed, she struggled and even kicked—but Jack was firm and kind and led her inside. There, in the inner cave, he gave her a juicy turnip, fresh-pulled from his grandfather's farm the night before. Daisy was pleased. She chewed it all up, and was quite good when she was led back through the passage once more.

The second time she made a fuss again, but did not kick, nor did she bellow quite so loudly. The third time she seemed quite pleased to go, because she knew by now that a fine turnip awaited her in the cave. The fourth time she even went into the cave by herself and made her way solemnly to the passage at the far end.

"It's an awfully tight squeeze," said Mike, from the back. "If Daisy grows any fatter she won't be able to get through, Jack."

"We won't meet our troubles half-way," said Jack cheerfully. "The main thing is, Daisy likes going into the cave now, and won't make a fuss if ever the time comes when she has to be put there in a hurry."

July passed into August. The weather was thundery and hot. Two or three thunderstorms came along, and the children slept in Willow House for a few nights. Jack suggested sleeping in the cave, but they all voted it would be too hot and stuffy. So they settled down in Willow House, and felt glad of the thick green roof above them, and the stout, heather-stuffed walls.

The wild raspberries ripened by the hundred. Wild strawberries began to appear in the shady parts of the island—not tiny ones, such as the children had often found round the farm, but big, sweet, juicy ones, even nicer than garden ones. They tasted most delicious with cream. The blackberries grew ripe on the bushes that rambled all over the place, and the children's mouths were always stained with them, for they picked them as they went about their various jobs.

Jack picked them on his way to milk Daisy, and so did Mike. Peggy picked them as she went to get water from the spring. Nora picked them as she went to feed the hens.

Nuts were ripening, too, but were not yet ready. Jack looked at the heavy clusters on the hazel-trees and longed for them to be ripe. He went to have a look at the beans.

They were ready to be picked! The runners grew up the brambles, and the long green pods were mixed up with the blackberry flowers and berries.

"Beans for dinner today!" shouted Jack. He went to fetch one of the many baskets that Peggy knew how to weave from willow twigs, and soon had it full of the juicy green beans.

Another time Jack remembered the mushrooms that used to grow in the field at the end of his grandfather's farm. He and Mike set off in the boat one early morning at the end of August to see if they could find some.

It was a heavenly morning. Mike wished they had brought the girls, too, but it would not do to take a crowd. Someone might see them. It was just sunrise. The sun rose up in the east and the whole sky was golden. A little yellow-hammer sang loudly on a nearby hedge, "Little bits of bread and no cheese!" A crowd of young sparrows chirruped madly in the trees. Dew was heavy on the grass, and the boys' bare feet were dripping wet. They were soaked to the knees, but they didn't mind. The early sun was warm, and all the world was blue and gold and green.

"Mushrooms!" said Jack, in delight, pointing to where two or three grew. "Look—fresh new ones, only grown up last night. Come on! Fill the sack!"

There were scores in the field. Jack picked the smaller ones, for he knew the bigger ones did not taste so nice and might have maggots in them. In half an hour their sack was full and they slipped away through the sunny fields to where they had moored their boat.

"What a breakfast we'll have!" grinned Jack. And they did! Fried mushrooms and fried eggs, wild strawberries and cream! The girls had gone out strawberry hunting whilst the boys had gone to look for mushrooms.

Nora learnt to swim well. She and Peggy practised every day in the lake till Jack said they were as good as he and

Mike were. They were soon like fish in the water, and tumbled and splashed about each day with yells and shrieks. Jack was clever at swimming under water and would disappear suddenly and come up just beside one of the others, clutching hard at their legs! What fun they had!

Then there came a spell of bad weather—just a few days. The island seemed very different then, with the sun gone, a soft rain-mist driving over it, soaking everything, and the lake-water as cold as ice.

Nora didn't like it. She didn't like feeding the hens in the rain. She asked Peggy to do it for her. But Jack heard her and was cross.

"You're not to be a fair-weather person," he told her. "It's all very well to go about happily when the sun is shining and do your jobs with a smile—but just you be the same when we get bad weather!"

"Ay, ay, Captain!" said Nora, who was learning not to be such a baby as she had been. And after that she went cheerfully out to feed the hens, even though the rain trickled down her neck and ran in a cold stream down her brown back.

They were rather bored when they had to keep indoors in Willow House when it rained. They had read all their books and papers by that time, and although it was fun to play games for a while, they couldn't do it all day long. Peggy didn't mind—she had always plenty of mending to do.

She showed the boys and Nora how to weave baskets. They needed a great many, for the baskets did not last very long, and there were always raspberries, strawberries, or blackberries to pick. Mike, Jack and Nora thought it was fun to weave all kinds and shapes of baskets, and soon they had a fine selection of them ready for sunny weather.

Then the sun came back again and the children lay

about in it and basked in the hot rays to get themselves warm once more. The hens fluffed out their wet feathers and clucked happily. Daisy came out from under the tree which gave her shelter, and gave soft moos of pleasure. The world was full of colour again and the children shouted for joy.

The beans, radishes, lettuces, and mustard and cress grew enormously in the rain. Jack and Mike picked a good crop, and everyone said that never had anything tasted so delicious before as the rain-swollen lettuces, so crisp, juicy, and sweet.

All sorts of little things happened. The hole in the boat grew so big that one day, when Mike went to fetch the boat from its hiding-place, it had disappeared! It had sunk into the water! Then Jack and Mike had to use all their brains and all their strength to get it up again and to mend it so that it would not leak quite so badly.

The corn for the hens came to an end, and Jack had to go and see if he could find some more. There was none at his grandfather's farm, so he went to Mike's farm—and there he found some in a shed, but was nearly bitten by a new dog that had been bought for the farm. The dog bit a hole in his trousers, and Peggy had to spend a whole morning mending them.

Another time there was a great alarm, because Nora said she had heard the splashing of oars. Jack rushed off to get Daisy, and Mike bundled the hens into a sack—but, as nothing more seemed to happen, Peggy ran to the top of the hill and looked down the lake.

No boat was in sight—only four big white swans, quarrelling among themselves, and slashing the water with their feet and wings!

"It's all right, boys!" she shouted. "It's only the swans! It isn't a boat!"

So Daisy was left in peace and the hens were emptied

out of the sack again. Nora was teased, and made up her mind that she would make quite certain it *was* a boat next time she gave the alarm!

One day Jack slipped down the hillside when he was reaching for raspberries and twisted his ankle. Mike had to help him back to the camp on the beach. Jack was very pale, for it was a bad twist.

Peggy ran to get some clean rags and soaked them in the cold spring water. She bound them tightly round Jack's foot and ankle.

"You mustn't use it for a while," she said. "You must keep quiet. Mike will do your jobs."

So Jack had to lie about quietly for a day or two, and he found this very strange. But he was a sensible boy, and he knew that it was the quickest way to get better. Soon he found that he could hop about quite well with a stout hazel stick Mike cut for him from the hedges—and after a week or so his foot was quite all right.

Another time poor Peggy overbalanced and fell into a gorse bush below her on the hill. She was dreadfully scratched, but she didn't even cry. She went to the lake and washed her scratches and cuts, and then got the supper just as usual. Jack said he was very proud of her. "Anybody else would have yelled the place down!" he said, looking at the scratches all over her arms and legs.

"It's nothing much," said Peggy, boiling some milk. "I'm lucky not to have broken my leg or something!"

So, with these little adventures, joys, and sorrows, the summer passed by. No one came to the island, and gradually the children forgot their fears of being found, and thought no more of it.

Jack Does Some Shopping

The summer passed away. The days grew gradually shorter. The children found that it was not always warm enough to sit by the camp-fire in the evenings, and they went to Willow House, where they could light the lantern and play games. Willow House was always cosy.

They had had to stuff the walls again with heather and bracken, for some of it crumbled away and then the wind blew in. All the willow stakes they had used in the making of the walls had put out roots, and now little tufts of green, pointed leaves jutted out here and there up the sticks! The children were pleased. It was fun to have walls and a roof that grew!

One day Mike got a shock. He went to get another candle for the lantern—and found that there was only one left! There were very few matches left, too, for although the children were careful with these, and only used one when the fire had gone out, they had to use them sometimes.

"I say, Jack, we've only got one candle left," said Mike.

"We'll have to get some more, then," said Jack.

"How?" asked Mike. "They don't grow on trees!"

"Jack means he'll go and get some from somewhere," said Peggy, who was mending a hole in Jack's shirt. She was so glad she had been sensible enough to bring her work-basket with her to the secret island. She could stop their clothes from falling to pieces by keeping an eye on them, and stitching them as soon as they were torn.

"But where could he get candles except in a shop?" said Mike.

"Well, I've been thinking," said Jack seriously. "I've been thinking very hard. The autumn is coming, when we shall need a better light in the evenings. We shall need another blanket, too. And there are all sorts of little things we want."

"I badly want some more mending wool and some black cotton," said Peggy. "I had to mend your grey trousers with blue wool yesterday, Jack."

"And I'll have to have some more corn for the hens soon," said Nora.

"And it *would* be nice if we could get some flour," said Peggy. "Because if I had a bag of flour I could make you little rolls of bread sometimes—I just long for bread, don't you!"

"It would be nice," said Jack. "Well, listen, everyone. Don't you think it would be a good idea if I took the boat and went to the village at the other end of the lake and bought some of the things we badly need?"

The others all cried out in surprise.

"You'd be caught!"

"You haven't any money to buy things with!"

"Oh, don't go, Jack!"

"I shouldn't be caught," said Jack. "I'd be very careful. No one knows me at that village. Anyway, if you're afraid, I'll go on to the next village—only it's five miles away and I'd be jolly tired carrying back all the things we want."

"But what about money, Jack?" said Peggy.

"I'd thought of that," said Jack. "If Mike will help me to pick a sackful of mushrooms early one moning, I could bring them back here, arrange them in the willow baskets we make, and then take them to the village to sell. With the money I get I'll buy the things we want."

"Oh, that *is* a good idea, Jack," said Peggy. "If only you don't get caught!"

"Don't worry about that, silly," said Jack. "Now we'd better make out a list of things we want, and I'll try and get them when I go."

"I wish we could have a book or two," said Peggy.

"And a pencil would be nice," said Nora. "I like drawing things."

"And a new kettle," said Peggy. "Ours leaks a bit now."

"And a few more nails," said Mike.

"And the flour and the wool and the black cotton," said Peggy.

So they went on, making up a list of things they would like to have. Jack said them all over, and counted them up so that he wouldn't forget them.

"Mike and I will get the mushrooms from the field over the water tomorrow morning," he said.

"And I say, Jack—do you suppose you could sell some wild strawberries if you took them?" asked Nora eagerly. "I know where there are lots. I found a whole patch yesterday, ever so big, and very sweet!"

"That's a splendid idea," said Jack, pleased. "Look here, we'll make lots of little baskets today, and then we will arrange the mushrooms and strawberries neatly in them and I'll take them in the boat to sell. We should make a lot of money!"

The children were really excited. Mike went off to get a supply of thin willow twigs, and Peggy ran to get some rushes. She had discovered that she could make dainty baskets from the rushes, too, and she thought those would be nice for the strawberries.

Soon all four children were sitting on the sunny hillside among the heather, weaving the baskets. The boys were as good at it as the girls now, and by the time the sun was sinking there was a fine array of baskets. Peggy counted them. There were twenty-seven!

106

"I say! If we can fill and sell all those, Jack, you will have plenty of money to buy everything," said Mike.

The children went to bed early, for they knew they would have to be up at dawn the next day. They had no watches or clocks, and the only way to wake up early was to go to bed early! They knew that. It was a warm night, so they slept in their outdoor bedroom among the gorse bushes, lying cosily on their heather beds. Nothing ever woke them now, as it had done at first. A hedgehog could crawl over Jack's legs and he wouldn't stir! A bat could flick Mike's face and he didn't even move.

Once a little spider had made a web from Peggy's nose to her shoulder, and when Nora awoke and saw it there she called the boys. How they laughed to see a web stretching from Peggy's nose, and a little spider in the middle of it! They woke Peggy up and told her—but she didn't mind a bit!

"Spiders are lucky!" she said. "I shall have some luck today!" And so she did—for she found her scissors, which she had lost the week before!

The children awoke early, just as the daylight was putting a sheet of silver over the eastern sky. A robin was tick-tick-ticking near by and burst into a little creamy song when the children awoke. He was not a bit afraid of them, for they all loved the birds and fed them with crumbs after every meal. The robin was very tame and would often sit on Peggy's shoulder whilst she prepared the meals. She liked this very much.

They all got up and had their dip in the lake. Peggy thought of one more thing they wanted—a bar of soap! Their one piece was finished—and it was difficult to rub dirt off with sand, which they had to do now they had no soap. Jack added that to the list in his mind—that made twenty-one things wanted! What a lot!

"Mike and I won't be very long picking mushrooms," he

said, as he got into the boat and pushed off. "You and Nora go and pick the strawberries, Peggy. Have a kettle boiling on the fire when we come back so that we can have something hot to drink. It's rather chilly this morning."

How busy the four children were as the sun rose! Mike and Jack were away in the mushroom field, picking as many mushrooms as they could, and stuffing them into the big sack they carried. Nora and Peggy were picking the wild strawberries on the island. Certainly the patch Nora had found was a wonderful one. Deep red strawberries glowed everywhere among the pretty leaves, and some of the berries were as big as garden ones.

"Don't they look pretty in our little green baskets?" said Peggy, pleased. The girls had taken some of their baskets with them, and had lined them with strawberry leaves first. Then neatly and gently they were putting the ripe strawberries in.

"I should think Jack could sell these baskets of strawberries for sixpence each," said Peggy. "They are just right for eating."

The girls filled twelve of the rush baskets, and then went back to light the camp-fire. It was soon burning well, and Peggy hung the kettle over the flames to boil. Nora went to feed the hens.

"I'll milk Daisy, I think," said Peggy. "It is getting about milking-time, and the boys won't have time this morning. Watch the fire, Nora, and take the kettle off when it boils."

Soon the boys were back, happy to show the girls such a fine collection of white mushrooms. Peggy had finished milking Daisy and there was soon hot tea for everyone. The tin of cocoa had long been finished, and was added to the list that Jack had in his mind.

Whilst the boys were having breakfast of fried eggs and mushrooms, with a few wild strawberries and cream to follow, the two girls were busy arranging the fine mushrooms in the willow baskets, which were bigger and stronger than the rush strawberry ones. There were more than enough to fill the baskets.

Peggy and Nora carried the full baskets carefully to the boat. They put them safely at the far end and covered them with elder leaves so that the flies would not get at them. The flies did not like the smell of the elder leaves.

The boys set off in the boat. It had been arranged that they should both go to the far end of the lake, but that only Jack should go to sell their goods and to shop. One boy alone would not be so much noticed. Mike was to wait in the boat, hidden somewhere by the lakeside, till Jack returned. Mike had some cold cooked fish and some milk, for it might be some hours before Jack came back.

"Here's a good place to put the boat," said Jack, as he and Mike rowed up the lake, and came in sight of the village at the far end. An alder tree leaned over the water by the lakeside, and Mike guided the boat there. It slid under the drooping tree and Jack jumped out.

"I can easily find my way to the village from here," he said. "I'll be as quick as I can, Mike."

Jack had two long sticks, and on them he threaded the handles of the baskets of mushrooms and strawberries. In this way he could carry them easily, without spilling anything. Off he went with his goods through the wood, and Mike settled down in the boat to wait for his return.

Jack was not long in finding the road that led to the little village—and to his great delight he found that it was market-day there! A small market was held every Wednesday, and it happened to be Wednesday that day!

"Good!" thought Jack. "I shall not be so much noticed if there is a crowd of people—and I should be able to sell my goods easily!"

The boy went to the little market-place, calling "Fine

mushrooms! Ripe wild strawberries!" at the top of his voice.

When people saw the neat and pretty baskets of mushrooms and strawberries they stopped to look at them. Certainly they were excellent goods, and very soon Jack was selling them fast. Shillings and sixpences clinked into his pocket, and Jack felt very happy. What a fine lot of things he would be able to buy!

At last his sticks held no more baskets. The people praised him for his goods and the cleverly woven baskets, and told him to come again. Jack made up his mind that he would. It was a pleasant way of earning money, and he could buy all the things he needed if only he could get the money!

He went shopping. He bought a very large bag of flour. He bought wool and cotton for Peggy. He bought scores of candles and plenty of matches. He bought a new kettle and two enamel plates. Peggy was always wishing she had more dishes. He bought some storybooks, and two pencils and a rubber. A drawing-book was added to his collection, some nails, soap, butter for a treat, some bars of chocolate, some tins of cocoa, tea, rice—oh, Jack had a load to carry before he had done!

When he could carry no more, and his money was all gone, he staggered off to the boat. He kept thinking what fun everyone would have that night when he unpacked the bags and boxes!

Mike was waiting for him impatiently. He was delighted to see Jack, and helped him to dump the things into the boat. Then off they rowed, home to the secret island.

Jack Nearly Gets Caught

What fun it was that evening, unpacking all the things Jack had brought! Mike helped Jack to take everything to the beach, and Nora and Peggy jumped up and down and squealed with excitement.

"Flour! What a lot! I can make you rolls now to eat with your fish and eggs!" cried Peggy in delight. "And here's my wool—and my cotton!"

"And *two* pencils for me—and a rubber—and a drawing-book!" cried Nora.

"And butter—oh, and *chocolate*!" yelled Mike. "I've forgotten what chocolate tastes like!"

"Oh, Jack, you are clever," said Peggy. "Did you sell all the mushrooms and strawberries?"

"Every single basket," said Jack. "And what is more, the people told me to bring more next week—so I shall earn some more money, and lay in a good stock of things for the winter! What do you say to that?"

"Fine, Captain!" shouted everyone joyfully. "We shall be as cosy as can be with candles to see by, nice things to eat, books to read, chocolate to nibble! Hurrah!"

"Have you brought the corn for my hens, Jack?" asked Nora anxiously.

"Yes, there it is!" said Jack. "And what about this new kettle and enamel dishes, Peggy? I thought you'd like those."

"Oh, Jack, isn't it all exciting?" cried Peggy. "Look here—shall we have supper now—and look at all the things again afterwards—and then put them away

111

carefully? You and Mike will have to put up shelves in Willow House for all these new stores!"

Talking all at once and at the tops of their voices the children set to work to get supper. This was a rabbit stew, with runner beans picked by Nora and a baked potato each, with raspberries and cream afterwards. And as a special treat Jack gave everyone half a bar of the precious chocolate! The children were so happy—they really felt that they couldn't be any happier! The girls had been lonely all day without the two boys, and it was lovely to be all together again.

After supper they cleared away and washed the dishes, and then stamped out the fire. They took everything to Willow House, and lighted the lantern that hung from the roof. Jack also lighted another candle to make enough light to see clearly all the treasures he had brought.

"I say! What a nice lot of matches!" said Mike. "We'll have to store those carefully in a dry place."

"And look at the books!" squealed Peggy. "Jack can read them out loud to us in the evening. *Robinson Crusoe*, and *Stories from the Bible* and *Animals of the World* and *The Boy's Book of Aeroplanes*. What a lovely lot! It will be fun to read about Robinson Crusoe, because he was alone on the island, just as we are. I guess we could teach him a few things, though!"

Everyone laughed. "He could teach *us* a few things, too!" said Jack.

Jack had really shopped very well. He had even bought a tin of treacle, so that sometimes, for a treat, Peggy could make toffee! He had got sugar, too, which would be nice in their tea and cocoa. Their own sugar had been finished long ago.

"And we needn't be too careful now of all our things," said Jack, "because I can go each week and sell

112

mushrooms and strawberries and earn money to buy more."

"But what will you do when the mushrooms and strawberries are over?" asked Peggy.

"Then there will be blackberries and nuts," said Jack. "They won't fetch so much money, but at any rate I can get enough to store up plenty of things for the winter. If we can get flour, potatoes, rice, cocoa, and things like that, we shall be quite all right. Daisy can always give us milk and cream, and we get lots of eggs from the hens, fish from the lake, and a rabbit or two. We are really very lucky."

"Jack, read to us tonight," begged Nora. "It's so long since I heard a story."

"We'll begin *Robinson Crusoe* first, then," said Jack. "That seems sort of suitable. By the way, Nora, can you read yourself?"

"Well, I wasn't very good at it," said Nora.

"I think it would be a good idea if we all took a night each to read out loud," said Jack. "It's no good forgetting what we learnt. I'll read tonight—and you shall read tomorrow night, Nora."

So, by the light of the two candles, Jack began reading the tale of Robinson Crusoe to the others. They lay on the heather, listening, happy to be together, enjoying the tale. When Jack shut up the book they sighed.

"That was lovely," said Peggy. "My goodness, Jack, I guess we could write an exciting book if we wrote down all our adventures on the island!"

"Nobody would believe them!" laughed Jack. "Yet it's all true—here we are, living by ourselves, feeding ourselves, having a glorious time on a secret island that nobody knows!"

The next day Jack and Mike rigged up some shelves on which to keep some of their new stores. It was fun arranging everything. The children soon began to make out their next list of things for Jack to buy when he went to market.

"We shall have to keep the days pretty carefully in future," said Jack. "I don't want to miss Wednesdays now because Wednesday is market-day at the village. I shall get better prices then."

So, the next Wednesday, once again there was a great stir just about dawn, and the four children hurried to their tasks of picking mushrooms and strawberries. They had made plenty of baskets again, and Jack and Mike set off two or three hours later with the boat, taking the full baskets with them.

For three or four weeks Jack went to market, sold all his goods, and bought a great many stores for the winter. He and Mike decided to store the bags and sacks of goods in the inner cave of the hillside, as there they would be quite dry—and, as the children would probably have to live in the caves in the winter, the stores would be quite handy there.

As the weeks went by there were not so many wild strawberries to be found. Mushrooms stopped growing in the field, and other market goods had to take their place. The children went nutting in the hazel trees and struck down great clusters of ripe nuts, lovely in their ragged green coats and brown shells. The girls picked baskets of big ripe blackberries, and Jack took these to the market instead of mushrooms and strawberries.

People soon grew to know him at the market. They wondered where he came from, but Jack never told them anything about himself.

"I just live by the lakeside," he said, when people asked him where he lived. They thought he meant somewhere by the lake—they did not know he meant by the lakeside on the secret island—and certainly Jack was not going to tell them!

One day, for the first time, Jack saw a policeman in the village. This struck him as strange, for he had never seen one there before, and he knew that the village was too small to have a policeman of its own. It shared one with the village five miles away. Jack's heart sank—could the policeman have been told that a strange boy was about—and could he be wondering if the boy was one of the lost children! Jack began to edge away, though his baskets of nuts and blackberries were only half sold.

"Hi, you!" called the policeman suddenly. "Where do you come from, boy?"

"From the lakeside, where I've been gathering blackberries and nuts to sell," said Jack, not coming near the policeman.

"Is your name Mike?" said the policeman.

And then Jack knew for certain that the policeman had been told that maybe he, Jack, *was* one of the four runaway children—and he had come to find out.

"No, that's not my name," said Jack, looking very innocent. "Buy some nuts, Mister Policeman?"

"No," said the policeman, getting a strip of paper out of his pocket, and looking at a photograph there. "Come you here, my lad. I think you're one of the runaway children —let's have a look at you."

Jack turned pale. If the policeman had a picture of him, he was caught! Quick as lightning the boy flung down the two sticks on which he had a dozen or so baskets strung, and darted off through the crowd that had gathered. Hands were put out to stop him, but he struggled away, tearing his jacket, but not caring for anything but to escape.

He slipped round a corner and into a garden. He darted round the cottage there and peered into the back garden. There was no one there—but there was a little henhouse at the side. Jack made up his mind quickly. He opened the door of the henhouse, slipped inside, and crouched down in the straw there, hardly daring to breathe. There were no hens there—they were scratching about in the little run outside.

Jack heard the sound of shouting and running feet, and he knew that people were looking for him. He crouched lower, hoping that no one had seen him dart into the cottage garden.

The running feet went by. The shouting died down. No one had seen him! Jack let out a big breath, and his heart thumped loudly. He was really frightened.

He stayed in the henhouse all day long. He did not dare to move out. He was hungry and thirsty and very cramped, but he knew quite well that if he slipped out he might be seen. He must stay there till night. He wondered what Mike would think. The girls would be anxious, too.

A hen came in, sat on a nesting-box and laid an egg. She cackled and went out again. Another came in and laid an egg. Jack hoped that no one would see him if they came looking for eggs that afternoon!

Someone did come for the eggs—but it was after tea and the henhouse was very dark. The door was opened and a head came round. A hand was stretched out and felt in all the boxes. The eggs were lifted out—the door was shut again! Jack hadn't been seen! He was crouching against the other side of the house, well away from the nesting-boxes!

The henhouse did not smell nice. Jack felt miserable as he sat there on the floor. He knew that by running away he had as good as told the policeman that he was one of the runaways. And now the whole countryside would be searched again, and the secret island would probably be explored, too.

"But if I hadn't run away the policeman would have caught me and made me tell where the others were,"

116

thought the boy. "If only I can get back to where Mike is waiting with the boat, and get back safely to the island, we can make preparations to hide everything."

When it was dark, and the hens were roosting in the house beside him, Jack opened the door and slipped out. He stood listening. Not a sound was to be heard except the voices of people in the kitchen of the cottage near by.

He ran quietly down the path to the gate. He slipped out into the road—and then ran for his life to the road that led to the wood by the lakeside where Mike was waiting.

But would Mike be waiting there? Suppose people had begun to hunt already for the four children—and had found Mike and the boat! What then? How would he get back to the girls on the island?

Jack forgot his hunger and thirst as he padded along at top speed to where he had left Mike. No one saw him. It was a dark night, for the moon was not yet up. Jack made his way through the trees to the lakeside.

And then his heart leapt for joy! He heard Mike's voice! "Is that you, Jack? What a time you've been! Whatever's happened?"

The Great Hunt Begins

Jack scrambled into the boat, panting. "Push off, quickly, Mike!" he said. "I was nearly caught today, and if anyone sees us we shall all be discovered!"

Mike pushed off, his heart sinking. He could not bear the idea of being caught and sent back to his uncle's farm. He waited till Jack had got back his breath and then asked him a few questions. Jack told him everything. Mike couldn't help smiling when he thought of poor Jack sitting with the hens in the hen-house—but he felt very frightened. Suppose Jack had been caught!

"This is the end of my marketing," said Jack gloomily. "I shan't dare to show my nose again in any village. They will all be on the look-out for me. Why can't people run away if they want to? We are not doing any harm—only living happily together on our secret island!"

After a bit Jack helped Mike to row, and they arrived at the island just as the moon was rising. The girls were on the beach by a big fire, waiting anxiously for them.

"Oh Jack, oh Mike!" cried Nora, hugging them both, and almost crying with delight, at seeing them again. "We thought you were never coming! We imagined all kinds of dreadful things! We felt sure you had been caught!"

"I jolly nearly *was*," said Jack.

"Where is your shopping" asked Peggy.

"Haven't got any," said Jack. "I had only sold a few baskets when a policeman spotted me. I've got the money for the ones I sold—but what's the good of money on this island, where you can't buy anything!"

Mike and Jack pulled hard at the oars

Soon Jack had told the girls his story. He sat by the fire, warming himself, and drinking a cup of hot cocoa. He was dreadfully hungry, too, for he had had nothing to eat all day. He ate a whole rice pudding, two fishes, and a hard-boiled egg whilst he talked.

Everyone was very grave and solemn. They knew things were serious. Nora was really scared. She tried her hardest not to cry, but Jack heard her sniffing and put his arm round her. "Don't be a baby," he said. "Things may not be so bad after all. We have all our plans laid. There is no real reason why anyone should find us if we are careful. We are all upset and tired. Let's go to bed and talk tomorrow."

So to bed in Willow House they went. Jack took off his clothes and wrapped himself in the old rug because he said he smelt like hens. Peggy said she would wash his things the next day. They did not get to sleep for a long time because first one and then another of them would say something, or ask a question—and then the talking would all begin again.

"Now, nobody is to say another word!" said Jack at last, in his firmest voice.

"Ay, ay, Captain!" said everyone sleepily. And not another word was spoken.

In the morning the children awoke early, and re-membered what had happened the day before. Nobody felt like singing or shouting or joking as they usually did. Peggy solemnly got the breakfast. Jack went off in his old overcoat to milk the cow, for his things were not yet washed. Mike got some water from the spring, and Nora fed the hens. It was not a very cheerful party that sat down to breakfast.

When the things were cleared away, and Peggy had washed Jack's clothes and set them out to dry, the children held a meeting.

"The first thing to do," said Jack, "is to arrange that someone shall always be on watch during the day, on the top of the hill. You can see all up the lake and down from there, and we should get good warning then if anyone were coming—we should have plenty of time to do everything."

"Shall we have someone on guard during the night?" asked Nora.

"No," said Jack. "People are not likely to come at night. We can sleep in peace. I don't think anyone will come for a few days, anyhow, because I think they will search around the lake-side first, and will only think of the island later."

"I think, as we are not going to the mainland for some time, we had better make a big hole in the boat and let her sink," said Mike. "I've always been afraid she might be found, although she is well hidden under the brambles. After all, Jack, if she is sunk, no one could possibly find her!"

"That's a good idea, Mike," said Jack. "We can't be too careful now. Sink her this morning. We can easily get her up again and mend her if we want her. Peggy, will you see that every single thing is cleared away that might show people we are here? Look, there's some snippings of wool, there—that sort of thing must be cleared up, for it tells a tale!"

"I'll see to it," promised Peggy. Jack knew she would, for she was a most dependable girl.

"Every single thing must be taken to the caves today," said Jack, "except just those few things we need for cooking, like a saucepan and kettle and so on. We can easily slip those away at the last minute. We will leave ourselves a candle or two in Willow House, because we can sleep there till we have to go to the caves."

"Jack, what about the hen-yard?" asked Nora. "It really

121

does look like a yard now, because the hens have scratched about so much."

"That's true," said Jack. "Well, as soon as we know we've got to hide, Mike can pull up the fence round the hen-yard and store it in Willow House. Then he can scatter sand over the yard and cover it with heather. It's a good thing you thought of that, Nora."

"There's one thing, even if we have to hide away for days, we've enough food!" said Peggy.

"What about Daisy, though?" said Mike. "She won't have anything to eat. A cow eats such a lot."

"We should have to take her out to feed at night," said Jack. "And by the way, Peggy, don't light the fire for cooking until the very last minute and stamp it out as soon as you have finished. A spire of smoke gives us away more than anything!"

"What about someone hopping up to the hill-top now?" said Mike. "The sun is getting high. We ought to keep a watch from now on."

"Yes, we ought," said Jack. "You take first watch, Mike. I'll give you a call when it's time to come down. We'll take turns all day long. Keep watch all round. We don't know from which end of the lake a boat might come, though it's more likely to be from the end I was at yesterday."

Mike sped up the hill and sat down there. The lake lay blue below him. Not a swan, not a moorhen disturbed its surface. Certainly no boat was in sight. Mike settled down to watch carefully.

The others were busy. Everything was taken up to the caves in the hillside and stored there. Nora left a sack by the hen-yard ready to bundle the hens into when the time came. She also put a pile of sand by the yard, ready for Mike to scatter after the fences had been pulled up. Nora was no longer the careless little girl she had been. Nor was she lazy any more. She had learned that when she did badly everyone suffered, so now she did her best—and it was a very good best too.

After a while Jack went up to take Mike's place on the hill-top. Mike set to work to sink the boat. She soon sank to the bottom of the water, under the bramble bushes. Mike felt sure that no one would ever know she was there.

Peggy went hunting round looking for anything that might give them away. She did not find very much, for all the children tidied up after any meal or game. Broken egg-shells were always buried, uneaten food was given to the hens, and it was only things like snippings of wool or cotton that the wind had blown away that could be found.

Peggy went on guard next and then Nora. It was dull work, sitting up on the hill-top doing nothing but watch, so Nora took her pencil and drawing-book and drew what she could see. That made the time go quickly. Peggy took her mending. She always had plenty of that to do, for every day somebody tore their clothes on brambles. After every stitch Peggy looked up and down the lake, but nothing could be seen.

That evening Mike was on guard, and he was just about to come down to get his supper when he saw something in the distance. He looked carefully. Could it be a boat? He called Jack.

"Jack! Come quickly! I can see something. Is it a boat, do you think?"

Everyone tore up the hill. Jack looked hard. "Well, if it's a boat, it's very small," he said.

"It's something black," said Nora. "Whatever is it? Oh, I do hope it isn't anyone coming now."

The children watched, straining their eyes. And suddenly the thing they thought might be a small boat flew up into the air!

"It's that black swan we saw the other day!" said Jack,

with a squeal of laughter. "What a fright it gave us! Look, there it goes! Isn't it a beauty?"

The children watched the lovely black swan flying slowly towards them, its wings making a curious whining noise as it came. Nora went rather red, for she remembered how frightened she had been the first time she had heard a swan flying over the island—but nobody teased her about it. They were all too thankful it was only a swan, not a boat.

"There's no need to keep watch any more tonight," said Jack, and they all went down the hill. Evening was almost on them. They sat by their fire and ate their supper, feeling happier than the day before. Perhaps after all no one would come to look for them—and anyway, they had done all they could now to get things ready in case anyone *did* come.

The next day the children kept watch in turn again, and the next. The third day, when Nora was on guard, she thought she saw people on the far side of the lake, where a thick wood grew. She whistled softly to Jack, and he came up and watched, too.

"Yes, you're right, Nora," he said at last. "There *are* people there—and they are certainly hunting for something or someone!"

They watched for a while and then they called the others. There was no fire going, for Peggy had stamped it out. They all crowded on to the hill-top, their heads peeping out of the tall bracken that grew there.

"See over there!" said Jack. "The hunt is on! It will only be a day or two before they come over here. We must watch very carefully indeed!"

"Well, everything is ready," said Peggy. "I wish they would come soon, if they are coming—I hate all this waiting about. It gives me a cold feeling in my tummy."

"So it does in mine," said Mike. "I'd like a hot-water bottle to carry about with me!"

That made everyone laugh. They watched for a while longer and then went down, leaving Jack on guard.

For two days nothing happened, though the children thought they could see people on the other side of the lake, beating about in the bushes and hunting. Mike went on guard in the morning and kept a keen watch. Nora fed the hens as usual and Jack milked Daisy.

And then Mike saw something! He stood up and looked—it was something at the far end of the lake, where Jack had gone marketing. It was a boat! No mistaking it this time—a boat it was, and a big one, too!

Mike called the others and they scrambled up. "Yes," said Jack at once. "That's a boat all right—with about four people in, too. Come on, there's no time to be lost. There's only one place a boat can come to here—and that's our island. To your jobs, everyone, and don't be frightened!"

The children hurried off. Jack went to get Daisy. Mike went to see to the hens and the hen-yard. Peggy scattered the dead remains of the fire, and caught up the kettle and the saucepan and any odds and ends of food on the beach to take to the cave. Nora ran to cover up their patches of growing seeds with bits of heather. Would they have time to do everything? Would they be well hidden before the boatload of people came to land on their secret island?

The Island Is Searched

Now that people had really come at last to search the island the children were glad to carry out their plans, for the days of waiting had been very upsetting. They had laid their plans so well that everything went smoothly. Daisy, the cow, did not seem a bit surprised to have Jack leading her to the inner cave again, and went like a lamb, without a single moo!

Jack got her safely through the narrow passage to the inner cave and left her there munching a turnip whilst he went to see if he could help the others. Before he left the outer cave he carefully rubbed away any traces of Daisy's hoofmarks. He arranged the bracken carelessly over the entrance so that it did not seem as if anyone went in and out of it.

Mike arrived with the hens just then, and Jack gave him a hand. Mike squeezed himself into the little tiny cave that led by the low passage to the inner cave, for it had been arranged that only Jack and the cow should use the other entrance for fear that much use of it should show too plainly that people went in and out.

Jack passed him the sack of hens, and Mike crawled on hands and knees through the low passage and into the big inner cave where Daisy was. The hens did not like being pulled through the tiny passage and squawked dismally. But when Mike shook them out of the sack, and scattered grain for them to eat, they were quite happy again. Jack had lighted the lantern in the inner cave, and it cast its dim light down. Mike thought he had better stay in the cave, in case the hens found their way out again.

So he sat down, his heart thumping, and waited for the others. One by one they came, carrying odds and ends. Each child had done his or her job, and with scarlet cheeks and beating hearts they sat down together in the cave and looked at one another.

"They're not at the island yet," said Jack. "I took a look just now. They've got another quarter-mile to go. Now, is there anything we can possibly have forgotten?"

The children thought hard. The boat was sunk. The cow and the hens were in. The fire was out and well scattered. The hen-yard was covered with sand and heather. The yard-fence was taken up and stored in Willow House. The seed-patches were hidden. The milk-pail was taken from the spring.

"We've done *every*thing!" said Peggy.

And then Mike jumped up in a fright. "My hat!" he said. "Where is it? I haven't got it on! I must have left it somewhere!"

The others stared at him in dismay. His hat was certainly not on his head nor was it anywhere in the cave.

"You had it on this morning," said Peggy. "I remember seeing it, and thinking it was getting very dirty and floppy. Oh, Mike dear! Where can you have left it? Think hard, for it is very important."

"It might be the one thing that gives us away," said Jack.

"There's just time to go and look for it," said Mike. "I'll go and see if I can find it."

He crawled through the narrow passage and out into the cave with the low entrance. He squeezed through that and went out into the sunlight. He could see the boat from where he was, being rowed through the water some distance away. He ran down the hill to the beach. He hunted there. He hunted round about the hen-yard. He hunted by the spring. He hunted everywhere! But he could *not* find that hat!

And then he wondered if it was anywhere near Willow House, for he had gone there that morning to store the hen-yard fences. He squeezed through the thickly growing trees and went to Willow House. There, beside the doorway, was his hat! The boy pushed it into his pocket, and made his way back up the hillside. Just as he got to the cave-entrance he heard the boat grinding on the beach below. The searchers had arrived.

He crawled into the big inner cave. The others greeted him excitedly.

"Did you find it, Mike?"

"Yes, thank goodness," said Mike, taking his hat out of his pocket. "It was just by Willow House—but I don't expect it would have been seen there, because Willow House is too well hidden among those thick trees to be found. Still, I'm glad I found it—I'd have been worried all the time if I hadn't. The boat is on the beach now, Jack; I heard it being pulled in. There are four men in it."

"I'm just a bit worried about the passage to this inner cave from the outer cave," said Jack. "If that is found it's all up with us. I was wondering if we could find a few rocks and stones and pile them up half-way through the passage, so that if anyone *does* come through there, he will find his way blocked and won't guess there is another cave behind, where *we* are hiding!"

"That's a fine idea, Jack" said Mike. "It doesn't matter about the other entrance, because no grown-up could possibly squeeze through there. Come on, everyone. Find rocks and stones and hard clods of earth and stop up the passage half-way through!"

The children worked hard, and before half an hour had gone by the passage was completely blocked up. No one could possibly guess there was a way through. It would be quite easy to unblock when the time came to go out.

"I'm going to crawl through to the cave with the small entrance and peep out to see if I can hear anything," said Jack. So he crawled through and sat just inside the tiny, low-down entrance, trying to hear.

The men were certainly searching the island! Jack could hear their shouts easily.

"*Some*one's been here!" shouted one man. "Look where they've made a fire."

"Trippers, probably!" called back another man. "There's an empty tin here, too—and a carton—just the sort of thing trippers leave about."

"Hi! Look at this spring here!" called another voice. "Looks to me as if people have been tramping about here."

Jack groaned. Surely there were not many footmarks there!

"Well, if those children are here we'll find them all right!" said a fourth voice. "It beats me how they could manage to live here, though, all alone, with no food, except what that boy could buy in the village!"

"I'm going over to the other side to look there," yelled the first man. "Come with me, Tom. You go one side of the hill and I'll go the other—and then, if the little beggars are dodging about to keep away from us, one of us will find them!"

Jack felt glad he was safely inside the cave. He stayed where he was till a whisper reached him from behind.

"Jack! We can hear voices. Is everything all right?"

"So far, Mike," said Jack. "They are all hunting hard — but the only thing they seem to have found is a few footmarks round the spring. I'll stay here for a bit and see what I can hear."

The hunt went on. Nothing seemed to be found. The children had cleared everything up very well indeed.

But, as Jack sat just inside the cave, there came a shout from someone near the beach.

"Just look here! What do you make of this?"

Jack wondered whatever the man had found. He soon knew. The man had kicked aside the heather that had hidden the hen-yard—and had found the newly scattered sand!

"This looks as if something had been going on here," said the man. "But goodness knows what! You know, I think those children *are* here somewhere. It's up to us to find them. Clever little things, too, they must be, hiding away all traces of themselves like this!"

"We'd better beat through the bushes and the bracken," said another man. "They may be hiding there. That'd be the likeliest place."

Then Jack heard the men beating through the bracken, poking into every bush, trying their hardest to find a hidden child. But not one could they find.

Jack crawled back to the cave after two or three hours and told the others what had happened. They listened, alarmed to hear that the hen-yard had been discovered even though they had tried so hard to hide it.

"It's time we had something to eat," said Peggy. "We can't light a fire in here, for we would be smoked out, but there are some rolls of bread I made yesterday, some wild strawberries, and a cold pudding. And lots of milk, of course."

They sat and ate, though none of them felt hungry. Daisy lay down behind them, perfectly good. The hens clucked, quietly, puzzled at finding themselves in such a strange dark place, but quite happy with the children there.

When the meal was over Jack went back to his post again. He sat just inside the cave-entrance and listened.

The men were getting puzzled and disheartened. They were sitting at the foot of the hill, eating sandwiches and drinking beer. Jack could hear their voices quite plainly.

"Well, those children *may* have been on this island, and I think they were—but they're not here now," said one man. "I'm certain of that."

"We've hunted every inch," said another man. "I think you're right, Tom; those kids have been here all right — who else could have planted those runner beans we found?—but they've gone. I expect that boy the policeman saw last Wednesday gave the alarm, and they've gone off in the boat."

"Ah yes, the boat!" said a third man. "Now, if the children were here we'd find a boat, wouldn't we? Well, we haven't found one—so they can't be here!"

"Quite right," said the first man. "I didn't think of that. If there's no boat here, there are no children! What about going back now? I'm sure it's no good hunting any more."

"There's just one place we haven't looked," said the quiet voice of the fourth man. "There are some caves in this hillside—it's possible those children may have hidden there."

"Caves!" said another man. "Yes—just the place. We'll certainly look there. Where are they?"

"I'll show you in a minute," said the fourth man. "Got a torch?"

"No, but I've got plenty of matches," said the other man. "But look here—they can't be there if there's no boat anywhere to be seen. If they are here, there must be a boat somewhere!"

"It's possible for a boat to be sunk so that no searcher could find it," said the fourth man.

"Children would never think of that!" said another.

"No, I don't think they would," was the answer.

Jack, who could hear everything, thought gratefully of Mike. It had been Mike's idea to sink the boat. If he hadn't sunk it, it would certainly have been found, for

131

the seach had been much more thorough than Jack had guessed. Fancy the men noticing the runner beans!

"Come on," said a man. "We'll go to those caves now. But it's a waste of time. I don't think the children are within miles! They've gone off up the lakeside somewhere in their boat!"

Jack crawled silently back to the inner cave, his heart thumping loudly.

"They don't think we're on the island," he whispered, "because they haven't found the boat. But they're coming to explore the caves. Put out the lantern, Mike. Now everyone must keep as quiet as a mouse. Is Daisy lying down? Good! The hens are quiet enough, too. They seem to think it's night, and are roosting in a row! Now nobody must sneeze or cough—everything depends on the next hour or two!"

Not a sound was to be heard in the big inner cave. Daisy lay like a log, breathing quietly. The hens roosted peacefully. The children sat like mice.

And then they heard the men coming into the cave outside. Matches were struck—and the passage that led to their cave was found!

"Look here, Tom," said a voice. "Here's what looks like a passage—shall we see where it goes?"

"We'd better, I suppose," said a voice. And then there came the sound of footsteps down the blocked-up passage!

The End Of The Search

The children sat in the inner cave as though they were turned into stone. They did not even blink their eyes. It seemed almost as if they did not even breathe! But how their hearts thumped! Jack thought that everyone must hear his heart beating, even the searchers outside, it bumped against his ribs so hard.

The children could hear the sound of someone fumbling his way along the narrow passage. He found it a tight squeeze, by his groanings and grumblings. He came right up to the place where the children had piled rocks, stones, and earth to block up the passage.

"I say!" the man called back to the others, "the passage ends here in what looks like loose rocks. Shall I try to force my way through—pull the rocks to see if they are just a fall from the roof?"

"No!" cried another man. "If you can't get through, the children couldn't! This is a wild-goose chase—we'll never find the children in these caves. Come back, Tom."

The man turned himself round with difficulty and began to squeeze back—and at the very moment a dreadful thing happened!

Daisy the cow let out a terrific moo!

The children were not expecting it, and they almost jumped out of their skins with fright. Then they clutched at one another, expecting the men to come chasing along at once, having heard Daisy.

There was an astonished silence. Then one of the men said, "Did you hear that?"

"Of course!" said another. "What in the wide world was it?"

"Well, it wasn't the children, that's certain!" said the first, with a laugh. "I never in my life heard a child make a noise like *that*!"

"It sounded like a cow," said another voice.

"A cow!" cried the first man, "what next? Do you mean to say you think there's a cow in the middle of this hill, Tom?"

"Of course there can't be," said Tom, laughing. "But it sounded mighty like one! Let's listen and see if we hear anything again."

There was a silence, as if the men were listening—and at that moment Daisy most obligingly gave a dreadfull hollow cough, that echoed mournfully round and round the cave.

"I don't like it," said a man's voice. "It sounds too queer for anything. Let's get out of these dark caves into the sunshine. I'm perfectly certain, since we heard those noises, that no children would be inside those caves! Why, they'd be frightened out of their lives!"

Jack squeezed Nora's hand in delight. So old Daisy had frightened the men! What a glorious joke! The children sat as still as could be, glad now that Daisy had given such a loud moo and such a dreadful cough.

There was the sound of scrambling about in the outer cave and then it seemed as if the men were all outside again. "We'd better just hunt about and see if there are any more caves," said one man. "Look that seems like one!"

"That's the cave where we put the hens when the trippers came!" whispered Jack. "It's got no passage leading to our inner cave here. They can explore that all they like."

The men did explore it, but as it was just a cave and

134

nothing else, and had no passage leading out of it, they soon left it. Then they found the cave with the low-down, tiny entrance—the one the childen used to squeeze into when they wanted to go to their inner cave—but, as Jack had said, the entrance was too small for any grown up to use, and, after trying once or twice, the men gave it up.

"No one could get in there except a rabbit," said a man's voice.

"Children could," said another.

"Now look here, Tom, if we find children on this island now, I'll eat my hat!" said the first man. "There's no boat, to begin with—and we really haven't found anything except runner beans, which might have been dropped by birds, and a funny sort of sandy yard—and you can't tell me children are clever enough to live here day after day, and yet vanish completely, leaving no trace behind, as soon as we come! No, no—no children are as clever as that!"

"I think you're right," said Tom. "Come on, let's go. I'm tired of this island with its strange noises. The sooner we get back home, the better I'll be pleased. Where those children have gone just beats me. I wish we could find them. There's such a surprise waiting for them!"

The voices grew distant as the men went down the hill to the beach, where they had put their boat. Jack crept quietly through the low passage into the small cave with the tiny entrance. He put his ear down to the entrance and listened. The sound of voices floated up to him. He heard the sound of oars being put ready. He heard the sound of the boat being pushed on to the water. Then came the sound of splashing.

"They're going!" he called. "They really are!"

The others crowded round Jack. Then, when he thought it was safe, they all squeezed out of the tiny cave entrance and crept out on the hillside. Well hidden in the

135

tall bracken, they watched the boatful of men being rowed away—away—away! The splashing of the oars, and the men's voices, came clearly to the four children as they stood there.

Nora suddenly began to cry. The excitement had been so great, and she had been so brave, that now she felt as if she must cry and cry and cry. And then Peggy began—and even Mike and Jack felt their eyes getting wet! This was dreadful—but oh, it was such a glorious feeling to know they had not been discovered, and that their dear little island, their secret island, was their very own again.

A low and mournful noise came from the inside of the hill—it was poor old Daisy the cow, sad at being left alone in the cave.

The children couldn't help laughing now! "Do you remember how Daisy frightened those men!" chuckled Jack.

"She frightened me too," said Peggy. "Honestly, I nearly jumped out of my skin—if my dress hadn't been well buttoned up I believe I would have jumped *right* out of myself!"

That made the others laugh still more—and half-laughing, half-crying, they sat down on the hillside to wait till the boat was out of sight.

"I really thought they'd found us when that men got up to the part we had blocked up," said Jack.

"Yes—it was a jolly good thing we *did* block it up!" said Peggy. "We would most certainly have been found if we hadn't!"

"And it was a good thing Mike sank the boat," said Nora. "If they had found a boat here they would have gone on looking for us till they'd found us."

"I wonder what they meant when they said that such a surprise was waiting for us," said Mike. "It couldn't have been a nice surprise, I suppose?"

"Of course not!" said Peggy.

"They're almost out of sight," said Nora. "Do you think it's safe to get up and do a dance or something, Jack? I'm just longing to shout and sing and dance after being shut up in the cave for so long!"

"Yes, we're safe enough now," said Jack. "They won't come back. We can settle into the caves for the winter quite happily."

"Shall we light a fire on the beach and have a good hot meal?" said Peggy. "I think we could all do with one!"

"Right," said Jack, and they set to work. Nora sang and danced about as she helped to fetch things. She felt so happy to think that they were safe, and that their secret island was their very own once more.

Soon they were eating as if they had never had a meal in their lives before. Then a loud moo from the hillside reminded them that Daisy was still there. So, leaving the girls to clear up, Jack sped off with Mike to get out Daisy and the hens.

"You're a good old cow, Daisy," Jack said to her, rubbing her soft nose. "We hoped you wouldn't moo when those men were hunting for us—but you knew better, and you mooed at them—and sent them off!"

The days were much shorter now, and night came early. It did not seem long before the sun went and the stars shone out in the sky. The children fetched the lantern from the cave and, taking their book, they went to Willow House. It was Nora's turn to read, and they all lay and listened to her. It was pleasant in Willow House with the lantern shining down softly, and the smell of the heather and bracken rising up. It was nice to be together and to know that the great hunt was over and they were safe.

"I'm sleepy," said Jack, at last. "Let's have some chocolate and a last talk and go to bed. You know, we shall soon have to think seriously of going to live in the caves. It won't be nice weather much longer!"

"We'll decide everything tomorrow," said Mike sleepily, munching his chocolate.

They were soon asleep, for the day's excitement had quite tired them out. But how lovely it was to wake the next day and know that the hunt was over and that they were safe for the winter. How they sang and joked and teased one another as they went down to bathe!

"Oooh!" said Nora, as she slipped into the water. "It's getting jolly cold to bathe in the lake, Jack. Have we got to do this all the winter?"

"Of course not," said Jack. "We'll have to give it up soon—but it's nice whilst it's warm enough."

That week the weather became really horrid. Storms swept over the lake and the children thought it looked just like the sea, with its big waves curling over and breaking on the beach with a crash. The waves ran right up the beach and it was impossible to make a fire there. The children got soaked with rain, and they had to dry their clothes as best they could by a fire they lighted outside the big cave. This was a good place for a fire, because the wind usually blew from the other direction and the fire was protected by the hill itself.

"I think we'll have to give up Willow House now and go to live in the caves," said Jack one morning, after a very wild night. The wind had slashed at the trees all night long, the rain had poured down, and, to the children's dismay, a little rivulet of rain had actually come into Willow House from the back and had soaked the heather bed Peggy and Nora were lying on. The girls had had to get up in the middle of the night and go to the front room, where the boys slept. This was a squash, but the front room was dry.

The leaves were falling from the trees. Every tree and

bush had flamed out into yellow, crimson, pink, brown or orange. The island was a lovely sight to see when the sun came out for an hour or two, for then its rays lighted up all the brilliant leaves, and they shone like jewels. But now the leaves were falling.

Leaves were dropping down in Willow House from the branches that made the roof. It was funny to lie in bed at night and feel a leaf drop lightly on to your cheek. Willow House looked different now that there were so few green or yellow leaves growing on the roof and walls. It was bare and brown.

Nora caught a cold and began to sneeze. Jack said they must move to the caves at once, or they would all get cold—and if they were ill, what would happen? There was no doctor to make them well!

They dosed Nora with hot milk and wrapped her up in the two new blankets Jack had bought in the village one week when he had been marketing. They set her at the back of the outer cave, with a candle beside her, for it was dim in that corner. She soon got better, and was able to help the others when they made their plans for living in the cave.

"We'll make this outer cave our living-room and bedroom!" Jack said, "and the inner one shall be our storeroom. We'll always have a fire burning at the entrance, and that will warm us and cook our food. This is going to be rather fun! We shall be cave-people this winter!"

Days In The Cave

That week the children made all their plans for passing the winter in the cave. Already all their stores were safely placed in the inner cave. It was just a question of getting the outer cave comforable and home-like. Peggy was wonderful at this sort of thing.

"You two boys must make a few shelves to put round the cave," she said. "You can weave them out of stout twigs, and put them up somehow. We will keep our books and games there, and any odd things we want. You must somehow manage to hang the lantern from the middle of the roof. Then, in the corner over here we will have our beds of heather and bracken. You boys can bring that in, too. If it's wet we'll dry it by the fire. The bracken is getting old and dry now—it should make a fine bed."

Peggy swept up the floor of the cave with a brush made of heather twigs, and then she and Nora threw fine sand on it which had brought from the beach. It looked very nice. The boys brought in the heather and bracken for the beds. Peggy arranged them comfortably, and then threw a blanket over each bed but one. There were only three blankets—two new ones and one old one—so it looked as if someone must go without.

"What's the fourth bed going to have for a blanket?" asked Jack.

And then Peggy brought out a great surprise! It was a fur rug, made of rabbit skins that she had carefully cleaned, dried, and sewn together! How the others stared!

"But how lovely, Peggy!" said Jack. "It's a most

beautiful fur rug, and will be as warm as toast. We'll take it in turns to have it on at night."

"Yes, that's what I thought," said Peggy, pleased to find the others admired her rabbit rug so much. "It was very hard to sew the skins together, but I did it at last. I thought it would be a nice surprise for when the cold weather came!"

Soon the cave began to look very homely indeed. The shelves were weighed down with the books and games. The lantern swung in the middle, and they all knocked their heads against it before they became used to it there! The beds lay neatly in the corners at the back, covered with blankets and the rabbit rug. In another corner stood the household things that Peggy was always using—the kettle, the saucepans, and so on.

And then Jack brought out a surprise—a nice little table he had made by himself! He had found the old plank the children had brought with them months ago when they first came to the island, and had managed, by means of a saw he had bought during his marketing, to make a good little table for Peggy!

It was a bit wobbly. The four legs were made of tree branches, the straightest Jack could find, but it was difficult to get them just right. He had sawn the plank into pieces, and nailed them together to make a square top to the table, and this was very good. Peggy was delighted!

"Now we can have meals on the table!" she cried. "Oh, that will be nice! And I can do my mending on the table, too—it will be much easier than crouching on the floor!"

"But what about chairs?" asked Nora. "You can't sit up to the table without chairs!"

"I'm making stools," said Jack—and so he was! He had found an old tree broken in two by the wind on the other side of the hill. With his saw he was sawing up the trunk, and each piece he sawed out was like a solid stool—just a piece of tree-trunk, but nice and smooth to sit on!

The days passed very happily as they made the cave into a home. It was fun to sit on their little stools beside Jack's table and eat their meals properly there. It was fun to watch the fire burning at the entrance of the cave, getting brighter and brighter as night came on. It was lovely to lie on a soft heathery bed at the back of the cave, covered by a warm blanket or rabbit rug, and watch the fire gradually die down to a few glowing embers.

It was very cosy in the cave when the wind howled round the hillside. The light from the lantern shone down, and sometimes Peggy had an extra candle beside her when she sewed. The boys scraped at a bit of wood, carving something, or played a game with Nora. Sometimes they read out loud. The fire burnt brightly and lighted up the cave brilliantly every now and again when extra big flames shot up. It was great fun.

There was always plenty to do. Daisy still had to be milked each morning and evening. She seemed quite happy living in the grassy field, and the boys had built her a sort of shelter where she went at night. There were the hens to feed and look after. They were in a yard near the cave now. They were not laying so many eggs, but the children had plenty of stores and did not worry about eggs.

There was the usual cooking, washing, and clearing-up to do. There was water to be got from the spring. There was firewood to hunt for and pile up. Peggy liked to find pine-cones because they burnt up beautifully and made such a nice smell.

November passed by. Sometimes there were lovely fine days when the children could sit out on the hillside and bask in the sun. Sometimes there were wind-swept days when the rain pelted down and the clouds raced across the sky, black and ragged. Then the lake was tossed into white-topped waves.

Mike and Jack had got the boat up again and mended it. They had pulled it up the beach as far as they could to be out of reach of the waves.

When December came, the children began to think of Christmas. It would be strange to have Christmas on the island!

"We'll have to decorate the cave with holly," said Jack. "There are two holly-trees on the island, and one has red berries on. But there is no mistletoe."

"Christmas will be funny with only just ourselves," said Peggy. "I don't know if I will like it. I like hearing carols sung, and seeing the shops all full of lovely things, and looking forward to Christmas stockings and crackers, and things like that."

"Before our Daddy and Mummy flew off in their aeroplane and got lost, we used to have Christmas with them," Nora said to Jack. "It was lovely then. I remember it all!"

"I wish Daddy and Mummy hadn't gone away and got lost for ever," said Mike. "I did love them—they were so jolly and happy."

Jack listened as the three children told him all they had done at Christmas time when their father and mother had been with them. He had always lived with his old grandfather, who had never bothered about Christmas. To Jack this all seemed wonderful. How Mike, and Nora, and Peggy must miss all the happy and lovely things they used to do when they had their father and mother with them!

The boy listened and made up his mind about something. He would take the boat and row off to the end of the lake just before Christmas. He still had some money —and with that he would buy crackers, a doll for Nora, a new work-box for Peggy, something for Mike, and some oranges and sweets! They should have a fine Christmas!

143

He said nothing to the others about it. He knew that they would be terribly afraid that he might be caught again. But he did not mean to go to the same village as before. He meant to walk to the one five miles away, where he would not be known, and buy what he wanted there. He was sure he would be safe, for he meant to be very careful indeed!

December crept on. The days were dull and dreary. Jack planned to go off in the boat one morning. He would tell the others he was just going for a row to get himself warm. He would not tell them about his great surprise for them!

A good day came when the pale wintry sun shone down, and the sky was a watery blue. Peggy was busy clearing up after breakfast. Mike meant to rebuild Daisy's shelter, which had been rather blown about by the wind. Nora was going to look for pine-cones.

"What are *you* going to do, Jack?" asked Peggy.

"Oh," said Jack, "I think I'll take the old boat out and go for a row to get myself warm. I haven't rowed for ages!"

"I'll come with you, Jack," said Nora.

But Jack didn't want anyone with him! "No, Nora," he said, "you go out and look for cones. I shall be gone a good while. Peggy, could you let me have some food to take with me?"

"Food!" said Peggy in amazement. "However long are you going for, Jack?"

"Oh, just a few hours," said Jack. "Some exercise will do me good. I'll take my fishing-line, too."

"Well, put on your overcoat, then," said Peggy; "you'll be cold out on the windy lake."

She put some rolls and a hard-boiled egg into a basket, together with a bottle of milk. Jack said goodbye and set off down the hillside. Nora came with him, half sulky at not being allowed to go in the boat.

"You might let me come, Jack," she said.

"You can't come today, Nora," said Jack. "You will know why when I come back!"

He pushed off and rowed out on to the lake, which was not very rough that day. He rowed hard, and Nora soon left the beach and went to seek for cones. She thought she would try and see where Jack was fishing, after a time, and went to the top of the hill—but, try as she would, she could see no sign of the boat. She thought that very strange.

Hours went by, and Jack did not come back. The others waited for him, wondering why he had gone off alone and why he had not come back.

"Do you think he's gone to the village again to get anything?" asked Peggy at last. "Nora says she couldn't see his boat anywhere on the lake when she looked—and if he was fishing anywhere near, we should easily see him!"

"Oh, dear!" said Mike, worried. "If he goes to that village he'll be caught again!"

But Jack hadn't been caught. Something else had happened—something very extraordinary!

Jack Has A Great Surprise

We must go back to Jack and find out what had been happening to him. He had been such a long time away from the island—far longer than he would have been if he had just gone shopping. What could have kept him?

Well, he had got safely in the boat to the far end of the lake, and had tied the boat up to a tree. Then he had slipped through the wood, and taken the road that led to the distant village, five miles away. It would take him nearly an hour and a half to get there, but what fun it would be to do a bit of shopping again!

The boy padded along the wintry road. It was muddy and cold, but he was as warm as toast. He jingled his money in his pocket and wondered if he could buy all he wanted to. He did badly want to get a doll for Nora, for he knew how much she would love it!

He carried the food Peggy had given him, and, when he got near the village, he sat up on a gate and ate it. Then off he went again. He did not think anyone would know him to be one of the runaways, for surely people had forgotten all about them by now! It was half a year since they had first run off to the island! But he was keeping a sharp look out in case he saw anyone looking at him too closely!

He went into the village. It was a big, straggling one, with a small High Street running down the middle. There were about six shops there. Jack went to look at them. He left the toy and sweet shop till last. He looked at the turkeys in the butcher's shop, some with red ribbons on.

146

He looked into the draper's shop and admired the gay streamers that floated all about it to decorate it for Christmas. It was fun to see shops again.

And then he came to the toy shop. It was lovely! Dolls stood in the window with their arms stretched out as if they were asking people to buy them. A railway train ran on lines. A little Father Christmas stood in the middle, carrying a sack. Boxes of chocolate, tins of toffee, and big bottles of brightly-coloured sweets were in the shop, too.

Jack stood gazing, wondering which doll to buy for Nora. He had already seen a nice little work-basket for Peggy, and had spied a book for Mike about boats. There was a box of red crackers at the back of the window, too, which he thought would do well for Nora. It would be such fun to pull them on Christmas Day in the cave, and wear paper hats there!

Jack went into the shop. It had two or three other people there, for the shop was a post office, too, and people were sending off Christmas parcels. The shop assistant was weighing them—and it was a long business. Jack waited patiently, looking round at all the toys.

The people in the shop were talking to one another. At first Jack did not listen—and then he heard something that made him prick up his ears.

This is what he heard:

"Yes, it's a great pity those children were never found," said one woman. "Their father and mother are quite ill with grief, I've heard."

"Poor things," said the second woman. "It's bad enough to come down in an aeroplane on a desert island, and not be found for two years—and then to come back safe to see your children—and learn that they've disappeared!"

Jack's eyes nearly dropped out of his head. What did this mean? Could it possibly—possibly—mean that Mike's father and mother had turned up again. Forgetting all

147

about being careful, Jack caught hold of the arm of the first woman.

"Please" he said, "please tell me something. Were the three children you are talking about called Mike, Peggy and Nora—and is it *their* father and mother that have come back?"

The woman in the shop stared at the excited boy in astonishment. "Yes," said the first woman. "Those were the children's names. They disappeared in June with another boy, called Jack, and have never been found. And in August the missing father and mother were found far away on a Pacific Island, and brought back safely here. Their aeroplane had come down and smashed, and they had been living there until a ship picked them up."

"But their children had gone," said the shop assistant joining in, "and it almost broke their hearts, for they had been worrying about them for months and longing to see them."

"What do *you* know about all this?" suddenly said one of the women. "You're not one of the children, are you?"

"Never mind about that," said Jack impatiently. "Just tell me one thing—where are the father and mother?"

"They are not far away," said the shop assistant. "They are staying at a hotel in the next town, hoping that the children will still be heard of."

"What hotel?" said Jack eagerly.

"The Swan Hotel," said the shop assistant, and then the women stared in amazement as Jack tore out of the shop at top speed, his eyes shining, and a look of the greatest excitement on his brown face!

He ran to the bus-stop. He knew that buses went to the town, and he had only one thought in mind—to get to the Swan Hotel and tell Mike's father and mother that their children were safe! Never in his life had Jack been so excited. To think that things would all come right like this, and he, Jack, was the one to tell the father and mother!

He jumped into the bus, and could not keep still. He leapt out of it when it rumbled into the town and ran off to the Swan Hotel. He rushed into the hall and caught hold of the hall-porter there.

"Where are Captain and Mrs. Arnold?" he cried. Mike had often told him that his father was a captain, and he knew the children's surname was Arnold—so he knew quite well whom to ask for.

"Here, here, not so fast, young man," said the porter, not quite liking the look of the boy in the old overcoat, and worn-out shoes. "What do you want the Captain for?"

"Oh, tell me, please, where are they?" begged Jack—at that moment a man's voice said:

"Who's this asking for me? What do you want, boy?"

Jack swung round. He saw a tall, brown-faced man looking down at him, and he liked him at once, because he was so like Mike to look at.

"Captain Arnold! I know where Mike and Peggy and Nora are!" he cried.

The Captain stared as if he had not heard aright. Then he took Jack's arm and pulled him upstairs into a room where a lady sat, writing a letter. Jack could see she was the children's mother, for she had a look of Peggy and Nora about her. She looked kind and strong and wise, and Jack wished very much that she was his mother, too.

"This boy says he knows where the children are, Mary," said the Captain.

What excitement there was then! Jack poured out his story and the two grown-ups listened without saying a word. When he had finished, the Captain shook hands with Jack, and his wife gave him a hug.

"You're a fine friend for our children to have!" said the

149

Captain, his face shining with excitement. "And you really mean to say that you have all been living together on that little island and nobody has found you?"

"Yes," said Jack, "and oh, sir, is it true that you and Mrs. Arnold have been living on an island, too, till a ship picked you up?"

"Quite true," said Captain Arnold, with a laugh. "Our plane came down and smashed—and there we were, lost on an island in the Pacific Ocean! Little did we know that our children were going to live alone on an island, too! This sort of thing must be in the family!"

"John, we must go at once to them," said Mrs. Arnold, who was almost crying with joy. "Quickly, this very minute. I can't wait!"

"We'd better get a proper boat," said Jack. "Our old boat is a leaky old thing now."

It wasn't long before a car was brought round to the door, and Jack, Captain and Mrs. Arnold were motoring to the lakeside. They hired a big boat from a fisherman there, and set off to the secret island. Jack wondered and wondered what the children would say!

Meanwhile the three children were getting more and more worried! It was past tea-time now, and getting dark. Where *could* Jack be?

"I can hear the splash of oars!" cried Peggy at last. They ran down to the beach, and saw the outline of the boat in the twilight coming near to the island. And then Mike saw that it was a bigger boat than their own—and there were three people in it, instead of one!

"That means Jack's been caught—and these people have been sent to get us!" he thought, and his heart sank. But then, to his amazement, he heard Jack's clear voice ringing out over the darkening water.

"Mike! Peggy! Nora! It's all right! I've brought a Christmas present for you!"

The three children stared. Whatever could Jack mean? But when the boat landed, and Captain and Mrs. Arnold sprang out, they soon knew!

"Mummy! Oh, Mummy! And Daddy!" shrieked the children, and flung themselves at their father and mother. You couldn't tell which were children and which were grown-ups, because they were all so mixed up. Only Jack was alone. He stood apart, looking at them—but not for long. Nora stretched out her hand and pulled him into the crowd of excited, happy people.

"You belong, too, Jack," she said.

Everyone seemed to be laughing and crying at the same time. But at last it was so dark that no one could see anyone else. Jack lighted the lantern that Mike had brought down to the beach, and led the way to the cave. He badly wanted Captain and Mrs. Arnold to see how lovely it was.

They all crowded inside. There was a bight fire crackling just outside, and the cave was warm and cosy. Jack hung the lantern up and placed two wooden stools for the children's parents. Peggy flew to heat some milk, and put out rolls of bread and some potted meat she had been saving up for Christmas. She did so want her mother to see how nicely she could do things, even though they all lived in a cave!

"What a lovely home!" said Mrs. Arnold, as she looked round and saw the shelves, the stools, the table, the beds, and everything. The cave was very neat and tidy, and looked so cosy and friendly. How they all talked! How they jumped up and down and laughed and told first this thing and then the other! Only one thing made Captain and Mrs. Arnold angry—and that was the tale of how unkind Aunt Harriet and Uncle Henry had been.

"They shall be punished," said Captain Arnold, and that was all he said about them.

Daisy chose to moo loudly that night, and Captain Arnold laughed till the tears came into his eyes when he heard about the night that poor Daisy had had to swim behind the boat to the island! And when he heard how she had mooed and frightened away the people who had come to look for them, he laughed still more!

"Someone will have to write a book about your adventures," he said. "I never in my life heard anything like them. *We* didn't have such thrilling adventures on *our* island! We just lived with the native people there till a boat picked us up! Very dull indeed!"

Jack disappeared at that moment, and when he came back he carried a great load of heather. He flung it down in a corner.

"You'll stay with us tonight, won't you, Captain?" he said. "We'd love to have you. Please do."

"Of course!" said Captain Arnold. And Mrs. Arnold nodded her dark head. "We will all be together in the cave," she said. "Then we shall share a bit of your secret island, children, and know what it is like."

So that night the children had visitors! They all fell asleep on their heather beds at last, happy, excited, and very tired. What fun to wake up tomorrow with their own father and mother beside them!

The End Of The Adventure

Mike awoke first in the morning. He sat up and remembered everything. There were his father and mother, fast asleep on their heathery bed in the corner of the cave! It was true then—he hadn't dreamt it all! They were alive and well, and had got their children again—everything was lovely.

Mike crept out to light the fire. He could not possibly go to sleep again. The day was just creeping in at the cave entrance. The sky was a very pale blue, and the sun was trying to break through a thin mist in the east. It was going to be fine!

When the fire was crackling merrily everyone woke up. Nora flung herself on her mother, for she could not believe she really had a mother again, and had to keep hugging her and touching her. Soon the cave was filled with talk and laughter.

Peggy and Nora got the breakfast. Mike showed his father the inner cave and their stores. Jack flew off to milk Daisy. The hens clucked outside, and Nora fetched in four brown eggs.

Fish from Jack's line, eggs, rolls, the rest of the potted meat, and a tin of peaches made a fine breakfast, washed down with hot tea. The fire died down and the sunshine came in at the cave entrance. Everyone went outside to see what sort of a day it was.

The lake sparkled blue below. The bare trees swung gently in the breeze. Nora told her mother all about the wild raspberries and strawberries and nuts, and Peggy chattered about the seeds they had planted, and the baskets they could make.

153

And then Captain Arnold said, "Well, I think it's about time we were going."

The children looked up at him. "Going! What do you mean, Daddy? Leave our island?"

"My dears," said Captain Arnold, "you can't live here always—besides, there is no need for you to, now. You are not runaways any more. You are our own children that we love, and we must have you with us."

"Yes," said Mrs. Arnold. "We must all go back to a proper home, and you must go to school, my dears. You have been very brave and very clever—and very happy, too—and now you can have a lovely home with us, and we will all be happy together."

"But what about Jack?" asked Nora, at once.

"Jack is ours, too," said Mrs. Arnold. "I am sure his grandfather will be glad for us to have him for always. He shall have me for his mother, and your father shall be his, too! We will all be one big family!"

Jack wanted to say such a lot but he couldn't say a single word. It was very strange. His face just went red with joy, and he held Nora's hand so tightly that he hurt her without meaning to. He was just about the happiest boy in the world at that moment.

"Mummy, I shall so hate leaving our dear, dear island," said Nora. "And Willow House, too—and our cosy cave and the bubbling spring—and everything."

"I think I might be able to buy the island for you," said Daddy. "Then, in the holidays you can always come here and run wild and live by yourselves if you want to. It shall be your very own."

"Oh, Daddy!" shouted the children, in delight. "We shan't mind going to school and being proper and living in a house if we've got the island to go back to in the holidays! Oh, what fun it will be!"

"But I think you must leave it now and come back home

for Christmas," said Mrs. Arnold. "We have our own old home to go back to—you remember it, don't you? Don't you think it would be nice to have Christmas there—and a Christmas pudding—and crackers—and stockings full of presents?"

"Yes, yes, yes!" shouted all the children.

"It's just what I longed for!" said Nora.

"I was going to buy you some red crackers yesterday, Nora," said Jack, "but I heard the great news before I had bought anything!"

"You shall all have red crackers!" said Captain Arnold, with a laugh. "Now, what about getting off in the boat?"

"Just give us time to say good-bye to everything," said Peggy. "Mummy, come down and see Willow House. We made it ourselves and it's so pretty in the summer, because you see, it's a *live* house, and grows leaves all the time!"

In an hour's time everyone was ready to leave. The hens were bundled once more into a sack and were most annoyed about it. Daisy was left, and Captain Arnold said he would send a fisherman over for her. It was too cold for her to swim behind the boat. Most of the children's stores were left, too. They would be able to use them when they next went to the island.

Peggy took the rabbit-rug she had made. That was too precious to leave. They brought the books too, because they had got fond of those. They had stored everything carefully in the inner cave, and thrown sacks over them in case of damp. They couldn't help feeling a bit sad to leave, although they knew they were going to their own happy home again.

At last everyone was in the boat. Captain Arnold pushed off and the sound of oars came to Daisy's ears as she stood pulling at the thin winter grass. She stood watching the boat as it bobbed away on the waves.

"Good-bye, dear secret island," said Nora.

"Good-bye, good-bye!" said the others. "We'll come back again! Good-bye, Daisy, good-bye, everything!"

"And now let's talk about all we're going to do at Christmas," said Mrs. Arnold, cheerfully, for she saw that the children were sad at leaving their beloved little island.

It was not long before the four children and their father and mother (for Jack counted them as his parents too, now) were settled happily in their own home. There was such a lot of excitement at first, for the children had to have new dresses, new suits, new underclothes, new socks, new shoes! Mrs. Arnold said that although Peggy had really done her best to keep them tidy, they were quite dropping to pieces!

So off they went shopping, and came back feeling as grand as kings and queens, all dressed up in their new things! Peggy looked fine in a blue coat and skirt with a little blue hat. Nora wore red, and the two boys had suits and overcoats of dark blue.

Jack felt queer in his. It was the first time in his life he had ever had anything new of his own to wear, for he had always gone about in somebody's old things before! He felt very grand indeed.

The children looked at one another and burst out laughing.

"How different we look now!" said Mike. "Think of our dirty old rags on the island! But it's good to be really properly dressed again—and the girls *do* look nice!"

It was strange at first to sleep in a proper bed again. The girls slept in a pretty room and had a little white bed each. The boys slept in the next room, and had two brown beds. At first they all wondered where they were when they awoke in the morning, but after a few days they got used to it.

Christmas drew near. They all went out to buy presents

for one another. It was most exciting. They went to London and marvelled at the great shops there. They watched all kinds of ships and boats sailing along in a big tank. They saw model trains tearing round and round a little countryside, going through tunnels, stopping at stations, just like a real train. It was all very exciting after living such a peaceful life on the island.

Christmas was lovely. They hung up their socks at the end of their beds—and in the morning what fun they had finding the things packed tightly in the long stockings! Tiny dolls in the girls', oranges, sweets, nuts, needle-books and balls—and in the boys' were all kinds of things, too. Bigger presents were at the foot of the bed, and *how* excited all the children were unpacking them!

"This is better than Christmas in the cave!" said Nora, unpacking a great big smiling doll with curly golden hair. "Oh, Jack! Did you really buy this for me? Oh, how lovely, lovely, lovely!"

Soon the bedrooms were full of dolls, books, trains, balls, aeroplanes and motor-cars! It was the loveliest Christmas morning the children had ever had—and certainly Jack had never in his life known one like it! He just simply couldn't believe his luck.

"You deserve it all, Jack," said Nora. "You were a good friend to us when we were unhappy—and now you can share with us when we are happy."

There was a Christmas-tree after tea, with more presents—and as for the crackers, you should have seen them! Red ones and yellow ones, blue ones and green ones! Soon everyone was wearing a paper hat, and how the children laughed when Captain Arnold pulled a cracker and got a tiny aeroplane out of it!

"Well, you can't fly away in *that*, Daddy," cried Peggy.

"You won't ever fly away again, Daddy, will you?" said Nora, suddenly frightened in case her father and mother should fly off again and be lost, so that the four children would be alone once more.

"No, never again," said her father. "Mummy and I have made such a lot of money out of our flying now, that we can afford to stay at home and look after you. We shall never leave you again!"

It was four happy children who went to bed that night. The boys left the door open between their room and the girls', so that they might all talk to one another till they fell asleep. They could not get out of this habit, for they had always been able to talk to one another in bed on the island.

"It's been a lovely day," said Peggy sleepily. "But I do just wish something now."

"What?" asked Mike.

"I do just wish we could all be back in our cosy cave on our secret island for five minutes," said Peggy.

"So do I," said everyone, and they lay silent, thinking of the happy days and nights on the island.

"I shall never, never forget our island," said Nora. "It's the loveliest place in the world, I think. I hope it isn't feeling lonely without us! Good-night, secret island! Wait for us till we come again!"

"Good-night, secret island!" said the others. And then they slept, and dreamt of their island—of the summer days when they would go there once more, and live merrily and happily alone, in the hot sunshine—of winter days in the cosy cave—of cooking over a camp fire—and sleeping soundly on heathery beds. Dear secret island, only wait, and you shall have the children with you once again!

THE END

The Secret of Spiggy Holes

First published in a single volume in hardback in 1940 by Basil
Blackwell Ltd.
First published in paperback in 1964 in Armada

Off For The Holidays

One morning, at the beginning of the summer holidays, four children sat in an express train, feeling tremendously excited.

"Now we're really off!" said Mike. "My word—think of it—two months in a little house by the sea! Bathing, paddling, fishing, boating—what fun we shall have!"

"All the same, I wish Mummy and Daddy were coming with us," said Nora, Mike's twin sister. "I shall miss them —especially after being away at school all term, and only seeing them once."

"Well, they couldn't take the whole lot of us with them on their lecture tour!" said Peggy sensibly. "They will join us at Spiggy Holes as soon as they can."

"Spiggy Holes! Doesn't that sound an exciting name for a holiday place?" said Jack. "Spiggy Holes—I wonder why it's called that. I suppose there are holes or caves or something."

The four children had come home from school the day before. Nora and Peggy had arrived back from their girls' school, and Mike and Jack from their boys' school. They had spent the night at home with their father and mother, and now they were off, all alone, to Spiggy Holes.

Jack was the most excited of the four, for he had never been to the sea before! He was not really the brother of Mike, Nora, and Peggy, and had no father and mother of his own.

But the children's parents had taken him for their own child, because he had helped Mike, Peggy, and Nora so much when they had run away from an unkind aunt and uncle. Captain Arnold, the children's father, had left them at a farm with his sister, whilst he and his wife had tried to fly to Australia in a tiny aeroplane.

Captain and Mrs. Arnold had been lost for months on a desert island, and when it seemed as if they would never come back, the children's aunt treated them unkindly. They had made friends with Jack, who had helped them to run away to a secret island in a lake, and there the children had lived together until they had heard that their parents had been found and had come back to England to look for them.

As Jack had no people of his own, and was very fond of Mike, Nora and Peggy, Captain and Mrs. Arnold had said that he should live with them just as if he were another of their children—and Jack had been very happy.

He had gone to boarding school with Mike, and now here they all were together again for the summer holidays. At first they had been sad to hear that Captain and Mrs. Arnold were to go to Ireland to lecture there all about their flying adventures—but now that they were on their way to Cornwall together, to live in a house on the cliffs, and do just what they liked, the children couldn't help feeling excited and happy.

"Who's going to look after us at Spiggy Holes?" asked Jack.

"Somebody called Miss Dimity,' said Nora. "I don't know anything about her except that Mummy says she is nice."

"Miss Dimity!" said Peggy. "She sounds sort of timid and mouse-like. I shall call her Dimmy."

The others laughed. "You wait till you see what she's like!" said Mike. "She might be tall and strict and have a loud voice."

The train roared on and on. Jack looked at a map on the

wall. "I say!" he said. "It looks as if Spiggy Holes isn't so very far from our secret island! I wonder if we could go over and see it. Dear little secret island—I expect it's looking grand now."

"It's a good distance," said Mike, looking at the map. "About forty miles, I should think. Well, we'll see. I'd just love to see our secret island again."

"Let's have our dinner now," said Peggy, undoing the luncheon basket. "Look what Mummy's given us!"

There were chicken sandwiches, tomato sandwiches, biscuits of all kinds, lemonade to drink, and apples and bananas.

"Jolly good," said Mike, taking his share of the lunch. "Mummy's great. She always knows what we like!"

"How long is it before we get to Spiggy Holes?" asked Nora, eating her chicken sandwiches hungrily.

"We get to the nearest station at half-past four this afternoon," said Mike. "But that's six miles from Spiggy Holes. There's to be a car or something to meet us."

The time passed rather slowly. They had their books to read, and they played games of counting the signal-boxes and tunnels—but long before half-past four came they all felt tired, dirty, and hot.

"I'm going to sleep," said Nora, and she put her feet up on the seat.

"Sleep!" said Mike scornfully. "I couldn't possibly go to sleep now."

All the same, he was fast asleep in a few minutes! So were they all, whilst the train thundered along through the sunny countryside, rushing under bridges, past stations and through tunnels at a tremendous speed.

The children only awoke as the train was slowing down in a station. Mike leapt up and looked out of the window.

"I say! Our station is the next one!" he yelled to the others. "Wake up, you sleepy-heads, wake up! Get your things down from the rack, and make yourselves a bit tidy. You look dreadful."

So they all cleaned themselves up, and got down their things. They were just ready when the train slowed up again and it was time to get out.

They jumped out, one after the other. Mike called to a porter, "We've two trunks in the van. Will you get them out, please?"

The porter ran to do so. Jack wandered out into the yard to see if any car had come to meet them. But there was none. Only a sleepy brown horse stood there, with a farm wagon behind him. A farm-lad stood at his head.

"Are you Master Arnold, sir?" he said to Jack. "I'm meeting a party of four children to take them to Spiggy Holes."

"Good," said Jack. He called to the others. "Hie, Mike! Nora! Peggy! There's a wagonette here to take us all. Hurry!"

The porter wheeled out the two trunks. The children piled themselves and their belongings into the wagonette and grinned at the farm-lad, who looked a jolly sort of fellow. He got up into the driving-seat, cracked his whip and off they went trundling over the six miles to Spiggy Holes.

It was wonderful country that they passed through. The sea lay on one side, far down the cliff, as blue as the sky above. The cliffs were magnificent, and the coast was very rocky. Here and there the sea splashed around enormous rocks, and washed them with white spray.

On the other side were fields and hills. Poppies blazed by the roadside, and blue chicory flowers shone as brightly as the sky. The children were thrilled with everything.

"Hope the weather keeps on being sunny and warm like this," said Mike. "I shall live in a swimsuit!"

"So shall I," said the others at once.

166

The horse trotted on. The children could hear the sound of the waves breaking on the shore far below. They were driving along a high, winding cliff road, and the sea-wind blew hard in their faces. It was a very pleasant breeze, for the sun was hot, and still high in the sky.

"What's our house called?" Mike asked the farm-lad, who was driving.

"It's called Peep-Hole," said the lad.

"Peep-Hole!" said Jack, surprised. "What an odd name!"

"You'll be seeing it in a minute," said the lad. "There it be!"

He pointed with his whip—and the four children saw the queer little house that was to be their home and the centre of their strange adventures for the next few weeks.

It was a funny crooked house, with a queer little tower built on one side of it. It was set in a hollow in the cliffs, and was turned towards the sea.

"It's called Peep-Hole because it really is a kind of peep-hole out to sea, set in the middle of those two cliffs," said the farm-lad. "And from the tower you can see the tower of the old house set back on the cliff behind those tall trees there. They do say that in smugglers' days someone in the Peep-Hole used to flash signals to someone watching in the tower of the Old House."

"I say! This sounds exciting," said Jack. "Smugglers —and towers—and flashing lights—and I suppose there are caves too."

"Scores of them," said the lad, grinning. "You mind you don't get lost in some of them, or get caught by the tide. This is a rare dangerous coast for children."

"Here's the Peep-Hole," cried Nora, as they drew up outside the funny house with its one tall tower. "And look—that must be Miss Dimity at the door! And she's just as mouse-like as you said, Peggy!"

167

All the children looked at Miss Dimity. She was a small, oldish woman, with neat grey hair, a little smiling face, and big grey eyes that looked timid and kind.

"Welcome to the Peep-Hole, children!" she cried in a little bird-like voice.

"Thank you, Miss Dimity!" said the children, and they each shook hands politely.

"I hope you'll have a good time here," said Miss Dimity, leading the way indoors. "Your rooms are in the tower. I thought you would like that."

"In the tower!" cried Nora, with a squeal that made Miss Dimity jump. "Oh, how lovely, lovely, lovely!"

Miss Dimity led the way to a funny little spiral staircase that went up and up and round and round to the top of the tower. In the tower were two rooms, one above the other. They were not very large and were perfectly round.

"Now you can wash and brush your hair and then come down to tea," said Miss Dimity, in her firm, gentle voice. And she added again, "I do hope you will have a good time here."

She didn't guess what a *strange* time the children would have—poor Miss Dimity!

At Spiggy Holes

The children washed and tidied themselves. They chattered loudly all the time. The boys had the top room, and as it had four windows, one on each side of the round tower, they had four different views.

"This window looks over the sea for a long way," said Jack, peering out. "And the next one looks on the cliffs—and this one looks overland and has a jolly good view of that old house up there—and this one just looks over the roofs of Peep-Hole."

"That old house looks rather interesting and mysterious," said Mike. "It's very big. I wonder who lives there."

"Come along, children!" called Miss Dimity. "Tea is ready."

They all ran downstairs, laughing at the queer little winding staircase. They felt so happy. It was such fun to be all together again, after three months at school—it was nice to think of the lovely long weeks stretching before them, full of sunshine and fun.

There was a splendid tea, with three kinds of home-made cakes, and some delicious honey made by Miss Dimity's own bees. There was no tea to drink—just big mugs of cold creamy milk.

Miss Dimity sat at the head of the table, and asked them about their journey down. The children liked her. She laughed at their jokes, and didn't seem to mind how many cakes they ate.

"I made them all," she said. "So it's nice to see them being eaten. I know you like them then."

"We certainly do, Dimmy," said Nora. The others giggled and looked at Miss Dimity. Was she going to be cross at being called Dimmy?

"Dear me," she said, "that's what I was called at school. It *is* nice to hear that old name again!"

So after that they all called her Dimmy, and the name suited her beautifully.

When they had eaten their tea Dimmy got up to clear away. She did all the cooking and housework herself.

"Would you like us to help you?" asked Peggy politely.

"Oh no, thank you," said Dimmy, stacking up the cups and saucers. "You've come here to have a holiday, not to help *me*. But there are one or two rules I want you to keep, all of you."

"What are they?" asked Mike, rather alarmed. This sounded a bit like school to him.

"Oh, nothing very much," said Dimmy, smiling. "You must make your own beds each morning. You must be in good time for meals—though if you want to picnic out of doors you can tell me and I'll put you up lunch or tea any time you like. And the third thing is something your mother asked me—that is, you must be in bed by half-past eight."

"All right, Dimmy," said Mike. "We'll keep the rules. We've all got watches, so we know the time. Now can we go and explore a bit?"

"Yes—go out for an hour, then come back in time for bed," said Dimmy. "I'll unpack for you, if you like."

"Oh goody!" said Peggy, pleased. "Thanks very much. Come on, you others!"

They all trooped out of the house and ran to the path that led down to the beach. It was a steep path, made of steps that were cut into the rock itelf.

"It winds down like our tower staircase!" said Mike. "Isn't it a steep cliff—and I say, just *look* at the colour of the sea! I've never seen such a blue."

The sun was sinking in the west. To the east the sea was deep blue and calm. To the west it was full of a dancing golden light. The children laughed for joy and jumped down the last steps to the golden sand. It was studded with shells of all sorts.

"I'll be able to make a fine collection of shells," said Mike, who loved to make collections of all kinds of things.

"I say! Look at those caves!" suddenly said Jack, and he pointed to the cliff behind them. The others looked. They saw big and small holes in the cliffs.

"Let's go and see them," said Nora. She ran up to the cliff and peered inside one cave.

"Oooh!" she said. "It's cold and dark in there." She was right. It was. The sunshine could not get inside the deep caves, and they felt damp and mysterious.

"I wonder how far they go back," said Mike. "It would be fun to bring a torch and see."

"We'll do that one day," said Peggy. "Now what about a paddle? Come on!"

They took off their sandals and splashed into the water. It was warm. They danced about in glee, and played 'catch' in the water. Nora fell over and wetted her frock.

Peggy squeezed it out, and then looked at her watch.

"Goodness, it's time we went back!" she said. "We must hurry. Come on!"

They ran back to the cliff and climbed up the steep, narrow path in the rock, panting and puffing, for they were not yet used to it. Then down the garden they ran to the side-door of Peep-Hole. Miss Dimity was setting a simple supper for them of green lettuce and brown bread and butter, and barley water.

"Good old Dimmy!" cried Mike. "Oh, this is a lovely place, Dimmy. There are dozens of caves down there on the beach."

"I know," said Dimmy. "They are called the Spiggy

Holes after a famous smuggler called Spiggy, who lived a hundred and fifty years ago. He used to live in that old house higher up the cliff. It is said that he used *this* house as a spy-place so that he might know when his smuggling boats were coming in."

"Oooh! How exciting!" said Mike. "Good old Spiggy!"

"He wasn't good," said Miss Dimity sternly. "He was very bad."

"I wish there were smugglers nowadays," said Peggy. "Then perhaps we could spy on them and discover them. It would be most exciting."

"Well, there are no smugglers in Spiggy Holes," said Dimmy. "Have you finished your supper? It is quite time you went up to bed. I suppose you can be trusted to wash and clean your teeth and all that without me seeing that you do?"

"Dimmy dear, *do* you suppose our teachers at school come and see that we do all that?" said Jack. "It may surprise you to know that we are all of us over five years old."

"It doesn't surprise me at all, you cheeky boy," said Dimmy, smacking him with a spoon, as he ran by her. "Go along with you!"

They all went upstairs giggling. "Dimmy is a good sort," said Nora, as she undressed in her little round tower room with Peggy. "She likes a bit of fun. Oh, I *do* like this funny bedroom, with its four windows, don't you, Peggy?"

"Yes," said Peggy. "But the boys have got the best room—so high up like that. Let's go and say good-night to them."

They slipped on their dressing-gowns and climbed the winding stairs to the boys' room. Both the boys were in bed. "We've come to say good-night," said Peggy. "Isn't this a lovely place to stay in, Mike?"

"Lovely," said Mike, with a huge yawn. "I like a room

172

where the sun shines in from dawn to dusk, and has four windows to peep through!"

Peggy went to the window that looked up the cliff, away from the sea.

"That old house looks queer," she said. "I don't think I like it. Do you see its big tower, Mike? It is just like this little one, but taller and bigger. It seems as if that big tower is frowning down at ours."

"You do have silly ideas, Peggy," said Mike sleepily. "We'll go and explore the grounds of the Old House sometime—and wouldn't it be fun if the house was empty and we could go inside and see what the tower there was like!"

"I wonder what Spiggy the Smuggler was like," said Nora.

"You'll have Dimmy after you with a hair-brush to spank you with if you don't go to bed," said Jack, burying his head in his pillow. "I can't think why you are so wide awake. Do go to bed."

"All right," said Peggy. "Good-night. See you tomorrow, sleepy heads!"

She and Nora slipped down the winding stairs into their own room. They got into bed. They were tiny little beds, but very comfortable.

"Now I'm going to think about all we've done today," began Nora. But before she had thought more than twelve words her mind floated off into sleep, and she didn't move until the morning. The sun came in from the opposite window then, and Peggy and Nora were awakened by somebody tickling them.

"Oooh, don't!" squealed Nora. "Mike, stop! What do you want?"

"Come and bathe before breakfast," said Mike. "Get up, lazybones. It's seven o'clock. Breakfast isn't till eight, so we've lots of time."

Nora and Peggy sat up, quite wide awake. They looked round their sunny room with its four quaint windows. They could see four bits of bright blue sky, and they could hear the sound of the waves breaking at the cliff-foot. They felt so full of happiness that they had to sing.

"Here we are at Spiggy Holes,
Here we are at Spiggy—
Here we are at Spiggy Holes,
Pop goes the weasel!"

yelled Nora to the tune of "Pop goes the Weasel."

The others took up the silly song and they all went downstairs in their swimsuits, roaring the tune. Miss Dimity put her head out of the kitchen.

"Dear me, it's you!" she said. "I thought it was the canary singing."

The children squealed with laughter and rushed down the steep path to the beach. They flung themselves into the water.

"Now our holidays really *have* begun!" said Mike, as he splashed Peggy. "What fun we're going to have!"

Inside The Old House

The first few days of the summer holiday slipped away happily. The children explored the beach, which was a most exciting one, but rather dangerous. The tide came right up to the cliffs when it was in, and filled most of the caves.

"We shall have to be careful not to get caught in any of these caves when the tide is coming in," said Jack. "It would be very difficult to get out."

Miss Dimity warned them too, and told them many stories of people who had explored the caves, forgetting about the tide, and who had had to be rescued by boats when they found that they could not get out of the caves.

The bathing was lovely at low tide. The children had to promise not to bathe at high tide, for then the waves were very big, and Dimmy was afraid the children might be dashed against the rocks. But it was lovely to bathe at low tide. The rock pools were deep and warm. The sand was smooth and golden, and felt pleasant to their bare feet.

"You need not wear your shoes here," Dimmy told them. "No trippers ever come to Spiggy Holes, leaving their litter and broken glass behind them!"

So they went barefoot, and loved to feel the sand between their toes. The farm-lad, who came to do Dimmy's garden for her, lent them his boat, and the four children had a wonderful time at low tide, boating around the rocks and all about the craggy coast.

One day there was a very high tide indeed. The waves splashed against the cliffs and all the caves were full of

It was fun playing in the rock pools.

water. There was nothing to do down on the beach, because, for one thing, there *was* no beach, and for another Dimmy said it was dangerous to go down the cliff-path when the tides were high because the spray made the path slippery, and they might easily slip down and fall into the high water.

"Well, what shall we do then?" said Jack, wandering out into the garden, and picking some pea-pods. He split the pods and emptied the peas into his mouth. Dimmy had a lovely garden—full of peas and beans and lettuces and gooseberries and late cherries and early plums. None of the children could help picking something as they went through it every day.

"I know what we'll do!" said Mike. "We'll go and explore the garden of the Old House. Come on!"

They passed the farm-lad, George, who was busy digging up some potatoes. Nora called to him.

"Hallo! We're going to explore the garden of the Old House. Nobody lives there, do they, George?"

"That house has been empty this twenty years," said George. "Maybe more. The garden is like a forest!"

"It will be fun to explore it then," said Peggy. They ran up the slope of the cliff towards the Old House. They were all in sun-suits and shady hats, but even so they were very hot. Soon they came to a high wall that ran all round the big garden of the Old House.

"We can't climb over this," said Jack, looking up at the wall, which was three times as tall as he was. "What are we going to do?"

"What about going in through the gates?" said Mike, with a grin. "Or do you feel it would be more exciting to break your leg trying to climb that wall, Jack?"

Everybody laughed. "Well, it *would* be more exciting to climb the wall," said Jack, giving Mike a friendly punch. "But we'll go and find the gates."

177

The gates were locked, but the children easily climbed over them. They jumped to the ground on the other side.

There was a long, dark drive in front of them, winding its way below tall, overhanging trees to the front door. The drive was completely overgrown with nettles and thistles, and the children stopped in dismay.

"I say!" said Jack. "We want to be dressed in macintoshes and boots to make our way through these stinging, prickly things! If we push through them we shall get terribly stung!"

"Well, look," said Nora, pointing to the left. "There's a better way off to the left there—only just tall grass, and no nettles. Let's go that way."

So they went to the left, making their way through shrubberies and over-grown beds. It was a very large garden, and very exciting, for there were all kinds of fruit trees that had not been pruned for years, but whose fruit was sweet and delicious.

The children picked some ripe plums and enjoyed the sweet juice. "Nobody lives here, so it can't matter having a few plums," said Nora. "The wasps would have them if we didn't. Isn't it hot in this garden!"

"Let's go and see what the house is like," said Jack. So they pushed their way through the long sprays of over-grown rose-bushes and went up to the house. It was built of white stone, and was very solid and strong. It had rather small windows, very dirty indeed, and the rooms looked dark and dreary when the children looked through the glass.

They came to the round tower built on to one side of the house, just as the tower of Peep-Hole was built on to Miss Dimity's house.

"This is an enormous tower," said Mike, in surprise. "It's three times as big as ours! My word, I'd like to go up it! The view over the sea must be marvellous!"

"Let's see if we can get into the house," said Peggy. She tried some of the windows, but they were fast shut. Mike tried a door set deep into the wall of the tower but that was locked and bolted inside.

Then Jack gave a shout. He had found an old broken ladder lying on the ground and had set it up beside the wall of the round tower. It just reached to a small window.

"I believe that window could be opened," said Jack. "Come and hold the ladder, Mike. The rungs don't look too good to me."

Mike held the ladder and Jack went carefully up it.

One of the rungs broke as he trod on it and he nearly fell. The ladder wobbled dangerously, but Mike was holding it tightly, so Jack was quite all right.

He climbed up to the window-sill and tried to pull the window open. "The catch is broken!" he said. "I believe I can get the window open if I try long enough. It's stuck hard."

"I'll hold the ladder tight," Mike shouted back. "Shake the window and bang the bottom part, Jack. Nora, help me to hold the ladder. Jack's shaking the window so hard that the ladder is swinging about! I don't want him sitting on my head suddenly!"

There was a shout from above and the ladder wobbled again. "I've got it open!" cried Jack. "It came up with a rush!"

"We'll climb up the ladder then," said Nora, in excitement.

"No," said Jack, leaning out of the window. He had climbed in through it. "That ladder's too dangerous for you all to use. I'll pop down and unlock the door in the tower, just near you."

"Right," said Mike, and he took the ladder away and threw it down on the ground again. Jack disappeared. They could hear him running down the stairs of the tower.

Then they heard him undoing bolts, and turning a rusty key. He pulled at the door and Mike pushed. It opened so suddenly that Jack sat down in the dust, and Mike flew in through the door as if he were running a race!

The girls followed, laughing at the two boys. Jack got up and dusted himself. "Let's go up the tower first," he said. "Look at the walls! They seem about four feet thick! My word, they knew how to build in the old days!"

The tower was very solid indeed. It had a small winding staircase that ran round and round as it went upwards. There were four rooms in the tower, one on top of the other.

"They are all quite round," said Jack. "Just as ours are in the Peep-Hole tower. I say! What a magnificent view you get over the sea from this top room!"

The children stood in silence and looked out of the window over the sea. It shimmered there for miles in the sun, purple blue, with tiny white flecks where the water washed over hidden rocks.

"You can see the tower of Peep-Hole very well from here," said Mike. "The two towers must have been built in these special positions so that the smugglers could signal to each other. If one of us were in our tower today we could easily wave a hanky to the others here, and it would be seen perfectly.'

"Mike! Jack! I can hear something!" said Nora suddenly. She had very sharp ears.

The others looked startled. "Whatever do you mean, Nora?" said Jack. "I can hear things too—the birds singing, and the far-away sound of the sea!"

"I don't mean those," said Nora. "I am sure I heard voices."

"Voices! In an old empty house that hasn't been lived in for years!" said Jack, laughing.

"I tell you I *did*," said Nora. She suddenly pointed out

through one of the tower windows. "Just look down there!" she said. "You can see the front gate from here—look at it!"

The others looked, and their eyes opened wide in surprise.

"The front gate is open!" said Mike. "And it was fast locked when we climbed over it! Nora is right. She must have heard somebody."

"Perhaps it is somebody come to look over the house to buy it," said Nora. "Oh dear—we oughtn't to be here, I'm sure. And I wish we hadn't eaten those plums now. Let's go quickly."

The others could hear the voices very clearly now too. Jack looked alarmed. "I believe they're in the tower already," he said. "They must have come into the house by the front door and gone round to the tower."

"They are coming up the stairway!" whispered Peggy, her hand half over her mouth. "Sh! Don't talk any more. Maybe they won't come right up to the top."

The voices came clearly up the stairway. One was a man's and one was a woman's.

"This tower is the very place," said the man's deep voice, which did not sound quite English.

"Nobody would ever guess," said the woman's voice, and she laughed. It was not a kind laugh. The strangers went into the room below the top one and the woman exclaimed at the view.

"Isn't it marvellous! And so lonely too. Not a house within miles except that little one down there—it's called the Peep-Hole, isn't it? And the old farmhouse four miles off. It's just right for us, Felipe."

"Yes," said the man. "Come along—we've seen all we need."

The children breathed a sigh of relief. So the people weren't coming up to their room after all.

"Well, I'd very much like to see the view from the topmost room of all," said the woman. "Also, that's the room we'd use, isn't it?"

"Very well. Come along, then," said the man. "But hurry, please, because we haven't long."

The footsteps came up and up. The children didn't know what to do, so they simply stood together and waited for the small but strong door to be opened. It swung inwards, and they saw a golden-haired woman looking at them, and a man with a very dark skin behind her.

"Well!" said the woman in astonishment and anger. "What are *you* doing here?"

"We just came to have a look at the garden and the tower of the Old House," said Jack. "We are staying at the Peep-Hole."

The man came into the room and scowled at them. "You've no right to get into empty houses. We are going to buy this house—and if we catch any of you in the house or garden again we'll give you a good whipping. Do you understand—because we mean it! Now clear out!"

The children were frightened. They tore down the winding staircase and out into the sunlight without a word. They had seldom been spoken to like that before.

"Let's go and tell Dimmy," said Nora. "Do hurry!"

Can They Be Smugglers?

The four children rushed out of the front gate and didn't stop till they got to the Peep-Hole. How nice and friendly it seemed, and how kind Dimmy looked as she stood picking peas for supper in the garden!

"Dimmy!" cried Nora, rushing up to her. "Some people are going to buy the Old House."

Dimmy looked astonished. "Whatever for?" she asked. "It's no use except for a school or for a hotel or something like that—it's so lonely for an ordinary family."

"Dimmy, they are odd people," said Jack, and he told what had happened. "Do you suppose they really *would* punish us if we go there again?"

"Quite likely," said Dimmy, going indoors with the peas. "If they are buying the house it will be theirs. So keep away from it. Surely you've got plenty to do without going wandering over *that* old place!"

"Well, you see, it's a mysterious sort of place, somehow," said Jack. "It looks as if anything might happen there. I keep looking at it and wondering about it."

"So do I," said Nora. "I don't like the old house—but I can't help thinking about it."

"Rubbish!" said Miss Dimity. "No doubt these people will move in and make it a holiday place, and it will be just as ordinary as Peep-Hole."

"Let's go and bathe," said Mike suddenly. "Don't let's think about it any more. They are horrid people, and we'll forget them."

They fetched their towels in silence. They had all had a shock, for never had they thought that anyone could speak to them so fiercely, or threaten them so unkindly. However, when they were splashing in the warm water they forgot the strange old house and the strange couple that were going to buy it, and shouted happily to one another.

But they had another shock when they went in to their tea that afternoon. They saw a car outside the door, and inside it was sitting the same yellow-haired woman they had seen in the old house! She looked at them without smiling.

The children went indoors, puzzled—and they walked straight into the dark-skinned man! He was standing just inside the sitting-room door, listening to Dimmy.

"Oh! Sorry!" said Jack. "I didn't know you had a visitor, Dimmy."

"He's just going," said Dimmy, who looked quite worried. "Go and tidy yourselves for tea."

As the children turned to go they heard the man speak again.

"But why will you not sell me this little house? I am offering far more money to you for it than you will ever get when you want to sell it!"

"It has been in my family for two hundred years," said Dimmy firmly. "It is true that I only live here in the summer-time, but I love it and I will not part from it,"

"Well, will you rent it to me for twelve months?" asked the man.

"No," said Miss Dimity. "I have never let it, and I don't want to."

"Very well," said the man angrily. "Do as you please. But I think you are very foolish."

"I'm afraid I don't really mind what you think about me," said Dimmy with a laugh. "Now, please go. The children want their tea."

"Oh, the children—yes, that reminds me," said the man

sternly. "Keep them out of the Old House from now on, or they will get into serious trouble. I'm not going to have badly-behaved children running all over my house and grounds."

"They are not badly behaved," said Dimmy, "and they didn't know you were going to buy it till today. Good-day."

She showed the man out of the door. He went to the car frowning, started it with a great noise and roared off down the country lane.

"Sort of fellow who likes a car to sound like a hundred aeroplanes," said Mike in disgust, looking out of his tower window. "You know, Jack, there's something funny about that man. Why does he want to buy the Old House—*and* the Peep-Hole, too? Do you suppose he's going to do something that he wants no one to know of? This would be a marvellous place to do a bit of smuggling, for instance."

"People use aeroplanes for that sort of thing nowadays," said Jack. "No—I just can't imagine what he's going to do here—but I'd dearly like to find out. And if Mr. Felipe, or whatever his name is, is up to something funny, I vote we find out what it is!"

"Yes, let's," said Nora excitedly. She and Peggy had come up to the boys' room to brush their hair. "I feel as if something is going to happen. Don't you?"

"I do rather," said Jack. "Though it may all turn out to be quite ordinary."

"Children! Are you never coming down to tea?" called Miss Dimity. "I suppose you don't want any jam-scones today?"

"Yes we do, yes we do!" yelled the children, rushing down the winding stairs. "Is there cream with them?"

There was. Dimmy poured out their milk and handed the new scones thickly spread with raspberry jam.

185

"Dimmy, who was that man?" asked Jack.

"He said his name was Mr. Felipe Diaz," said Dimmy, eating a scone. "Fancy him thinking I'd let him have the Peep-Hole! I certainly wouldn't sell my old home to a person like Mr. Diaz!"

"We think he's up to no good," said Jack, taking a second scone. "And if he is, Dimmy, *we* are going to find out what's wrong!"

"Now don't you do anything of the sort," said Dimmy at once. "He's a man of his word, and if he says he'll punish you if you trespass on his grounds you may be sure you'll get into trouble if you disobey. Keep away from the Old House. Don't even peep over the wall."

The children said nothing. They didn't want to make any promises, because they never broke a promise, and it would spoil things if they had to promise Dimmy never to go near the Old House.

They ate a huge tea, and not a single scone or cake was left. "You made too few scones, Dimmy dear," said Jack, getting up.

"Oh no, I didn't," said Dimmy. "You ate too many! I am just wondering whether I shall bother to think about supper for you—I am sure you couldn't possibly eat any more today."

The children laughed. They knew Dimmy was only teasing them. "We're going out in George's boat," said Jack. "Why don't you come with us, Dimmy? We'd love to have you."

Dimmy shook her head. "I've plenty to do," she said. "Go off and enjoy yourselves and see if you can possibly get an appetite for supper!"

The children shot off to get George's boat. He kept it tied to a rough little wooden pier in a cove nearby. He used it for fishing and it was a good, strong little boat.

"George, did you see anything of the people who are going to buy the Old House?" asked Jack eagerly.

"Yes," said George, who was mending his fishing lines. "They came and asked me to tidy up the garden a bit and to get a couple of women from the nearest village to scrub down the house. And they wanted to know a tidy lot about the coast around here!"

"Did they? What for?" asked Mike.

"That's what *I'd* like to know!" said George, with a laugh. "That man's up to no good, I reckon! He wanted me to sell him my boat too, when I told him it was the only one hereabouts."

"Oh, George! You didn't sell it to him, did you?" cried Jack in dismay.

"Of course not," said George. "I wouldn't part with my boat, not for a hundred pounds! I don't think they wanted the boat to use themselves though—I just think they didn't want me rowing round about this coast for a bit."

"George! Do you think they are smugglers then?" cried Mike. "I thought smugglers used aeroplanes, not boats nowadays."

"They've got some little game on," said George, packing up his nets neatly into the bottom of the boat. "But I'm not going to help them by selling my boat, I'm going to keep my eyes open."

"So are we, George, so are we!" cried the four children excitedly. They told him all about their adventure in the Old House that day. George listened. He got into his boat, which was floating by the side of the little pier, and beckoned to the children to get in.

"You come along with me and I'll show you something," he said. They all tumbled in, and Jack and Mike took an oar each. George had two. They rowed out on the calm sea, bumping a little on the waves that ran round the rocks here and there.

"We've got to row a good way," said George. "I reckon we can just do it before supper. Right round the cliff there, look—and beyond it—and then round the next crag too. It's a goodish way."

It was lovely on the sea in the evening. The children took turns at rowing. The sun sank lower. The boat rounded the big cliff, went across the next bay, and rounded a great craggy head of rock that stood well out into the sea. Beyond that the cliff fell amost down to sea-level before it rose again.

George took the boat well out to sea then—and suddenly he pulled in his oars, shaded his eyes with his hand, and looked over the land to the north-west.

"Now you look over there," he said, "and tell me what you can see."

The children looked. Jack gave a shout. "Why, we can see the topmost window of the Old House from here—and we can see the topmost window of our own tower too! The cliffs seem to fall away in a more or less straight line from here, and the towers can just be seen."

"Yes," said George. "And in smuggling days a ship could come and anchor out here, right out of sight of Spiggy Holes, and could come in at night when a light shone in those towers! Old man Spiggy used to light the lamp when it was safe, and it used to wink out at the smuggling ships here, and in they'd ride on the tide, unseen by anyone!"

"It does sound exciting," said Jack. "Do you suppose Mr. Felipe Diaz is going to use the tower for the same thing, George?"

"Oh no!" said George. "But we'll keep our eyes open, shall we?"

"Yes, rather!" cried all the children, and rowed back to supper as fast as they could.

The Light In The Tower

The next few days the children kept a sharp eye on the Old House. They saw smoke rising from two of the chimneys and guessed that women were at work cleaning the big place. George also went up and tried to clear the weeds from the drive, and he told the children that the new people were coming in the very next week.

"They seem in a mighty hurry to come in," he said. "Why, that place wants painting from top to bottom—and they're not going to have anything done except that the big boiler is to be put right!"

The children bathed and paddled, fished and boated as much as ever, but the day that the new people moved into the Old House all four of them went to hide themselves in an enormous oak tree that grew not far from the gates.

They climbed up into the tree, settled themselves down on two broad branches, leaned comfortably against the trunk of the tree, and sat there, whispering and waiting.

Presently a large removal van came along the road, and then another—but that was all.

"Funny!" said Jack, in surprise. "Only two vans of furniture for that enormous house! They must just be furnishing a small part of it."

The vans moved in through the gates, stopped in front of the house, and the men began to unload. Then the big car belonging to Mr. Felipe Diaz came tearing along, and, just under the tree where the children hid, it had to stop, to allow a tradesman's van to pass out of the gates.

In the car was Mr. Diaz, the yellow-haired woman, a

chauffeur as dark as Mr. Diaz, and a sleepy-eyed young man who lolled back in the car, talking to the woman.

"Well," said Mr. Diaz, hopping out of the car, and beckoning to the young man to come with him. "Here we are! You go on to the house, Anna. Luiz and I are just going to walk round the walls of the place to see that they are all right."

The car moved in through the gates. The two men stood underneath the tree, talking in low tones. The children could hear every word.

"This is as safe a place as anywhere in the country," said Mr. Diaz. "See that tower? Well, the boat can hang about right out of sight till we light a signal in the tower. Then it can come slipping in, and nobody will ever know. We shall be copying the old smugglers, Luiz—but our goods are not quite the same! Ha, ha!"

Luiz laughed too. "Come on," he said. "I want to see the place. When are the dogs coming?"

Mr. Diaz murmured something that the children couldn't hear, and the two went off round the walls of the Old House's garden. The children, who had hardly dared to breathe whilst the men had stood beneath the tree, looked at one another in the greatest excitement.

"Did you hear?" whispered Mike. "They're going to use a boat—and put a signal into the tower! It's just like the old days!"

"But are they smugglers then?" asked Nora, puzzled. "And what are the 'goods' they spoke of?"

"*I* don't know," said Mike. "But I'm jolly well going to find out. This is about the most exciting thing that has happend to us since we ran away long ago to our secret island!"

"I love adventures," said Jack. "But look here—we've got to be jolly careful of these people. If they think we even *guess* that they're up to something, there'll be a whole heap of trouble for us!"

190

"We'll be careful," said Nora, and she began to climb down the tree. "Come on! I'm tired of being up here."

"Nora! Don't be an idiot!" whispered Jack, as loudly as he dared. "Come back—we haven't looked to see if it's safe to get down!"

But Nora slipped at that moment, slid down the last bit of tree trunk, and landed on her hands and knees on the ground below the tree. And at that very moment Mr. Diaz and Luiz came back from their walk round the high walls of the grounds!

They saw Nora, and Mr. Diaz frowned. "Come here!" he shouted. Nora was too afraid to go to him, and too afraid to run away! She just stood there and stared. The others up the tree stayed as still as mice, wondering what Nora was going to do.

Mr. Diaz came up to poor Nora and shouted at her. "What are you doing here? Didn't I say that you children were not to come round the Old House?" He took hold of Nora's shoulder and shook her.

"Where are the others? Are they anywhere about?"

Nora knew that Mr. Diaz hadn't seen her fall from the tree, and she was glad. If only he didn't look up and see the others!

"Please let me go," she said, half crying. "I just came for a walk up here. I haven't been inside the gates."

"You just try coming inside the grounds!" said Mr. Diaz fiercely. He gave her another shake. "Now, go home. And tell the others that if *they* come for walks up here they will soon feel very sorry for themselves. I keep a cane for tiresome children!"

"I'll go and tell the others," said Nora, and she sped away down the slope of the cliff as if she were going to find Peggy, Jack, and Mike straightaway.

"That's given her a good fright," said Luiz, with a sleepy grin. "We don't want any sharp-eyed kids about,

Felipe! Well, when the two dogs come they'll keep everyone away. They'll bite anyone at sight!"

The two men went through the gate laughing together. When they were safely out of sight, Jack spoke.

"A nice pleasant pair, aren't they?" he whispered to the others. "Nora was pretty sharp the way she shot off like that—it looked exactly as if she was going to find us—and yet there we were above dear Mr. Diaz's head all the time! He'd only got to look up and see my big feet!"

"I want to get down as soon as I can," said Peggy, who felt that if anyone *did* happen to see them up the tree they would be well trapped. "Is it safe to slip down now, Jack?"

Jack parted the leaves and peered all round. "Yes," he said. "Come on, down we go!"

One by one they slipped down, and then shot off down the slope, keeping behind the big gorse bushes as much as they could in case any of the people of the Old House caught sight of them. They guessed that Nora would be waiting for them at the Peep-Hole.

She was—but she was crying bitterly.

"Don't cry, Nora," said Jack, putting his arm round her. "Were you very frightened?"

"I'm n-n-n-ot crying b-b-b-because I was frightened," sobbed Nora, "I'm c-c-c-rying because I was such an idiot —slipping down out of the tree like that, and nearly spoiling everything."

"Well, that was really very silly of you," said Mike. "But you didn't give us away, thank goodness—you were quite sharp, Nora. So cheer up—but you'd better be careful next time."

"Jack shall be captain," said Peggy. "He always was on the secret island—and he shall be now. He shall take charge of this adventure, and we'll do what he says."

"All right," said Nora, cheering up and putting away her hanky. "I'll always do what the captain says."

"Do you think we ought to tell Dimmy about this adventure?" said Mike.

"No, I don't," said Jack at once. "She is awfully nice—but she might be frightened. She might even forbid us to try and find out anything. We'll keep this secret all to ourselves—though perhaps we might get George to help us later on."

"Did you hear what they said about the boat coming in?" said Mike. "We'll watch for that, anyway! We can take it in turns to sit up each night in the top bedroom of our own tower and watch for a light in the tower of the big house. When we see it, we'll slip down to the beach, hide in a cave, and watch the boat coming in—and maybe we'll see what the mysterious 'goods' are that Mr. Diaz is smuggling in!"

"It's getting very exciting," said Peggy, not quite sure whether she liked it or not. "We shall have to be awfully careful that we're not seen or caught."

George told the children that the furniture had been put into only eight of the twenty rooms of the Old House.

"The tower rooms have been furnished," he said. "I found that out from one of the women who is cleaning the place. So they are going to use the tower."

"Yes—they are going to use the tower!" said Mike, looking at the others. But they did not tell George what they knew. He was very nice—but he was almost grown-up and he might think, perhaps, they should tell Miss Dimity—and they did so want to follow the adventure themselves and find out everything before any grown-ups came into it.

That night the children undressed in great excitement. Jack was to take the first watch, from ten o'clock to twelve o'clock. Then Mike was to watch from twelve to two and Nora from two to four. By that time it would be daylight and there would be no need to watch.

The next night Peggy was to begin the watch. "We must sit by this window, and keep our eyes on the tower of the Old House," said Jack. "If any of us sees a light flashing or burning there, he must wake the others at once—and then we'll all creep down to the beach, hide in a cave and see if we can spot the boat coming in."

Peggy and Nora went down to their bedroom. They found it difficult to go to sleep. Mike got into bed and talked to Jack, but they both fell asleep very soon. Jack had set the alarm clock to wake him at ten.

"R-r-r-r-r-r-ring!" It went off shrilly at ten o'clock. Jack sat up and switched it off. "Good thing Dimmy gave us our rooms right away in this tower," he thought to himself. "She would be waked too, if we slept anywhere near her. Mike, are you awake? Well, go to sleep again. I'm going to watch now, and I'll wake you at twelve."

Jack put on a dressing-gown, and sat down by the window that looked towards the tower of the Old House. It was a dark, cloudy night. Jack could not make out the tower, stare as he might.

"Well, I should see it if it had a light in it," he thought.

An owl hooted in a distant wood. A moth fluttered in a corner near Jack's head and made him jump. He yawned. After the first five minutes, it was rather boring to sit and look at dark nothingness.

He was glad when it was time to wake Mike. Mike stumbled sleepily out of bed, dragged on his dressing-gown, and went to sit by the window. Jack tumbled into bed thankfully and was asleep in a second.

Mike sat and stared sleepily at the tower of the Old House. He could just see it now, for the sky had cleared. The tower was dark. Mike felt his eyes closing and he jerked his head up. He got up to walk about, afraid that he might fall asleep in the chair.

When his two hours were almost up, he heard a sound

in the bedroom, and a hand touched his shoulder. Mike almost jumped out of his skin. He hit out and struck something soft.

"Oh!" said Nora's voice. "You hurt me, Mike! I've just come up to tell you it's my turn to watch."

"Well, what do you want to come creeping in like that for, and make me jump!" said Mike crossly. "I thought you were a smuggler or something!"

Nora giggled and took her seat by the window. "Get into bed," she said. "It's my turn now. Oooh, I do feel important!"

That night nothing happened—neither did anything happen the next night or the next—but on the fourth night there was great excitement. A light flashed in the tower at midnight! There it was, as plain as could be!

A Strange Discovery

It was Peggy who first saw the light flashing in the tower of the Old House. Mike had had the first watch that night, and Peggy had come up from her room about one minute before midnight to take her turn at watching.

She whispered a few words to Mike, and took her seat by the window.

'There hasn't been a sign of anything," Mike said in a low voice, and he threw off his dressing-gown to get into bed. "This is the fourth night we've watched—it's a bit boring, I think. Do you suppose that . . .'

But just at that moment Peggy gave such a loud squeal that Mike jumped. "Mike! Oooh, look! Mike! There's a light in the tower. It's just come, this very moment!"

Mike ran to the window, almost falling over a chair on the way. Jack awoke at the noise.

'Yes!" said Mike. "It's a light! Jack! Jack! Come and look!"

Jack jumped out of bed and ran to the window. Sure enough, there was a light in the distant tower—a light that dipped and flashed and dipped and flashed.

"They are signalling," said Jack, in excitement. "The boat must be standing out to sea watching for the signal, right beyond that rocky crag we sailed round."

"Shall we get on our things and slip down to the beach?" said Mike, so excited that he could hardly stand still.

"Yes," said Jack. "Peggy, wake Nora. There's no hurry, because if that light has only just shone out of the tower, it will take some time for the boat to get round to Spiggy Holes. We've plenty of time to dress properly.'

Peggy flew down the winding staircase to tell Nora, who was still sleeping soundly. Peggy shook her, and Nora woke up in a hurry.

"Nora! The light's in the tower! Hurry and get dressed, because we're all going to creep down to the beach and hide in a cave to watch," said Peggy. Nora almost fell out of bed in her excitement. They put on their clothes in the dark, for Jack had forbidden lights of any sort in their tower, in case they should be seen from the Old House.

"If we can see their light, they could see ours," said Jack.

"True, Captain!" said Mike and dressed himself at top speed. He put on both his socks inside out, and buttoned his coat up wrong—but who minded?

They were all ready in five minutes. Jack took his torch and gave one to Peggy for the girls. They all crept down the staircase, out of the little tower door, and down the garden path, where the smell of honeysuckle came to them.

"Nora's got on her bedroom slippers," said Peggy, with a giggle. "She couldn't find her others."

"Sh!" said Jack sharply. "Other people may be about, remember. We mustn't be seen or heard."

They went as quietly as they could down the rocky path to the beach. The tide was half in and half out. The moon swam out from behind a cloud and lighted up the shore for the children. Jack stopped and looked out over the sea.

"No sign of any boat yet," he whispered. "Let's get into one of the nearest caves and get settled before anyone arrives. I expect the people from the Old House will come down to the beach soon."

The children went into a small cave not far from the steep cliff path. They thought that if they hid there they could easily see who came or went up the cliff. They sat on the dry sand on the floor of the cave and waited, speaking in whispers. Nora was shaking with excitement. She said her knees wouldn't keep still.

Suddenly the children heard voices, and they stiffened in surprise. The voices were to the right of them. Jack cautiously peeped out of the cave when the moon went behind a cloud.

"I believe it's the man called Felipe Diaz and that sleepy-looking chap called Luiz," whispered Jack.

"But, Jack, how in the world did they get on to the beach?" whispered back Mike. "We didn't see them come down the cliff-path—and that's the only way down on to the beach for a couple of miles! The cliffs are much too steep anywhere else to get down to the shore."

"That's funny," said Jack. "They couldn't have been here already, surely, or we'd have seen them. Perhaps they were waiting in a cave. Good gracious, I hope they didn't spot *us*!'

Nora went hot and cold when she heard Jack say that. Mike shook his head.

"If they'd seen us they'd have rushed us off the beach at once," he said. "They wouldn't want us to see what was happening tonight. Listen! What's that!"

The children listened—and over the black and silver water they heard the sound of a low humming.

"It's a motor-boat!" said Jack, in an excited whisper. "It's been waiting out yonder, round the crag, for the signal. Now it's coming in! Watch out, everyone. See all you can."

The children stood up and craned their necks round the rocky edges of the cave. The moon came out for a moment, and coming nearer and nearer to the shore a large motor-boat could be seen, glinting in the moonlight. Its hum was loud in the stillness of the night.

The motor-boat roared away

It shut off its engine and ran gently into the little cove where George kept his boat. The children could no longer see it.

"It must be by George's small wooden jetty," whispered Jack. "Well, we shall see what kind of goods the smugglers are bringing in, when they pass us on their way to the cliff-path."

They all waited impatiently. The sound of hushed voices came to them, and the thud of the boat against the wooden pier. The children waited and waited. Then there came the sound of humming once again, and the motor-boat slid out of the cove and made its way swiftly out to sea and round the rocky headlands.

"They'll be coming by in a second," said Jack. "Now be quiet as mice, everyone—don't sneeze or cough for goodness' sake!"

Nora at once felt as if she was going to sneeze. She took out her hanky and buried her face in it. How dreadful if she gave their hiding-place away just at this most important moment!

But the sneeze didn't come—and nobody came. Not a shadow passed in front of the children's cave. Not even a voice could be heard now.

After half an hour, the children became impatient.

"Jack, what's happened, do you suppose?" whispered Nora.

"Can't imagine," said Jack. Then a thought struck him. "I say! I wonder if the boat came to fetch anyone! We shouldn't see them come by if they'd gone in the boat!"

"Well, then, we might as well go out and look round a bit," said Mike. "Can we, Jack?"

"All right," said Jack. "But for goodness' sake be quiet!"

They made their way softly to the little cove where the wooden pier stood. George's boat was beside it. Jack shone his torch on the ground and pointed out the footsteps in the sand.

"Let's follow them backwards and see where they come from," said Mike. "I simply can't understand how those men came down to the beach tonight without us seeing them pass."

So, with the help of the torches the children followed two pairs of footsteps from the cove, round the beach — and into a big cave!

"So they must have been hiding here all the time!" said Jack.

"Look," said Mike, in a puzzled voice, swinging his torch all over the sandy beach. "There are no more footsteps beyond this cave— they didn't come to the cave by the cliff-path, that's certain. Then how did they come?"

"Jack! Mike! There must be a secret passage from the Old House to the beach!" suddenly said Nora, in such a loud whisper that the others jumped.

"Sh!" said Jack. Then he too began to whisper loudly. "I believe Nora's right! Of course! There's a secret passage from the shore to the Old House! Why didn't I think of it before! My goodness, Nora, that was smart of you to think of that."

"The passage must begin in this cave, where the men's footsteps go," said Nora, pleased and excited to think that Jack thought she was smart. "Let's go in and explore."

"And walk straight into Mr. Diaz and his friend Luiz!" said Jack. "No, thank you. Besides, I'd prefer to do it in daytime. It's a bit too creepy now. Come on, let's go back to bed and talk."

They all went back up the steep cliff-path, through the scented garden and into their tower. The girls curled up in one bed in the top room and the boys in the other.

And they talked. *How* they talked! They were so thrilled with the night's adventure that it was dawn before they thought of really going to bed.

"You see, what happened was they signalled to the boat to come in with the smuggled goods, whatever they were," said Jack, for the twentieth time, "and Mr. Diaz and his friend slipped down from the Old House to the shore by the secret passage that leads to that cave—and then they took the goods up that way back to the Old House. So we never saw them."

"*When* can we explore the cave for that secret passage, Jack?" said Peggy longingly.

"Tomorrow!" said Jack, hugging his knees, as he sat in Mike's bed.

"Today you mean!" said Mike, with a laugh, and he pointed to where the eastern sky was beginning to shine with a silvery light. "It's today *now*. Come on, we really *must* go to sleep for a bit!"

The girls went down to their room. The boys settled into their beds and were asleep in a few seconds. It seemed as if they had only been in bed for a few minutes when Dimmy awakened them at half-past seven.

"Are you *never* going to wake today?" she said in amazement. "Did you keep awake half the night, you naughty children?"

"Perhaps we did, Dimmy, perhaps we did!" said Jack, with a laugh—and not another word would he say to explain why they were all such sleepyheads that morning!

The Secret Passage!

The children were half sleepy, half excited at breakfast-time. Dimmy couldn't make them out at all.

"I don't understand what's the matter with you all today," she said, as she passed them their cocoa. "First you yawn, then you giggle, then you rub your hands together in glee, then you yawn again. Are you planning any mischief?"

"Oh no, Dimmy," said everyone together.

"Well, see you don't," said Dimmy.

"Dimmy, would you give us a picnic lunch, please?" said Jack. "We'd like to be out till tea."

"Very well," said Dimmy. "You shall have some little veal and ham pies that I made yesterday, some ginger cake, and some ripe plums and lemonade. Will that do? Oh, and you can have some hard-boiled eggs, too, if you like."

"Lovely!" said everybody. Nora got up and hugged Dimmy. "You're a dear!" she said. "It's lovely staying with you!"

Dimmy prepared their lunch whilst the children collected electric torches, and also candles and matches in case their torches failed. They talked excitedly. It was lovely to be going to find a secret passage.

Dimmy gave them the lunch done up in two kit-bags. Jack put one on his back and Mike put the other on his. They called good-bye and ran off down the garden path to the cliff. Down the steep rocky steps they went, on to the beach.

The sea had been right up to the cliff and had washed away the footsteps of the night before. But the children knew which cave the men had come from and they made their way there, first looking to see that nobody else was on the beach too.

They came to the cave. The entrance was large and open. The cave ran back a good way, and was very dark and damp. Seaweed grew from the walls, and at the foot the red and green sea anemones grew, like lumps of jelly, waiting for the tide to sweep into the cave again so that they might open like flowers.

The children switched on their torches. They swung them here and there, all around the cave, looking for the passage that led from the cave.

At first they could find nothing at all. "It's nothing but walls, walls, walls," said Mike, flashing his torch round the damp rock that made the sides of the cave. "And at the back it just ends in rock too. Oh dear—I wonder if after all there *isn't* a passage!"

"Look here!" shouted Jack suddenly. "What's this?" He held his torch fairly high up one wall. The children crowded round eagerly. They saw rough steps hewn in the rock—and they could see that the seaweed that grew around had been bruised and torn.

"See that seaweed?" said Jack excitedly. "Well, somebody has trodden on that! That's the way—up there! Come on, everybody!"

With their torches flashing the children tried to climb up the steep rocky steps in the cave-wall. They were slippery, and it was very difficult.

Suddenly Peggy caught sight of something that looked like a black worm hanging down the wall, and she shone her torch on it.

"Here's a rope!" she said. "Look! Look! It must be to pull ourselves up by!"

204

The others stared at the rope. Mike caught hold of it. It hung down from a black hole at the top of the rocky wall, and as he pulled it, it held firm.

"Yes, that's what it is!" said Mike. "It's fastened to something overhead, and is meant to help anyone using this cave. I'll go up first with the rope's help, and you others can follow."

It was easy to get up the slippery, rocky steps with the rope to help them. Mike swung himself through the dark opening at the top of the sloping wall. He shone his torch around.

He was in another cave, but much smaller. A few boxes and barrels lay around, empty and half broken.

Mike called down excitedly. "This has been used by smugglers in the olden days! There are still the old boxes here that must have brought the brandy and silks and things that the smugglers hid. Come along, you others!"

One by one they scrambled up. Jack kicked the boxes. They were all empty. "Unpacked by smugglers years and years ago!" said Jack. He shone his torch round the cave. "Where do we go from here?" he wondered. "Ah, look—is that a door or something over there?"

"Yes," said Mike, who was nearest. "A good solid oak door too, fitted with bolts! I say, what a shame if it's locked."

He tried it—but it was not locked. It swung heavily into the cave, showing beyond it a narrow passage cut out of the rock itself.

"*Here's* the passage!" cried Mike, in the greatest excitement. "I say! Isn't this thrilling?"

"Mike, don't make such a row," said Jack. "We don't know if anyone is coming down the passage or not, and if they should be, they'll hear us easily! Let me go first. My torch is the brightest."

He went up the dark, damp passage. It was so low in

places that the children had to put down their heads in case they were bumped. The passage wound round and round and in and out, always going uphill, sometimes quite steeply. After a while it was not cut out of the rock, but out of sand and soil. It was quite dry by the time they had gone a few hundred yards.

Except for the noise that their feet made now and again the children were perfectly quiet. Presently they came to a wider piece of the passage and this widened out so much in a few moments that it became a kind of underground room. Here were more boxes, larger ones and much stronger looking. All were empty.

"Think of the old-time smugglers sitting here and having a feast, opening the boxes and barrels, selling the goods, going off again in the middle of the night!" said Peggy, looking round. The children could imagine it all very well.

"Aren't we nearly up to the Old House now, Jack?" asked Nora. "We seem to have come a long way, always going uphill!"

"I think we must be very near," said Jack, in a low voice. "That oak door over there in the corner must lead into the cellars, I should think."

"Let's open it and see," whispered Mike. He took hold of the iron handle of the door and pushed gently. It opened outwards, and Mike looked through it. There was a flight of stone steps beyond, leading steeply upwards.

The children went softly up them. There were eighteen of them.

At the top Jack swung his torch around. They were in a dark, underground cellar, set round with shelves. Empty bottles stood in rows. Barrels stood in corners.

"This is the cellar of the Old House, I'm sure," said Jack. "And look—there are the steps leading into the house itself!"

His torch showed a short flight of steps in the far corner, leading up to a door that stood ajar, for a faint crack of daylight came through.

"You stay here, and I'll slip up and see if I can hear anything," said Jack. The others stayed as still as mice. Jack went quietly up the steps. He swung the door a little farther open and listened.

He could hear nothing. He peeped through the door. A large stone-floored scullery lay beyond the door. Nobody seemed about at all. Jack tried to remember where the tower would be. Of course! It would be quite near the scullery —maybe a door would lead from the scullery into the tower, so that servants could take the meals there when necessary.

Jack slipped through the door and took a quick look round. Yes—there was a little stout door at the end of the big scullery, just like the door through which the children had gone into the tower! It must lead there.

Now that he had gone so far Jack felt as if he must go farther! He tiptoed through the scullery, and tried the little tower door. It opened! He slipped through and ran up the winding stairs of the tower. He went right to the top—and when he got there he stopped in amazement.

He could hear somebody crying inside the top room of the tower. It sounded like a child. Jack tried the door —but alas, that was locked! He knocked softly.

The person inside stopped crying at once. "Who is it?" said a voice.

But just as Jack was going to answer, he heard the sound of voices. Someone was coming up the tower stairs! What was Jack to do? He couldn't hide in the room at the top! But perhaps there was time to hide in the room below–if only they didn't come there!

He slipped quickly down the stairs and into the room below, which was roughly furnished with a rug and a chair and table. Jack hid behind the door.

The voices came nearer as the people came up the winding staircase. Jack trembled with excitement behind the door.

The footsteps stopped outside the room where Jack was hiding. "I'll just see if I left my papers in here," said the voice of sleepy-eyed Luiz. The door was pushed open a little farther, and Luiz looked in!

A Narrow Escape!

Jack was quite sure that Luiz would see him when he popped his head in by the door. His heart beat so loudly that he thought Luiz would hear it. But to his great astonishment and joy Luiz glanced over to the table by the window, and then shut the door and went on up the tower stairs.

"My papers are not there," Jack heard him say to his companion. The boy could hardly believe that he had not been seen. He waited until he heard the door of the room above unlocked, and then he quietly opened his own door, shot down the stairs at top speed, ran through the little door into the scullery and down the cellar steps, falling in a heap at the bottom.

"Jack!" whispered Mike in surprise. "What's the matter? What a long time you've been!"

"I was nearly caught!" said Jack, panting. "Tell you all about it in a minute. Let's get out of this cellar down into that underground room. Hurry!"

They all climbed down the eighteen steps to the underground room. They were longing to know what had happened to Jack.

"Let's sit down here for a minute," said Jack. They sat down on the old boxes and barrels. "I'll tell you what happened," said Jack. "I tiptoed through the scullery to the door that leads into the tower from there—and slipped up the winding staircase to the top—but the top door was locked. *And there was somebody crying behind it!*"

"Crying!" said Nora, in surprise. "Is there a prisoner in the tower, then?"

"Must be," said Jack. "And it sounds like a boy or a girl, too! Isn't it mysterious?"

"Perhaps they're not smuggling silks and things, then, but have got a prisoner," said Peggy seriously. "Perhaps it was the prisoner they brought in last night by that motor-boat and took through the secret passage to the tower."

"I think you're right, Peggy," said Jack. "Now we'll have to find out *somehow* who it is!"

"Well, I should think the prisoner will look out of the tower window sometime!" said Nora. "We could borrow Dimmy's field-glasses and keep a watch, couldn't we? Then we should see what sort of a prisoner it is."

"Good idea, Nora," said Mike. "We could easily take it in turns to keep watch for that."

"I feel jolly hungry," said Peggy. "Isn't it about time we had our dinner? All this exploring has taken ages. What's the time, Jack?"

Jack looked at his watch. "It's getting late," he said. "We'll go back to the beach and eat our dinner there. Come on! We don't want to eat in this dark, dismal room!"

They went back to the secret passage. It was easier going down it than up. Bending their heads down every now and again the children made their way down it, stumbling over the rough, rocky path underfoot. Nora's torch had no more light showing in it, so she walked close behind Jack, trying to see by the light of his.

At last they came to the cave that was over the shore cave. The rope hung down through the hole that led to the steps down the cave-wall. Jack got hold of it. He began to climb down—but he hadn't gone far before he gave a shout of dismay.

"I say! What do you think's happened?"

"What?" cried everyone anxiously.

"Why, the tide's come in whilst we've been exploring, and the shore cave is full of water!" shouted Jack. "It's almost up to the roof of the cave. We can't possibly get down this way."

He climbed back into the cave above. The children looked at each other gloomily by the light of their torches.

"What idiots we are!" said Mike. "We never thought about the tide. If we *had* thought we'd have known it was coming in and that we'd be nicely caught by it. It won't be out of this cave for ages."

"What are we going to do?" said Nora. "I'm so hungry. Can't we eat our dinner now?"

"It's damp and cold here," said Jack, with a shiver. "We shall all get chills if we sit in this cave. We'd better go back to that underground room. At least it's dry there. We can light our candles and eat our food by their light. Our torches won't last much longer if we use them such a lot."

So back they toiled up the secret passage till they came to the underground room. And there, where many a time the smugglers had sat and feasted and smoked, the four children undid their kit-bags and took out all the delicious things that Dimmy had put in for them.

Veal and ham pies had never tasted quite so good! And as for the ginger cake, the children could have done with twice as much! They finished up every scrap of everything, hard-boiled eggs and all, and then drank the sweet lemonade.

"That's better," said Jack, grinning round at the others by the light of four shining candles. "I *was* hungry."

Mike looked at his watch. "It's four o'clock,' he said. "I don't suppose that cave will be clear till at least half-past five—and even then the beach is washed by huge waves that might sweep us off our feet. What a bore!"

The cave was full of water

"I'm simply longing to have a look at the tower of the Old House from the window of *our* tower," said Nora. "I do want to see who the prisoner is. Wouldn't it be lovely if we could rescue him!"

"Jack, couldn't we escape through the grounds straightaway now?" said Peggy. "If we went up into the cellars again, and into the scullery, and down the tradesmen's entrance to the back gate we could easily get home in ten minutes—instead of waiting for hours for the tide to go out of the cave!"

"Well, we'll have to be jolly careful," said Jack, who also didn't want to wait for hours for the tide. "I'll go first as usual and see that all's clear."

They all went up the eighteen steps into the cellar. Jack slipped up the steps to the scullery. No one was there. He could hear voices in the kitchen, but he guessed that the maids there were having their tea.

Everything was quiet. Jack gave a low whistle and the others came up the steps quietly. They tiptoed to the back door, where a row of empty milk-bottles stood, waiting for the milkman.

And then they saw something that filled them with dismay! Two big Airedale dogs were roaming about the garden!

"Look!" whispered Jack. "They'll never let us pass. I'd forgotten that they'd got dogs to guard the place."

Nora looked as if she were going to cry. First it was the tide that stopped them—and now it was two dogs.

"Do you think they'd hurt us if we tried to slip out of the grounds?" said Peggy.

"No," said Jack, "but they'd bark the place down, and we'd be found at once. Wait a minute whilst I think what to do."

"Ay, ay, Captain!" said Mike. The others waited obediently. Jack was always good at thinking of ideas when they were in a fix.

213

"I know what," said Jack at last. "We'll go into this little wash-house here and hide behind that heap of sacks. They *must* call in the dogs when a tradesman comes, or they wouldn't get any goods. Well, we'll wait till someone comes—the milkman or the baker—and as soon as the dogs are called in, we will slip out! We won't go down the back path, we'll make for that tree over there and climb it. I believe we could drop on to the top of the wall from its branches and get down the other side quite safely."

"Good idea!" said Mike. They all crouched down in the little wash-house, first of all shutting the door so that no dog could wander inside and find them.

They waited. Jack sometimes popped his head up and peeped out of the window, but no one came. Then they heard the rattling of the milkman's van down the lane and Jack grinned at the others.

"Be ready," he whispered. The milkman got down from his van and rang a bell at the back gate. At once the two dogs set up a terrific barking. Luiz appeared round the house and called them. He tied the dogs to a tree and shouted to the milkman.

"All right! The dogs are tied. You can come in."

The milkman went up the path with some bottles and some butter. A voice came from the kitchen. "Come right in, please." He disappeared inside the scullery.

"Now's our chance!" whispered Jack. "Luiz is gone. The dogs are tied. Run!"

The four of them ran through the wash-house door and sprinted across the grass to the tree that Jack had pointed out. The dogs saw them and began barking again, pulling at their leads as if they would break them.

"Lie down and be quiet!" yelled a voice from somewhere around the house. The dogs went on barking —but in a minute or two the children were safely up the tree, hidden in the branches. Still the dogs went on barking and barking.

Luiz appeared again, and shouted at them. "Quiet, I tell you!" he yelled. "It's only the milkman!"

But the dogs knew that it wasn't and they barked till they were hoarse. The children waited till Luiz had gone again and then one by one they climbed from a branch to the top of the wall, and dropped down to the other side in safety.

How glad they were! How they tore down the slope to Peep-Hole, giggling as they went. What an adventure they had had!

"Secret caves and passages, and finding a prisoner, and nearly getting caught ourselves!" panted Mike, as they reached Peep-Hole. "It's all too exciting for anything!"

"And now we've got to find out *who* the poor prisoner is," said Nora. "That's what *I'm* longing to know!"

Dimmy met them in the hall. "So you're back again," she said. "Did you have a good picnic? What a lovely sunny day it has been, hasn't it?"

"Has it?" said the children, trying to remember—but all they could remember was darkness and dampness in the secret passage and caves and cellar! "We really didn't notice if the weather was sunny or not, Dimmy!"

"What nonsense you do talk!" said Dimmy. "Go and get ready for tea. I've got you the last of the big red eating gooseberries out of the garden!"

"Good old Dimmy-Duck!" yelled Mike, and he tore upstairs to wash—but before he washed he went to his window to look across at the tower window of the Old House. When would he see somebody looking out there?

215

The Prisoner In The Tower

The four children were in a great state of excitement. They could talk about nothing else but the secret passage and the prisoner in the tower, though when Dimmy was there they had to stop, and talk of other things.

"We simply *must* keep it all a secret," said Mike. "I'm quite sure Dimmy would be worried. The only thing I'm wondering about is—how are we going to keep a watch on the tower of the Old House in the daytime, without Dimmy wondering what we are doing? It was easy enough at night—but in the daytime it won't be so easy."

"Well, we'll *have* to be out of our rooms whilst Dimmy is cleaning them each day," said Peggy. "But as soon as the cleaning is done we could take it in turns to go into the top bedroom and watch, without Dimmy knowing. We could have fairly long watches—say three hours. We needn't keep our eyes on the tower *all* the time—we could read or something and keep looking up. I shall do my knitting."

"And I shall do my jigsaw," said Mike. "I can do that and keep looking up easily."

"We'll begin tomorrow morning," said Jack. "I hope Dimmy doesn't go up to our bedroom and find one of us there—she'll think we've quarrelled or something!"

They took a look at the tower in the distance as they went to bed that night. But there was nothing to be seen. Nobody looked out. A dim light shone, that was all.

"There must be somebody there *now*,' said Jack. "Or they wouldn't have a light. Goodness, I'm sure I shall never go to sleep tonight! My mind keeps thinking of secret caves!"

They did lie awake rather a long time, but at last they were all asleep and dreaming. They dreamt of caves and passages and towers and prisoners, and had just as exciting a time in their sleep as they had had in the daytime.

Mike looked at the distant tower as soon as he jumped out of bed next morning, but there was no one there. Jack took a glance as he was about to go downstairs—and he gave a cry.

"There's someone at the window!"

Mike came rushing to see—but Jack pushed him back. "Don't go too near our window. If we can see them they can see us—and it looks to me as if it's only Mr. Diaz."

The two boys kept back a little so that no one could see them. Yes—It *was* Mr. Diaz—and he was looking straight at their window.

"Keep quite still, Mike," he said. "He's just trying to find out how much we can see of his tower, I'm sure!"

Mr. Diaz drew back after a while. Dimmy rang the breakfast bell again downstairs, and Peggy came bounding up the winding staircase to find out what the boys were doing.

That day the children began their three-hourly watches —and it was just as Peggy was taking over from Jack about six o'clock that evening that they first saw the Prisoner!

Jack had been carving a wooden boat with his penknife, sitting patiently for three hours at one side of the window so that Mr. Diaz would not catch sight of him if he should happen to look out once more. Every minute or two Jack glanced over to the distant tower, but he had seen no one there.

Then Peggy came running up the stairs to take her turn at watching—and just as Jack was getting up from his

217

chair, and Peggy was picking up her knitting, they both happened to glance at the far window.

And they both saw the same thing!

"It's a little boy!" said Jack, in the greatest astonishment. "He doesn't look more than seven or eight!"

"He doesn't look English," said Peggy. "Even from here he looks very dark-haired and dark-eyed."

The little boy in the distant tower leaned on the window-sill. Jack took up the field-glasses that lay near at hand and looked through them. He could then see the little boy looking as near as if he were in the garden of Peep-Hole!

"He looks awfully pale and miserable," said Jack. "Almost as if he were crying!"

"Let *me* see," said Peggy. Jack gave her the glasses. She looked through them. "Yes," she said. "He certainly does look sad. I'm not surprised, either, if he's a prisoner!"

"Let's wave to him!" said Jack suddenly. "He'll be glad to see other children." Jack leaned right out of his window, and began waving violently.

At first the boy in the tower did not notice. Then Jack's moving arm attracted his attention, and he stared. Jack almost fell out of the window, because he waved so hard. Peggy squeezed beside him and waved too. The boy smiled and waved back. First he put one hand out of the window and then both, and waved them like flags!

"Good! He's seen us," said Jack, pleased. "Now the next thing is—how are we going to find out who he is?"

Peggy had a good idea. "If we did some big letters in black ink, and held them up at the window one after the other, to spell out words, he would know we were friends!"

"Good idea!" said Jack. "It looks as if it's going to be rainy tonight, so we could all come up here and do the letters then. Dimmy's got a friend coming in to see her, I know, so she won't mind us coming up here."

"I wonder if she's got some black ink," said Peggy. "We'll ask her. I've got some sheets of drawing paper we can use."

The little boy at the tower window suddenly disappeared and did not come back. "I expect somebody came into the tower room, and he came away from the window in case they guessed that he was signalling to someone," said Jack.

Mike and Nora came running in through the garden at that moment, for it was raining. They rushed up to the bedroom at the top of their tower to see why Jack hadn't come down to the beach.

When they heard about the boy prisoner in the tower of the Old House, they wished that they had seen him too. They were thrilled when Jack told them that they were all going to make giant black letters so that they might spell out words to the prisoner.

Peggy ran to see if Dimmy had any black ink, but she hadn't.

"I've only the ordinary blue ink," said Dimmy, rummaging in her desk. "But look—here's some black charcoal. Will that do instead?"

"Oh yes!" cried Peggy. "Thank you, Dimmy. You won't mind if we all play in Mike's bedroom this evening, will you? You are having a friend to keep you company, aren't you?"

"Oh yes," said Dimmy. "I'll be glad to have you four monkeys out of my way! You do what you like up there, but have the windows open so that you get plenty of fresh air."

"Oh, we'll be very particular about the windows, Dimmy!" said Peggy, laughing, and she ran off with the box of black charcoal.

She took the big white drawing sheets from her box, and went up to Mike's bedroom. She gave some to each of the children, and opened the box of black charcoal.

"We *shall* make our hands black!" she said. "Isn't the charcoal nice and black, Mike? The letters we make will show up well, and the prisoner will easily be able to read them."

"Make them about a foot and a half tall and as thick as you can," said Jack, sketching out a big letter A. "I'll do the first six letters, you do the next six, Mike, Peggy the next six, and Nora the next. Whoever has finished first can do the odd two letters left. Look at my big A! I guess the prisoner could easily see that from his window."

It was indeed a fine big A, nearly as high as the stool on which Jack was sitting. It was thickly done too, and surely anybody would be able to read it from quite a distance.

It did not take the children very long to finish all the letters. Peggy had done hers first, so she did Y and Z too, though she was sure they would not want to use the Z.

They had kept their eye on the tower window, but the boy had not appeared again. Now, with the rainy sky, the dark was coming down. A faint light appeared in the distant tower window. For a moment the children saw the outline of a boy's head and shoulders at the window, and then it was gone again.

"We can't do any signalling till tomorrow," said Jack. "What a pity! All the letters are ready!"

Again the next day the children kept a three-hourly watch, and about two o'clock in the afternoon Jack and Nora saw the boy prisoner. He came to the window and leaned out as far as he could.

"He's looking down into the grounds to make sure that nobody can see him waving to us," said Jack. "Sensible fellow!"

Jack waved from his window, and the boy saw him and

waved back. "Now we'll do a bit of letter-work!" said Jack excitedly. "Give me the letters I want, Nora, please, and I'll send him a message. I hope he can read!"

"What message are you sending?" asked Nora.

"Well, I think I'll just say 'WE ARE FRIENDS,'" said Jack. "Hand me the letters one by one."

So Nora handed Jack the big letters drawn in black on the white paper. First a big W, then a big E, and so on. The boy prisoner watched the letters eagerly.

He read the words as the letters made them and nodded his head and smiled and waved. Then he began making letters with his fingers—but Jack could not see them so far away. He snatched up the field-glasses and looked through them. The boy began his message again. He held up one finger first.

"That's 'I,'" said Jack. Then the boy slanted his two fingers together and crossed them with a middle finger.

"That's 'A,'" said Jack. Then the boy turned his hands the other way and made the letter M with four fingers.

"'M'!" said Jack. "'I AM' he has spelt out so far, Nora."

The boy went on making the letters very cleverly with his fingers—and he spelt out the message "I AM A PRIS-ONER."

By this time Mike and Peggy had come upstairs to get their swimsuits, which they had forgotten—but when they saw what was going on they sat down excitedly on Mike's bed, whilst Jack spelt out the prisoner's message.

"Jack, ask him who he is!" cried Nora, dancing up and down in excitement. So Jack spelt out the question with his black letters. And, dear me, *what* a surprising answer he got!

The Rope Ladder

Jack had been watching the boy's answer through the field-glasses. The others sat near him, waiting eagerly to know who the boy was. They could see him making letters with his fingers, but they could not see what letters they were for, unlike Jack, they had no glasses to help them.

"Who is he, Jack? Who is the prisoner?" cried Nora impatiently.

"Well," said Jack, turning to them, "he has just spelt out on his fingers that he is Prince Paul!"

The others stared at him in surprise.

"Prince Paul!" said Peggy. "A prince! What country is he prince of?"

"I don't know," said Jack. "I'll ask him. Where are the letters?"

But by the time he had got the first one, Prince Paul had disappeared. He went quite suddenly, as if someone had pulled him back. Jack darted back from his own window, and pulled Peggy with him. They almost fell on the floor and Peggy was quite cross.

"Don't, Jack," she began—but then she saw Jack's face, and she followed his eyes, and saw what he saw. Mr. Diaz and sleepy-eyed Luiz were both at the far tower window —and they were looking very hard indeed at the children's window.

"Did he see us, Jack?" said Peggy, speaking in a whisper, as if she was afraid that Mr. Diaz might hear her.

"No," said Jack. "We got away just in time. Maybe they went into the prisoner's room and caught him signalling.

Or maybe they just took him away from the window because they wanted to look out themselves. I'm sure they know this is our bedroom!"

"Jack, do you think we can possibly rescue that boy?" asked Nora eagerly. "And do you think he really is a prince?"

"We can't rescue him by using the secret passage," said Jack, "because even if we used it, it only takes us to the cellars, and Mr. Diaz keeps the tower-room locked. This is going to be difficult."

"We shall have to be very careful not to be seen by Mr. Diaz at our window," said Nora. "Perhaps he already thinks we know about the prisoner."

"He can't know that," said Jack. "He didn't see our messages."

"I say! I've got an idea!" said Mike. "What about us making a rope ladder and getting up to the tower-room on it at night?"

"But how could we get it up to the window?" said Nora.

"Well, if we can tell the prisoner about it he can help to pull it up," said Jack. "You know how to get a rope ladder up to a high window, don't you? First of all you tie a stone or something heavy on to a long piece of string. Then you tie the piece of string on to a thin twine. Then you tie the twine to the rope ladder. You throw the stone up to the window and the person there catches it, pulls up the string, pulls up the twine—and the rope ladder comes last of all! He fixes it safely to something and escapes!"

"That's a *grand* idea!" said the others.

"Let's try it," said Peggy.

"We'll have to get string and twine and rope," said Nora.

"George will let us have some," said Mike.

"Let's go and ask him now!" said Jack, jumping up. So down the stairs they rushed and out into the field where they knew George was working that day.

"George, George! Can you let us have lots of string and twine and rope?" yelled Jack.

"I dare say," said George. "What do you want it for?"

"It's a secret," said Mike. "We'll tell you later on."

"You can go to my old boat in the cove and open the locker there," said George. "There's a mighty lot of string and stuff all tangled up there. You can have the loan of it if you want it."

"Oh, thank you, George!" cried the four children, and they tore off to the cove. They found George's boat and opened the locker at one end of it. Sure enough there *was* a mighty lot of string and twine and rope there, that George used for mending and making fishing-nets.

"Goodness! It'll take some time to untangle all this!" said Peggy.

"Well, there's four of us to do it," said Jack. "We might as well sit here in the boat and get on with it now."

"What shall we make the rungs of the ladder with?" said Peggy.

"There's some little wooden stakes, quite strong, in Dimmy's garden shed," said Jack. "I saw them there the other day. They would be the very thing!"

"Look! Look!" said Peggy suddenly, in a low voice. The others looked up, and saw, coming across the sand towards them, the yellow-haired woman who had been with Mr. Diaz in the car, and who lived at the Old House.

"That must be Mrs. Diaz," said Nora. "Is she coming to talk to us, I wonder?"

"Leave *me* to do the talking," said Jack. "She's been sent to find out how much we know, I'm sure."

Mrs. Diaz came slowly over to them, holding a big sunshade over her head. She nodded to the children.

"You are very busy," she said. "What are you doing?"

"Oh, playing about in George's boat," said Jack.

"You are often on the beach?" asked the woman, putting down her sunshade. "You play all the time here?"

"Nearly all," said Jack. "We can't when the tide is in."

"Have you seen these exciting caves?" asked Mrs. Diaz, pointing to the caves with her sunshade. "Have you ever been in any, I wonder?"

"We don't like them because they are dark and damp," said Jack.

"Have none of the other children any tongues?" asked Mrs. Diaz, in a slightly sharp voice.

"They're rather shy," said Jack. "I'm their captain, anyway, so I do the talking."

"Oh," said Mrs. Diaz. She made a pattern in the sand with her sunshade point. "How long are you staying at Peep-Hole?" she asked.

"Oh, not long," said Jack.

"Your bedrooms are in the tower, aren't they?" asked Mrs. Diaz, looking straight at Jack. Jack looked straight back.

"Yes," he said. "They are."

"Can you see the Old House from your bedrooms?" asked the golden-haired woman.

"I'll look and see when we get back tonight," answered Jack.

Just then the children heard the sound of Dimmy's tea-bell and they scrambled up, glad to be able to get away from the strange woman's questions. Mike took a bundle of the rope with him, meaning to go on with the untangling of it at Peep-Hole. But Jack signalled quietly to him to leave it, so he put it down.

"Good-bye," said the children politely, and ran over the sands at top speed.

225

"Jack, you *were* clever at answering those awkward questions of hers!" panted Mike. "I don't know *what* I would have said if she had asked *me* if I could see the Old House from our bedroom window!"

"Jack said he'd look and see when we got back tonight!" giggled Peggy. "How *did* you think of that answer, Jack?"

"You know, they suspect us of knowing about their prisoner," said Jack. "They'll be on the look-out now, more than ever. I guess we shan't be able to do much more signalling to the prisoner boy."

"Why did you make me leave the bundle of rope behind?" asked Mike. "I thought if I took it with me that we could undo it and get on with the ladder here in our bedroom, after tea."

"But, Mike, Mrs. Diaz is sure to guess we're up to something if you go lugging bundles of rope about," said Jack. "We'd far better go back and get it after tea."

"You're right as usual, Captain," said Mike.

So after tea they went back to the boat to get the rope, and took it up to their room. The tide was in and there was nothing to do on the beach. It would be fun to make the ladder.

"What *are* you all doing up there?" called Dimmy, in surprise. "Aren't you going out this evening?"

"No, Dimmy. We've got a secret on," called back Nora. "You don't mind, do you?"

"Not a bit!" said Dimmy, and went back to her washing-up. The children worked hard at the rope. Soon they had a great deal of it untangled, and they found that it was good strong rope, knotted here and there. They chose two long lengths, and then Mike went down to get the little stakes from the shed. He soon came back with them. Jack showed the others how to knot the ends of the stakes firmly to the sides of the rope ladder. The stakes were the rungs. Soon the ladder took shape under their hands.

"Doesn't it look fine!" cried Peggy. "I'm simply *longing* to use it! Do let's use it tonight, Jack!"

Jack Has An Adventure

"We can't possibly use the rope ladder tonight to rescue Prince Paul," said Jack. "For one thing, there are those fierce dogs. They would never let us get into the grounds at night. They would bark the place down."

"Gracious! I forgot the dogs!" said Nora in dismay. "What can we do, then?"

"The only thing to do is to make friends with the dogs," said Jack.

The other three stared at him. None of them felt that they wanted to make friends with the two big dogs. Jack grinned.

"Don't look so scared," he said. "*I'll* be the one to make friends. Animals are good with me. Until I met you and came to live with you I lived on a farm, and I know all about animals and their ways."

"Oh, Jack!" said Nora. "You're marvellous! Will you really make friends with those dogs?"

"It's the only thing to do," said Jack. "And I'm going to begin tonight. As soon as those dogs will let me pass in as a friend. I'll be able to take the rope ladder in some night and get Prince Paul down."

"How are you going to make friends?" asked Mike.

"I'll get some meat and biscuits from Dimmy," said Jack.

"She *will* think you're hungry all of a sudden," said Mike with a grin.

Dimmy was surprised to hear that Jack wanted some meat and biscuits that evening. She had given the children a good supper of stewed raspberries, cream, and home-made bread and butter, and as Jack had had three helpings she really couldn't believe that he now wanted meat and biscuits.

"I think you must be going to have a midnight feast in your room," she said. "Well—for once in a way I'll let you have it."

Jack chuckled, and winked at the others. "It's for a midnight picnic all right!" he said. "But not in my bedroom, Dimmy."

Dimmy didn't hear the last bit, for she had gone out of the room. She made Jack some ham sandwiches and gave him a bag of biscuits. He was pleased.

"Thank you," he said. "That's jolly good of you, Dimmy."

"Well, if you feel ill tomorrow, it'll be your own fault," said Dimmy, with a laugh. She really was an awfully good sort.

When it got dark Jack put the sandwiches and biscuits into a bag and said good-bye to the others. They wanted to come too and wait outside the wall, but Jack wouldn't let them.

"No," he said. "If they smell you or hear you those dogs will bark their heads off. I must go alone. I'll come back in about two hours."

He slipped down the winding staircase and out into the garden without Dimmy seeing him. He set off quietly up the cliff towards the Old House, which loomed up large and dark against the night sky. He could quite well see the round tower on one side of it, and at the top was a faint light.

"I suppose poor Prince Paul is up there trying to read or something," said Jack to himself, feeling sorry for the little prisoner all alone in the tall tower. "How I wish we could rescue him quickly!"

He soon came to the wall. He wondered how to slip into the grounds without making the dogs bark too loudly. They were always loose at night and might come rushing at him if he went in by the gate.

And then a lucky thing happened. One of the maids came up the lane and turned in at the back gate, quite near to where Jack stood. At once the two dogs rushed up and began to bark madly at the woman.

She was used to them, however, and spoke sharply. "Don! Tinker! Be quiet! Don't you know me yet?"

A voice called from the house. "Is that you, Anna?"

"Yes, sir," answered the woman. "It's only me they're barking at."

"That was Mr. Diaz's voice," said Jack to himself. "Now's my chance. If I slip in now and the dogs go on barking, Mr. Diaz will simply think it's because of Anna. And maybe I can make them stop barking in a little while."

He slid in silently at the back gate like a black shadow. Both the dogs heard him and smelt him, and set up a great barking again.

"Quiet!" roared Mr. Diaz. "Quiet!"

The dogs paused in their barking. Mr. Diaz only said "Quiet!" when the visitor was a friend. The pause was enough for Jack.

"Don! Tinker!" he said in a low voice, and then he sat himself down on the ground beside a thick bush. The dogs heard their names and pricked up their ears. Don barked loudly again. Tinker looked as if he wanted to rush at Jack—but this boy was sitting down like a friend! It was strange!

Jack made no movement. He knew from his life on the farm that animals and birds are afraid of sudden quick movements, even from a friend. His heart beat loudly, for he was not at all sure that one or both of the dogs might not attack him.

Don barked again. Tinker ran up to Jack and sniffed at him. Jack sat perfectly still. The dog smelt the meat sandwiches and the biscuits and tried to get his nose in the bag. Both dogs were underfed, because Mr. Diaz thought they would be wide awake then, if they were hungry, and would not sleep well as a properly fed dog does.

"Good dog, Tinker, good dog," said Jack in a very low voice. The dog sniffed hungrily at the bag. Jack slowly and cautiously undid it. Don, the other dog, would not come near. He stood at a distance, very suspicious, growling softly.

"Growl all you like!" thought Jack. "But don't start that dreadful barking again. I don't want Mr. Diaz out here looking round!"

Tinker took a ham sandwich from Jack's hand. It was gone at a gulp, for the dog was very hungry indeed. He sniffed for another.

Jack slowly put out his hand to the dog's head and patted it gently. The dog was not used to being kindly treated and was surprised. He gave Jack's hand a quick lick.

"We're getting on!" thought the boy. He gave Tinker another sandwich, and that was swallowed at once. Don smelt the meat from where he stood. He decided that if Tinker was friendly to this strange boy, he could be too—and also he badly wanted that nice-smelling meat.

So he ran up, still growling softly. But Jack knew it was a pretend-growl, and he chuckled to himself. He gave the hungry animal a sandwich, and then another. The dog swallowed them both. There were only two more left, so Jack gave the dogs one each.

Then he stood up and took a few cautious steps towards the tower. The dogs did not seem to mind. They could now smell Jack's biscuits and they kept close to the boy as he walked. Tinker was very friendly indeed, and licked

231

Jack's hand when he found it near his nose. Don would not do that, but he no longer growled.

Jack walked to the foot of the tower and looked up. He gave each dog a biscuit, and wondered if by any chance the door at the foot of the tower was unlocked. If it was, dare he run up the winding stairway and try to talk to the prisoner? Maybe he could even unlock the door and get the boy out? But no—the dogs would not know Prince Paul and might bark and then they would both be caught.

He tried the door. It opened! Jack listened. No one seemed to be about at all. The dogs pressed against him, asking for another biscuit. He threw them each one a little way off and then slipped through the door leaving it open.

The dogs ate the biscuits, and then lay down by the door to wait for this unexpected friend to come back. They hoped he would have some more biscuits!

Jack stood at the bottom of the tower stairway and listened. The stone steps were dark. Not a sound was to be heard. Jack got out his torch and switched it on. Then, making no sound, the brave boy slowly went up the steps, only using his torch at the awkward parts, for he was afraid of slipping there and making a noise.

There were no lights in the rooms he passed. Only when he came to the top room did he see a streak of light under the door. He stood outside and listened. Somebody was crying inside. Jack looked for the keyhole and put his eye to it.

He could see a small boy sitting at a table with his head on his hands. He was crying quietly, and the tears fell on to a page of the book in front of him. Nobody else seemed to be in the room as far as Jack could see or hear.

Jack knocked very gently on the door. The boy inside raised his head.

"Who is there?" he asked.

"It's Jack, one of your friends!" answered Jack in a low

tone. "I'm one of the children you've seen waving to you in the tower. I've made friends with the two dogs and I've slipped up here to talk to you."

"Oh!" cried the boy, in a voice of great delight. "Can you let me out? Is the door locked on the outside? See if they have left the key."

Jack felt. He tried the door. It was locked and bolted. He could undo the bolts easily enough—but there was no key to unlock the door. It was hopeless.

"I can't rescue you tonight," said Jack. "But listen, please. We've made a rope ladder that will reach your window. If you hear a stone rattling up one night that falls into your room, pick it up at once. It will be tied to a string. Pull the string, and some twine will come up. Pull the twine and it will bring up the rope ladder. See? Fix the ladder to something and get down it."

"Oh, thank you!" said the boy. He pressed his face to the door and Jack could hear him sigh. "I am so tired of being shut up here."

"Why are you a prisoner?" asked Jack.

"It is a long story," said the boy. "My father is King of Baronia, and he is ill. If he dies, I shall be king—and my uncle does not want me to be. So he has paid some men to kidnap me and carry me away. Then, if my father dies and I am not there to become king, my uncle will seize the throne and make himself king before I can be found!"

"So you really *are* a prince!" said Jack. "We wondered *if* you were. What a wicked shame to keep you prisoner like this! Shall we tell the police, Paul?"

"Oh no," said Paul at once. "If Mr. Diaz and Luiz think that the police know about me they might harm me in some way—and certainly they would smuggle me down that secret passage and then you would never know where I had gone. Please try to rescue me yourself. What is your name?"

233

"I'm Jack," said Jack. "Look here, Prince, keep your eyes open for our letter-messages from our tower. We will let you know when we are coming at night with the rope ladder."

"You are very good," said the little prince. "I was so pleased when I saw you waving."

"I must go," said Jack. "I think I can hear something. I mustn't be caught. Good-bye!"

He slipped down the stairs, and tried to open the tower door—but it was now locked! Mr. Diaz had been along, found it open, and had locked it, although he had no idea that Jack was inside.

Jack stood inside the locked door, with his heart beating loudly. How could he get out? Perhaps the kitchen door could be opened without noise?

He went to the door that led from the tower to the scullery. There was no sound to be heard beyond it. Jack opened it cautiously. He stepped into the big, dark scullery, meaning to creep across to the back door, open it and escape through the grounds.

But, alas for Jack! He walked straight into a tin bath, and fell over it with a most tremendous clatter!

Another Narrow Escape

Jack picked himself up at once in a fright. The door into the scullery opened, and Anna looked in, switching on the light. She screamed when she saw Jack, and ran back into the kitchen, shouting for Luiz.

"Luiz! Luiz! There is a burglar in the scullery!"

Jack ran to the back door and tried to open it. But it was locked and bolted and even had a chain on it, too. The boy knew quite well that by the time he had undone everything he would be caught! He was in despair. Whatever could he do? It was no use to run back up the stairs to the tower-rooms, for he would be caught there too.

And then he thought of something. Of course! He could escape down the secret passage! He had his torch with him, and he could easily see the way.

He ran to the cellar door. Fortunately that was open. He leapt down the steps into the cellar just as Mr. Diaz and Luiz came tearing into the kitchen. He heard them shouting, "Where is he? Where is he?"

Jack sped to the eighteen stone steps that led down to the door of the underground room. He ran down them, using his torch. He opened the thick door at the bottom. He ran through the large underground room there to the secret passage.

His heart was beating fast and his breath was coming in pants. He made his way down the secret passage, bending his head every now and again when he came to the narrow, low parts. Soon he came to the damp piece, and knew that he would presently come to the small cave that lay above the large shore-cave.

He came to the oak door that led into the small cave. He pushed it open and made his way to where he knew the rope hung to help him down into the big beach-cave.

"Then all I'll have to do is to slip round the sands, up the cliff-path and into Peep-Hole," thought the boy thankfully.

But what a dreadful shock for Jack—once more the tide was in and the water filled the big cave. He could not possibly get home that way. He would have to wait till it went out.

"I only hope that they don't realise I've come down through the secret passage, and come after me," thought Jack. "I would be properly caught then. But I don't see how they can think anything else. After all, all the doors were locked, and I didn't get out through the tower door or the scullery door—so they'll know I *must* have come this way. And if they remember that the tide is in, they will be able to come along and catch me beautifully."

Jack really didn't know what to do. It was no use at all going back—and he certainly couldn't go forward unless he wanted to struggle with the tide in the cave.

"And I don't want to do that," thought the boy, listening to the smack and gurgle of the big waves that swept into the large cave below. "What in the world am I to do?"

He suddenly thought that he could hear someone coming down the secret passage. He looked round the small cave in despair. Could he lock the door that led into the cave? No—the lock was broken many years ago.

He flashed his torch round the little cave. He suddenly saw a small hole in one corner. He bent down and shone his torch into it. It was a hole big enough for a small man to get through—but where did it lead?

There was no time to be lost. Jack wriggled through the hole somehow. It widened out a little in a moment or two and dipped down into the next cave. But as that was also full of swishing waves Jack could go no farther. The hole was simply a connection between the two caves, it seemed.

"Well, I simply can't do anything but wait here," thought Jack. So he waited—and in a minute or two he heard the sound of people in the cave he had left, and heard voices.

"He's not here, Luiz," said the voice of Mr. Diaz. "And he couldn't possibly have gone down through the shore-cave, surely, or he would have been drowned."

"Maybe he has tried, though," said Luiz. "He might have been very frightened, and have leapt into the water and tried to swim away."

"Well, if so, he's gone," said Mr. Diaz. "I can't imagine that *any* one could swim down there! Listen to the water sucking in and out. It would be impossible even for a man to swim through that."

"Well, if he didn't go down there, where is he?" said Luiz rather sharply. "You don't suggest that he is hiding in any of these small boxes, do you?"

"That's enough, Luiz," said Mr. Diaz, in an angry tone. "I can't understand the whole thing—how did that boy get into the grounds and the house when the dogs were there? And how did he know about the secret passage? Where has he gone now? And what do you suppose he knows about the prince?"

"Well, if you really want to know what I think, I think that Anna the cook made a mistake," said Luiz, sounding very bored. "I think maybe something fell down in the scullery, and Anna rushed in—and *thought* she saw a boy! And she screamed and made a fuss."

"Well, maybe you're right," said Mr. Diaz. "Come on, let's go back. He's not here, anyway."

Jack heard their scrambling footsteps going from the cave.

Jack just managed to cling to the rocks

For a while he caught the sound of their voices as they went up the secret passage. Then there was silence.

"My word, that *was* a narrow escape!" thought Jack. "Good thing I found this hole. I wonder if the tide is going out? It sounds less strong."

He wriggled himself into a different position, and was then able to switch on his torch and see the cave below. It was the one next to the large cave, and was only small. The sea was leaving it.

"It's safe to get down," thought the boy, and he wriggled out of the small passage, slid down the cave wall and jumped down to the wet sand. A wave immediately ran into the cave and wetted Jack to the waist.

"You *would*!" said Jack to the wave. "Just waiting for me, I suppose!"

The wave ran out. Jack ran quickly to the cave entrance and looked up the beach. If he were quick, and dodged in between the big waves that ran up the sand and back, he could get up on the rocks, and climb along them to the cliff-path.

Another wave ran up and Jack ran back into the cave to escape it. It swirled around his knees and nearly knocked him over. As soon as it ran out Jack ran out after it. He jumped quickly up on the rocks at the foot of the steep cliff. Another wave swept up and wetted his legs—but Jack clung to the rock and was safe.

He climbed a bit higher on to the rocks. Now the sea could hardly reach him, and as it was going down he would soon be safe.

He clambered over the rocks, stumbling and slipping on the seaweed. He came to the cliff-path and put his feet on the steps cut out of the rock. He switched on his torch and went carefully up to the top of the cliff.

A wind was blowing there. Jack switched off his torch in case anyone saw its light, and made his way softly back to

Peep-Hole. The gate creaked as he opened it. He was safe home at last!

He ran up the winding staircase and into his bedroom at the top. The others were there, and they crowded round him at once.

"Jack! Jack! What an age you've been! Were you nearly caught again?"

"You just listen to what happened to me tonight!" said Jack. "I *have* had a time, I can tell you! My word, we had plenty of adventures on our secret island last year, but tonight's adventure was the most exciting of all!"

A Plan To Rescue Paul

Jack told the others of his adventures that night. They listened in silence. When he came to the part about how he escaped down the secret passage to the shore, and could not get down into the cave because of the tide, Nora took hold of his hand tightly.

"You're not to go on adventures alone any more, Jack," she said. "Suppose you had been caught! We wouldn't have known *where* you were! Please, please, let us all go together in future, when there is anything to be done."

"We'll see," said Jack. "Sometimes it's impossible for the whole lot of us to go together—we'd be noticed."

"All the same, Nora's right," said Mike. "I think we ought to go out in pairs, Jack. You *have* had a time. What's going to be our next move?"

"Bed," said Jack at once. "I'm so sleepy. I can't keep my eyes open! We'll decide tomorrow what is to be done."

The girls went down to their bedroom. Jack and Mike tumbled into their beds, and were soon asleep. Once again Dimmy had to wake them all, for they were *so* sleepy the next morning!

"You *have* turned into sleepyheads!" said Dimmy, in surprise. "You will be very late for breakfast, so hurry up, please."

The children put on their sun-suits, and raced downstairs. It was a beautiful sunny day, and they meant to bathe as soon as they could.

"Not till two hours after breakfast, remember," said Dimmy warningly. "It is dangerous to bathe after a big meal. Jack, I can trust you not to let the others do anything foolish, can't I?"

"Jack's our captain, Dimmy," said Nora. "We always do what he says."

They went down to the beach, taking with them a basket of ripe plums from the garden for their eleven o'clock lunch. They chose a rock far down the beach, that the tide was already lapping round, and sat on it.

"It's best to be in some place where we can't possibly be overheard," said Jack, looking all round. "Now that Mr. Diaz thinks one of us knows the secret of the prisoner in the tower, and all about the secret passage too, we shall have to be extra careful. I think Nora's right when she says we must go about together. Mr. Diaz and Luiz would be pleased if they could catch any of us and keep us prisoner too!"

"Let's talk about rescuing Prince Paul," said Nora, who was longing to get the boy out of the tower. "Couldn't we take the rope ladder along tonight, Jack? Now that you've made friends with the dogs, it would be easy."

"Well, I don't know if the dogs would be friends with you too," said Jack doubtfully. "We could try. No—I know what we'll do. I'll take Mike along with me to help, and you two girls can stay behind. We'll signal a message to Prince Paul with our big black letters today, then he will be ready to look out for the ladder tonight."

The girls were disappointed at the thought of being left behind, but they made no fuss. It was no use all of them going if the dogs barked at them and warned Mr. Diaz that they were about. Perhaps they would be all right with just Jack and Mike.

"I'll take some meat along with me too, tonight," said Mike. "You can go into the grounds first, Jack, and fuss the dogs a bit—and then you can bring them to where I am and try to make them understand I am a friend, too."

So it was all decided. The rescue was to take place that night. What fun! The children were so thrilled that they could hardly talk of anything else as they ate their plums at eleven o'clock, and then dug an enormous castle on the beach to sit on when the tide came in. It came swirling up the sand and soon surrounded their great castle.

They went back to Peep-Hole early, about noon, because for one thing the sea was rough and there was very little beach to play on, and for another thing they wanted to signal to Prince Paul. They got out their big letters and went to the window.

Prince Paul was in his tower, looking out. When he saw them he waved in delight. At once Jack began to send a message, holding out first one letter and then another. He spelt out quite a long message. Prince Paul hung half out of his window and waved as each word came to an end, to show that he had read it.

"Tonight look out for the rope ladder," Jack spelt out.

Prince Paul made three letters with his fingers, one after the other. "YES," he spelt out. They were difficult letters to make with his fingers, and Jack, who was looking at Paul through the field-glasses, would hardly have known what they were if Paul hadn't nodded his head all the time to show that he meant yes.

"Cheer up," Jack spelt out next. Paul waved and nodded again, then suddenly disappeared into the room. Jack at once came away from his window and pulled the others from it too.

"Somebody's come into Paul's room," he said. "He went away from the window so quickly. Yes—there's dear Mr. Diaz looking across to our tower. Oh no, Mr. Diaz, you won't see *us*! We're much too sharp for you!"

The others laughed. The dinner-bell went at that minute and they all rushed downstairs, only to be sent up

243

again because in their excitement they had quite forgotten to wash their hands and do their hair.

"Sorry, Dimmy," they said, when they arrived down clean at last. "We were doing something exciting and quite forgot to tidy ourselves."

"And what was this exciting thing you were doing?" asked Dimmy, ladling great helpings of garden peas on to their plates.

"It's a secret," said Jack. "A great big exciting secret, Dimmy! Wouldn't you love to know it?"

"I would," said Dimmy. "One of these days you will have to tell me."

The others laughed. They did not know that very soon they would *have* to tell Dimmy their great big exciting secret!

They went boating with George the rest of the day. They caught some fish, and Dimmy said she would cook them for their supper.

"You're a good sort, Dimmy," said Mike, giving her a hug. "Have you any meat-bones to spare? We'd like some tonight."

Dimmy stared in surprise. "What is all this mystery about meat at night?" she asked. "Are you keeping some stray dogs up in your bedroom or something?"

The children squealed with laughter. "No," grinned Jack. "It's all part of our secret, that's all, Dimmy."

"Well, I won't ask any questions," said Dimmy. "If you want secrets, you can have them. There's an old mutton-bone you may have. Get it when you want it. It's in the larder."

So Mike got the mutton-bone before he went to bed and put it into a bag. Jack was to carry the rope ladder. "I think we'd better get to bed and try and have a sleep first," said Jack, yawning. "I feel very sleepy after my night out last night, Mike. We can set our alarm clock for whatever time we like."

"Well, I'll set it for half-past twelve," said Mike. "The moon will be up then, and we can see where we're going and what we're doing."

So the alarm was set for half-past twelve and the four children settled into bed and went to sleep. The bell of the alarm clock rang loudly at half-past twelve and the two boys awoke. The girls heard it in their bedroom below, and slipped on their dressing-gowns ready to see the boys off.

Down the staircase went the children, Jack carrying the rope ladder and Mike carrying the mutton-bone. The girls whispered a good-bye and went back upstairs.

"Let's sit at the window of the boys' room," said Nora. "The moon is very bright now, and if we use the field-glasses we can easily see what happens. It would be fun to see Prince Paul climbing down the rope ladder we made!"

So Nora and Peggy pulled a blanket over themselves and sat at the window of the boy's bedroom, keeping a watch on the window of the tower up the cliff. They took it in turns to use the field-glasses. How they wondered what the boys were doing!

Mike and Jack went silently up the cliff to the Old House. When they got there Jack whispered to Mike to stay outside the back gate whilst he went in to see if the dogs remembered him.

He slipped in softly. Tinker and Don were roaming about loose as usual. They smelt him and Don growled softly. Tinker came running up and licked his hand.

"Good dog, good dog," said Jack in a low tone. He patted Tinker and then went softly to Don. Don sniffed round him, remembering the ham sandwiches and the biscuits that this boy had brought with him last time.

Jack took hold of the dogs' collars and led them to the back gate outside which Mike was waiting. The dogs growled when they saw Mike, but they did not bark. Mike held out the bone to them.

They were very hungry and they took the bone at once. They let Mike pat them. This boy seemed to be a friend of Jack's so they were not going to bark at him. They lay on the ground, growling and worrying at the big bone.

"Come on," whispered Jack. Mike went with him to the bottom of the tower. A faint light shone at the top. Mike picked up a smooth round stone and took aim at the tower to warn Prince Paul they were there. The windows of the tower were open. Mike hoped to goodness he wouldn't smash the glass and waken everyone! However, he was good at throwing, so the stone went through the open window and landed neatly inside.

At once Prince Paul appeared at the window. "Hallo," he said, in a low voice. "I'm ready."

Jack got hold of the stone to which the piece of string was firmly tied. It had a hole through the middle and the string was knotted through it. Jack took aim at the window.

The stone flew up in the air, carrying the length of thin string with it. It missed the window and fell down again. Jack picked it up. Once more he aimed—and this time the stone went right through the open window, just missing Paul, and landed on the floor.

Paul picked up the stone. He pulled at the string and it came up to the window pulling the strong twine behind it. Then Paul pulled at the twine, and the rope ladder began to unravel itself from Jack's hands and slip silently up the wall of the tower.

"There goes the ladder!" whispered Jack in excitement. "Paul's got it! He's only got to fix it firmly to something and escape down it!"

Mike pulled on it gently. It felt tight to his hand.

"Paul's fixed it!" he whispered. "It feels quite firm. I hope he gets a move on and comes down at once!"

But Paul didn't come! The boys waited and waited, but nobody came down the rope ladder. Whatever could have happened?

Mike Is Caught

"Why doesn't Paul come?" wondered Jack impatiently. "What a time he is! Surely the ladder is safe now."

Mike peered up. The moon shone brightly on the tower of the Old House, and the rope ladder hung against the wall, quite straight and firm.

"It's funny," said Mike. "Do you suppose he doesn't dare to risk himself down our ladder?"

"Can't imagine *what* he's doing," said Jack. "We can't stand here all night. I do wish he'd hurry."

The two dogs came running up. They had finished their bone. They nosed round the two boys, licking their hands. Jack patted them. "Don't you bark at Paul when he comes down the ladder," he warned them. "He's a friend of ours—so don't you dare to make a sound. Do you hear, Tinker? Do you hear, Don?"

The dogs wagged their tails. They did not understand what Jack was saying, but they liked to hear him talking to them. Jack looked impatiently up the ladder once more. He shook it—but still nothing happened.

"I'll climb up softly and see what's up," said Mike at last. "He may be waiting for one of us to tell him how to climb down."

"All right," said Jack. "I'll hold the ladder as firmly as I can. Good luck!"

Mike began to climb the rope ladder. He went up the side of the tower in the bright moonlight like a little black shadow. The girls at Peep-Hole could see him quite well through the field-glasses. They were puzzled to think why

248

Mike should go up the ladder instead of Prince Paul coming down.

Mike went up and up. At last he came to the window where Prince Paul had taken in the top of the ladder. He put his head cautiously above the window-sill—caught sight of a little boy sitting on a couch at the far side of the room, looking very scared—and then a voice said, "Got him!" and Mr. Diaz leaned out of the window and took firm hold of poor Mike!

Mike did not dare to struggle, for he was afraid of falling down the ladder. He had to let himself be hauled into the tower room. Mr. Diaz stood him on the floor and then quickly pulled up the rope ladder, jerking it roughly from Jack's hands below.

"And now we have two prisoners," said the soft sleepy voice of Luiz, and Mike saw that he was there too, standing behind Mr. Diaz.

Mike said nothing. He just stood there, looking angry. He glanced at Prince Paul. The little boy called out to Mike.

"I would have warned you, but I dared not. They came into the room and saw me fixing the ladder—and they made me sit over here whilst they waited to see if you would come up."

"And he came up," said Mr. Diaz. "And here he can stay. And tomorrow, Luiz, we will board up this window so that neither Paul nor this inquisitive boy can signal to the other tiresome children. They must do without his company until Friday, when we take Paul somewhere that is not crowded out with curious children, who get themselves into trouble through poking their noses into somebody else's business."

"You will have to miss a little of your holiday," said sleepy-eyed Luiz to Mike. "But Paul here will welcome your company, I am sure! Maybe this will teach you not to interfere another time in what is no business of yours!"

The two men went out of the tower-room, locked the door and bolted it, Mike shot to the window and leaned out.

"Jack! Jack!" he called in a low voice. "Are you there?"

"Yes," said Jack from behind a bush. "What's happened?"

"They've pulled up the ladder and made me a prisoner too," said Mike. "But they don't know you're outside, Jack. Go back to the others and tell them and see if you can think of some idea to get us out. You won't be able to signal tomorrow because this window is going to be boarded up. You'll have to be jolly clever to rescue us. They are taking Paul away somewhere else on Friday and I expect they'll set me free then; but we *must* be rescued before or we'll never know where Paul has gone."

Jack listened to this long whisper in silence. He was angry with himself for having let Mike go up the ladder. He might have thought that maybe someone was waiting up there to catch one of them. "All right, Mike, old chap," he said. "I'll get you both out somehow. Cheer up. I'm going back now."

He slipped through the bushes to the wall. He climbed up a tree, whilst the dogs whined below, sad to see him go, and then dropped on to the top of the high wall. He jumped from there to the ground, took a quick look round to see if anyone was about and then tore off in the moonlight to Peep-Hole.

The girls were waiting for him, both in tears, for they had seen all that had happened through their field-glasses.

"Oh, Jack, oh, Jack!" wept Nora. "How can we get poor Mike back? Oh, why did you let him go up? We could see somebody waiting at the side of the window, and we couldn't warn you."

"It was bad luck," said Jack gloomily. "I was an idiot to

let him go up. Somehow I never thought of anyone lying in wait for one of us up there."

"What are we going to do now?" asked Peggy, wiping her eyes. "We'll have to get Mike back somehow. What will Dimmy say tomorrow morning when he doesn't go down to breakfast?"

"Cheer up," he said. "After all, we do know where Mike is—and we've only got to go to the police and they'll get him back for us."

"There's only one fat old policeman here and he doesn't belong to Spiggy Holes," said Peggy. "And anyway we can't get him in the middle of the night."

"I want to tell Dimmy," said Nora suddenly. "We will have to tell her tomorrow morning anyhow—and I want to tell her tonight. I can't go to sleep unless we tell somebody grown-up about Mike being caught."

"But we can't wake Dimmy in the middle of the night!" said Jack. "We'd better wait till the morning. Mike will be all right tonight; there's a bed in that tower-room, I saw it through the key-hole last night."

"I want to tell Dimmy," wept poor Nora. "I do want to tell Dimmy."

The little girl felt that if only she could tell somebody grown-up something could be done. Grown-up people were powerful—she even had an idea that Dimmy might march up to the Old House straightaway and demand that Mike should be set free!

"Well, we'll go and wake Dimmy and tell her now, if you feel you must let her know tonight," said Jack, who secretly felt as if he would like to tell her as soon as possible too. "She may have a good idea."

So down the winding staircase of their little tower went the three children, through the tower door into the kitchen and then up the carpeted staircase to Dimmy's bedroom. They knocked on the door.

"Who's that?" said Dimmy's voice.

"It's us," said Nora. "Can we come in?"

"Of course," said Dimmy. "Is one of you ill?"

The children opened the door. Dimmy switched on the light and sat up in bed and looked at them. Her hair was in two long plaits over her shoulder, and she somehow looked different, but very kind and anxious.

"Where's Mike?" she said. "Is he ill?"

They sat on her bed, and first one and then another of the children told her the strange story of the Old House, the secret passage from the shore to the cellars of the Old House, the prince who was a prisoner in the tower—and then how Mike had been caught at the top of the rope ladder.

Dimmy listened in the greatest surprise and astonishment. She asked them questions, she exclaimed in amazement, she groaned with horror when she heard about Mike.

"Well!" she said, when the long story was finished, "so that was your great secret! And a most extraordinary one too. I have wondered what those people up at the Old House were up to—I knew it was something queer and not right. Poor little Prince! What a shame to keep him prisoner like that! I read in the paper how he had disappeared, and no one knew where he was—but little did I think he was so near!"

"How are we to get Mike back?" asked Nora, much happier now that Dimmy knew everything. "And Paul too—he must be rescued before Friday."

Dimmy thought for a long time. Then she said something that set the children's hearts beating with excitement.

"My grandfather once told me that there was a secret way between Peep-Hole tower and the tower of the Old House," she said. "It was often used by the old-time

252

smugglers when they wanted to get unseen from one house to the other. If we could find it, we could reach the tower of the Old House easily, and fetch back the two boys without anyone knowing."

"Oh, Dimmy!" cried the three children, their eyes shining brightly. "We *must* find it! We must, we must!"

"Well, we will hunt for it tomorrow," said Dimmy. "And I think we must get George to help us, because it will mean using a good deal of strength to find a passage that has been unused and hidden for years. As far as I remember, my grandfather said that a great stone had to be swivelled round in the wall of our tower—and certainly none of us could do that. George is very strong, and he can keep a secret too."

After talking for a little while longer the children were sent off to bed. Before they got into bed they were very much cheered by seeing Mike at the lighted window of the Old House tower, waving to them in the moonlight. He seemed quite cheerful, and Nora and Peggy were very glad to see him.

"Good old Mike," said Jack, getting into bed. "I hope he won't be too miserable."

"So do I," said Nora. "And, oh, I do hope we find the hidden way between our tower and the other tower. Won't George be surprised when he hears all we've got to tell him! Oh, tomorrow, do come quickly!"

Where Is The Secret Door?

The next morning when Jack rushed to the window to look at the tower of the Old House he found that Mr. Diaz had kept his word—the window was now boarded up! No messages could be given to the prisoners, and they could send no messages back.

Jack didn't like it. He had hoped that perhaps Mr. Diaz might have forgotten to block up the window. It made everything seem very serious, when he looked at that blind window with the boards across it.

The children went down to breakfast looking solemn. Nora gave a little sob when she looked at Mike's empty chair at the table. But Dimmy seemed very cheerful and patted her on the back.

"Don't worry," she said. "Now that you've told me, I'll do my best to help—and we'll rescue both boys, never fear!"

Nobody seemed to want much breakfast, although it was poached eggs, which they all loved. Nora was anxious to do something for Mike and Paul as soon as possible, and she wouldn't even let Dimmy wash up after breakfast.

"Please do let us see if we can discover the secret door out of our tower," she begged. "Leave the cups and things, Dimmy dear—we can do those afterwards."

So Dimmy left them, and the three children trooped up the winding stone staircase with her. They went to Jack's room and looked round the grey stone walls.

It seemed impossible to find any secret door in those great walls. They knocked on them, they pressed on them, they stood on chairs and pushed against the higher part of the walls, but nothing moved, nothing swung round to show a hidden passage in the thick stone walls.

At eleven o'clock they stopped their hunting, quite tired out. Dimmy looked at Nora's pale face, and was sorry for her.

"I'm going to make some cocoa for us all, and get some ginger cake," she said. "We need a rest."

She ran downstairs. Peggy went with her to help. Nora sat on Jack's bed and looked gloomy.

"Cheer up, Nora," said Jack.

"I'm quite, quite sure there's no hidden door in this room," said Nora, with a deep sigh.

"I feel as if there isn't too," said Jack anxiously. "Wouldn't it be dreadful if it were only a tale, and not true at all!"

"Don't, Jack," said Nora. "You make me feel worse."

Jack sat and thought for a few minutes. "I wonder if by any chance Dimmy has any old maps of Spiggy Holes in that big bookcase of hers downstairs," he said. "If she had, one of them might show where the hidden door is."

Dimmy came into the room at that minute, carrying a big jug of milky cocoa. Peggy followed with a dish of brown gingerbread. Everyone felt quite cheered by the look of it.

"Dimmy, I suppose you've no old books about Spiggy Holes, or old maps, have you?" asked Jack, munching his gingerbread.

Dimmy looked surprised. "Why didn't I think of that before?" she said. "Of course! There are two or three old books about this place, belonging to my great-grandfather. I believe they are very valuable. They are locked up in the big bookcase downstairs."

Jack almost choked over his cake in his delight. "Let's get them!" he said, jumping up.

"Finish your cake and cocoa," said Dimmy. "Then we'll go downstairs and look for them."

How the three children swallowed down their cocoa and gingerbread, in their eagerness to rush downstairs to find the old books! It wasn't more than a minute or two before they were all in Dimmy's rather dark little drawing-room, watching her whilst she unlocked the big old-fashioned bookcase there.

She moved aside some of the books on the top row, and behind them were some very old books, carefully covered in thick brown paper.

"There they are," said Dimmy. "This one is called *Spiggy Holes*—a record of smuggling days. And this one is called *Tales of Smugglers*, and Spiggy Holes is mentioned several times. This one is only an old cookery book—and this is a diary kept by my grandfather."

The children pounced eagerly on the first two books. The girls turned over the pages of *Spiggy Holes*, and Jack looked hurriedly through *Tales of Smugglers*.

"Look! Look! Here's a map of the secret passage we know!" cried Peggy suddenly. All the others crowded round her and peeped at the book she was holding. She laid it flat on the table. She pointed to a page on which was drawn a small map, showing Peep-Hole and the Old House and the shore. From the shore-cave to the Old House the secret passage was shown winding its way through the cliff underground to the cellars of the Old House.

"But there's no way shown from Peep-Hole to the Old House," said Jack in disappointment.

He was right. There was no hidden path between the two houses on the map. Eagerly Nora turned the pages to see if another map was shown, but there was none.

The two books were a great disappointment. Peggy, who was a good reader, hurriedly read through both of them to see if she could perhaps find anything written about the way between the two towers—but not a word was said.

"It must have been just a tale," said Nora in disappointment, closing the books.

"I feel sure it wasn't," said Dimmy, puzzled. "I remember so well how my grandfather told me about the secret. I wonder if he says anything about it in his old diary. He kept it when he was a boy, and it wasn't found until a year or two ago. The ink has faded, and it was so difficult to read that I didn't try more than a few pages. It was all about his days as a boy."

"Dimmy, let me have it," said Jack. "I will go away by myself and try to make it all out. It will take me a little time, but I'll use my magnifying-glass to help me to read your grandfather's tiny writing."

Dimmy gave the little paper-covered diary to Jack. He slipped off upstairs with it. The two girls looked at Dimmy.

"What shall *we* do?" asked Nora. "I don't feel like bathing or digging without Mike here."

"Then you can just come and help me to wash up those breakfast things and make the beds and dust and get dinner ready!" said Dimmy briskly. "It will do you good to think of something else for a while."

"It won't," said Peggy dismally. But Dimmy was right. Both girls felt much better about things when they set to work to wash up and to dust.

Dinner-time came. Peggy went up to fetch Jack. He was huddled in a corner with his magnifying-glass, trying to read every word of the old, old diary.

"Dinner-time," said Peggy. "Have you found anything interesting, Jack?"

"No," said Jack. "It's all about how he goes birds '-nesting and fishing and boating. He must have

257

been a nice sort of boy. He was a great one for playing tricks on people too. It says here how he put a toad into his aunt's bed, and she woke the whole house up to get it out!"

"Naughty boy!" said Peggy. "And poor old toad! It must have hated being squashed under the bedclothes. What else does it say?"

"Oh, lots of things," said Jack, flicking over the pages. "Tell Dimmy I'll be down in half a minute. I just want to finish the next few pages."

So Peggy went downstairs again, and Dimmy and the two girls began their meal without Jack. They were in the middle of it when they heard a tremendous shouting, and Jack's feet came tearing down the stone staircase. The door into the kitchen was flung open, and then the dining-room door flew back with a crash. The girls almost jumped out of their skin. Dimmy leapt to her feet.

"Whatever's the matter?" she cried.

"I've found it, I've found it!" yelled Jack, dancing round the room like a clown in a circus. "It's all here —there's a map of it and everything!"

The girls squealed. Dimmy sank down into her chair again. She wasn't used to these adventures!

"Show! Show us the map!" yelled Nora. She swept aside her plate and glass with a crash, and Jack set the old diary down on the tablecloth.

"Listen," he said. "This is Dimmy's grandfather's entry for the third of June, exactly one hundred years ago! He says, 'Today has been the most exciting day of my life. I found at last the old hidden passage between Peep-Hole and the Old House tower. A gull fell into the chimney of my room and I climbed up it to free the bird. Whilst I was there I pressed by accident on the great stone that swings round to open the passage in the wall of the tower.'"

"O-o-oh!" squealed Nora. "We can find it too!"

"Don't interrupt," said Peggy, her face pale with excitement. "Go on, Jack."

"He goes on to tell how he got into the passage, which runs down the walls of our tower to the ground, up the cliff to the Old House, branches off to join our own secret passage somewhere, and also goes on to the tower of the Old House, up and inside the thick walls there, and into the topmost room of the tower!" Jack could hardly speak, he was so thrilled at having found what he wanted.

"There's a rough map here that he drew after he had found out all about the passage. He kept the secret to himself, because he was afraid that if he didn't his father might have the passage blocked up."

Everyone pored over the map. It was faded and difficult to see, even under the magnifying-glass, but the children could plainly follow the passage from their tower, downwards in the wall right to the ground and below it, then underground to the Old House, up through the thick walls there, and into the top room of the Old House tower.

"I knew I was right! I knew I was right!" said Dimmy, quite as excited as the children.

"Let's go straight up and find it!" said Nora. "Come on! Oh, do come on!"

They all fled upstairs, tumbling over the steps in their haste. They *must* find that secret door in the chimney. Quick! Quick!

Another Secret Passage!

They all rushed into Jack's bedroom at the top of the tower—but at the first look round Peggy gave a cry.

"What sillies we are! There's no fireplace here!"

"Goodness—of course not," said Jack in dismay. "I'd completely forgotten that. But the map quite clearly shows that the passage starts somewhere in the chimney."

"Our room below has a big stone fireplace!" cried Nora. "It must be there that the passage starts. Hurry!"

Down they tore to Nora's room, where there was certainly a big, old-fashioned stone fireplace. Jack looked up it.

"Get me a stool or something," he said. "I can stand on that and grope about."

So, with the girls jigging impatiently about below, Jack stood on a stool and groped about in the dirty old chimney. At one side he felt what seemed to him to be narrow steps cut in the chimney. He told Miss Dimmy, looking down at her as black as a little sweep!

"Yes, that's right, there would be steps there," said Dimmy. "In the olden days small boys were sent up to sweep these big chimneys and sometimes steps were cut to help them. Can you get up them, Jack?"

Jack thought he could. So up he went, choking over the years-old soot. The steps were very small, and came unexpectedly to a little opening off the chimney itself. Jack was sure that the door to the hidden passage was somewhere in that opening!

The stones and bricks were intermixed there and were

rough to his hand. He pulled and pushed at each one, hoping it would swing round and show him an opening beyond. But not until he suddenly slipped and bumped against a certain stone did anything move at all!

His shoulder fell against a stone that stood out from the rest. It gave under his weight, and seemed to swing round, giving a click as it did so. Jack quickly shone his torch on to it, and saw a small hole appearing in the wall of the chimney. He put his hand into the hole and felt an iron ring.

"I've found the entrance! I've found it!" he yelled down the chimney. He pulled hard at the iron ring, and felt the stone to which it was fastened move a little; but no matter how hard Jack pulled he could not make the stone move any farther.

He climbed down the chimney, and the girls cried out in horror when they saw his black face and hands. He grinned at them, and his teeth shone white in his mouth.

"Dimmy, we'll have to get George to help us," he said. "I think the entrance-stone is stiff with the years that have gone by since it was last used. If we got George to bring a thick rope and fasten it to the iron ring I've found up there, we could swing the stone round all right and see the entrance to the passage. The stone has moved just a little—I can see the crack with my torch where it should come away from its place."

"George is working in the garden this afternoon," said Dimmy joyfully. "We can get him easily. No, Jack, no, don't *you* go and get him—you look so awful!"

But Jack was gone. He sped down the staircase and out into the garden. George was busy digging up potatoes. Jack burst on him, crying, "George, George, come quickly!"

George looked up in surprise, and saw a black, grinning creature running towards him. He got a tremendous shock

261

and dropped his spade. It took him quite a minute before he would believe that the black creature was his friend Jack!

Talking eagerly and telling George things that astonished the farm-lad greatly, Jack led him up the stone staircase to the girls' bedroom.

"Has he brought a rope?" cried Nora.

George nearly always had a rope tied two or three times round his waist. He gaped at the two girls and Miss Dimmy, and then said, "Where's Mike?"

"You haven't been listening!" said Jack impatiently. "I was telling you all the way up."

"Let *me* tell him," said Dimmy, seeing that George really was thinking that everyone was quite mad. So she told him the whole story as shortly as possible. George nodded his head solemnly every now and again. He didn't really seem astonished now that he knew everything, but his eyes gleamed when he heard that Dimmy wanted him to go up the chimney and tie his rope to the iron ring.

"I'd like to get Mike back all right," said George, undoing the rope round his middle. It proved to be very long and very strong. He disappeared into the chimney with Jack's torch. Jack tried to climb up after him, he was so impatient, but came down at once, his eyes and mouth full of soot kicked down by George's enormous boots.

George found the iron ring in the little opening and knotted his rope in it. The end fell down the chimney to the hearth like a brown snake. George jumped down.

"Now we'll all pull," he said, with his slow, wide smile. So they all pulled—and the rope gave a little as the big stone above swung round and back, leaving just enough room for anyone to squeeze through.

Jack climbed up the chimney again and gave a shout as he saw the dark opening. "Oh, the secret passage is here all right! Come on, all of you!"

Poor Dimmy! She was really horrified at seeing everyone go up that dirty, dark old chimney and getting black with soot—but even she went up too, just to see what kind of a secret passage it could be!

George had squeezed through the opening that was made when one big stone had swung out of its place. It had been cunningly built on a kind of swivel set in the next stone, and when weight was put on to the iron ring the stone swung round.

A very narrow way led round the back of the chimney—so narrow that George had to walk sideways to make himself small enough. Then he came to an iron ladder set at his feet, disappearing down into the darkness. He called back to the children.

"There's a ladder here, going downwards. I reckon there's an outer wall and an inner wall to part of this tower, and that's where the passage is! The rest of the tower wall is solid."

Down the narrow iron ladder they all went. They had to hold their torches in their teeth, for they needed both their hands. Dimmy had no torch, so she stood at the top of the ladder, waiting for them all to return.

The iron ladder went right down inside the wall and ended below the tower itself. A small room was at the foot of the ladder, and in it the children saw two old tops, a wooden hand-carved toy boat and some old, mildewed books.

"This must have been Dimmy's grandfather's hidey-hole when he was a boy," said Jack. "Look at his toys!"

From this small underground room, smelling so musty and queer, a narrow passage led up the cliff.

"This passage can't be so very far underground," said George, leading the way. "Hallo! Look there! Surely that is daylight?"

It was! A bright circle of daylight shone not far above their heads.

"I guess a rabbit has made its burrow above us," said Jack, with a laugh. "He must have burrowed from the surface down to this passage. What a shock for him when he fell through!"

"Well, the bunny has let some fresh air into this place, at any rate," said George. "Perhaps that is what has kept it fresh enough to breathe in."

They went along the passage, and then came to a stop. "What's up, George? Why have you stopped?" asked Jack.

"Because the passage has fallen in here," said George. "We'll have to get spades and dig it free again. The roof has fallen in, and we can't get any farther. We'll come back and dig it out. I reckon the passage goes on to the tower of the Old House, and then we'll find an iron ladder going up inside the walls just as we found at Peep-Hole."

The children squeezed back through the passage and went up the iron ladder to the chimney. Dimmy had got down again and was awaiting for them in the girls' room, having washed herself clean.

They told her excitedly what they had found. Jack ran down to the shed to get spades, and to find some biscuits for himself, for he had had no dinner.

"We shall be able to rescue Mike and Paul very soon now," said Peggy hopefully.

"Better clear the passage now and try to get to the boys tonight," said George thoughtfully. "You see, if we can rescue them at night there's not so much fear of us being heard, and we can get a good few hours' start of the folk at the Old House."

"Right, George," said Dimmy, who was just as excited as the children.

George and Jack went to clear the passage ready for the night's adventure. The girls went to wash themselves, and to pore once more over the exciting diary that had told them just what they wanted to know.

In an hour's time Jack and George came back, hot, dusty, sooty, and thirsty. Dimmy made them have a bath, and put on clean clothes—though George looked very comical in Mike's shorts and jersey! Then they all sat down to a good tea, which they really felt they had earned.

"This is getting more and more exciting!" said Peggy, spreading her bread and butter with Dimmy's homemade shrimp paste. "I feel as if I'm bursting with excitement. If only old Mike knew what we were doing!"

"He'll know soon enough," said Jack, with his mouth full.

"I reckon the strange folk up at the Old House will be pretty furious when they find Mike and the prince gone," said George rather solemnly. "I think you'd better all get away from here with Paul, whilst Miss Dimity and I tell the police and find out a bit more about this prince of yours."

"Get away from here?" said Jack. "But where could we go that was safe?"

No sooner had he said it than he and the girls had the most marvellous idea in the world.

"Our secret island! We'd be safe there! It's not far from here!" yelled Jack.

"The secret island!" cried Peggy and Nora.

"What's that?" asked George in astonishment.

"It's on Lake Wildwater, about forty miles from here," said Jack. "We lived on our secret island on the lake when we ran away once—it would be a wonderful place for the prince till he's safe from his enemies."

"Good idea!" said George. "I'll take you round the coast in my boat to Longrigg, where I've a brother who has a car. He can drive you to Wildwater—and you can do the rest!"

"Won't Mike be pleased, won't Mike be pleased!" shouted Nora. "Oh, I do feel so happy!" And she danced poor Dimmy round and round the room till Dimmy had to beg for mercy!

The Rescue Of The Prisoners

It was arranged that Mike and Paul should be rescued that night through the secret passage—if only the entrance at the other end could be used and was not too old or stiff!

"Jack and I went right along the passage to the Old House tower," said George. "There's an iron ladder there like ours. I reckon it leads up to the top room, to the fireplace."

"We had better plan everything carefully," said Dimmy. "George and Jack had better rescue the boys, and bring them safely back here. Then I and the girls will prepare plenty of food and take it down to George's boat. We will wait there for you."

"Yes, we shall need plenty of food on the secret island," said Nora. "There are wild raspberries there, and wild strawberries, but that's about all, unless we catch rabbits and fish as we did last year when we lived there!"

"You'll only be there a day or two until we can find out about Prince Paul and get someone to take charge of him till he goes back to his own land," said Dimmy. "I will stay behind here—and George will return to me, too, so that I shall be able to deal with the folk at the Old House. I shall simply say that you have all gone away."

"Dimmy, lets get the food ready for tonight," said Peggy eagerly. "We only need food—we don't need saucepans or kettles, or beds or anything like that—everything is neatly stored away in the dry caves on the secret island, ready for when we went there again. But we shall need plenty of food for five people."

So the two girls and Dimmy began to pack up all kinds of food. There was a joint of meat, two dozen tarts, a tin of cakes of all kinds, a tin of biscuits, some tins of soup and fruit, potatoes and peas from the garden, and a basket of ripe plums. Cocoa was put into the box of food, and tins of milk. Nora remembered the sugar, and Peggy thought of the salt. It was really exciting packing everything up.

George carried the big box down to the boat and stowed it there. Jack followed with two baskets. Dimmy hurriedly stuffed a box of black currant lozenges into one basket, in case any of them caught cold that night.

"I think that's everything," said Dimmy. "You must wear your coats tonight, for the weather is a bit colder. Good gracious me, what an adventure this is! I never thought I'd have such a time at my age!"

"Dimmy dear, I wish you were coming with us to our lovely secret island," said Peggy. "You'd love it so. You'll be lonely without us here, won't you?"

"Yes," said Dimmy. "But perhaps you'll soon be back again. Anyway, it will be nice to have Mike safe. I don't like to think of him up there in that tower all the time."

The night came quickly, for they had all been busy. It was arranged that George and Jack should go to rescue the two boys about half-past eleven. George had already been to the next village and had rung up his brother at Longrigg to tell him to have a car ready for the children. In fact, George was really marvellous.

"Now it's time to go," said George, looking at the enormous watch he kept in his waistcoat pocket. "Miss Dimity, you will go down to my boat with the girls, won't you, in a few minutes. Jack and I will bring the boys back here by the secret passage and slip down to the boat too. Then we can set off."

"Good luck, George!" said Nora. "Good luck, Jack!"

Dimmy and the girls went to the tower-room with them

and watched them climb up the chimney. They heard them groping round the narrow way behind the chimney to the iron ladder. Then there was silence.

"We'd better get Mike's coat and an extra coat for Prince Paul," said Dimmy. "Then we'll make our way to the beach and sit in the boat till the others come. I'll just give you both a drink of hot milk first, for I can see you are shivering!"

"It's with excitement, not with cold," said Nora. But she was glad of the hot milk all the same.

"I do wonder how George and Jack are getting on," said Peggy. "I wonder if they've reached the Old House tower yet."

George and Jack were getting on very well. They had climbed down the iron ladder, their torches between their teeth. They had gone through the little room below, where the old old toys still lay, and had made their way through the narrow passage underground that led to the Old House.

When they came to the part where they had cleared away the fallen roof that afternoon George shone his torch round. "It looks to me as if another bit of the roof will fall in at any moment," said George anxiously. "I hope it lasts till we get back."

"So do I," said Jack. "It would be awful to be caught because the roof fell in. Gracious, George—a bit of it's tumbling in now—some stones fell on my coat."

"Well, let's hope for the best," said George. "Come on."

On they went, and presently came to where another narrow passage forked off from the one they were following.

"That's the passage to the secret way between the shore-cave and the cellars of the Old House," said Jack. "It's a pity that is blocked up too, George, or we might have tried it."

The two had already seen that afternoon that the passage joining theirs to the shore-cave passage was blocked up with fallen stones, and they had not tried to clear it, for, as George said, it might be blocked up all the way. It was quicker to use the passage from one tower to the other, and to return to Peep-Hole and run down to the beach by the cliff-path.

They soon came to the iron ladder that led up the inside of the walls of the Old House tower. They climbed it as quietly as they could. They came to a narow ledge running round the back of a chimney-place. They squeezed round it, and found themselves in a small dark place with stone walls all around.

"Feel for an iron ring," whispered George. "There is sure to be one here. If we can find it, we'll slip my rope into it, and both pull hard. I reckon the stone will swivel round just like ours at Peep-Hole did."

So they felt about for an iron ring, and shone their torches here and there—and at last George found the ring! He slipped his rope into it and knotted it. Then he and Jack pulled this way and that way—and suddenly the stone in which the iron ring was set groaned a little, swung slowly round—and there, in front of George and Jack, was the entrance to the fireplace built in the top room of the Old House tower!

Voices came up from the room below. George and Jack stood perfectly still and listened. Mr. Diaz was speaking.

"At dawn tomorrow you will come with me, Paul—and we will leave Mike here for a few days, just to give him a lesson not to put his nose into things that don't concern him! Anna will see to him, and set him free next week."

"Where are you taking Paul?" asked Mike's voice.

"Wouldn't you like to know?" said Mr. Diaz in a mocking voice.

"Yes, I would," said Mike. "You've no right to make

270

any boy a prisoner, Mr. Diaz, and you'll get punished soon."

"Be careful I don't punish you first, you impudent boy!" said Mr. Diaz angrily. "Now go to bed, both of you—but you, Paul, must not get undressed, for you must be ready to come with me when I fetch you at dawn."

There was the sound of a door closing. George and Jack heard a key being turned and bolts being shot into their place. Then they heard footsteps going down the winding stone staircase.

"Wait a few minutes in case he comes back," whispered George, as he felt Jack move forward. They waited. They heard Mike comforting poor Paul. Jack felt furiously angry with Mr. Diaz. If only he could have him well punished!

"Now," whispered George. The two squeezed themselves through the narrow opening into the chimney. Below were rough steps. They felt for them with their feet.

Mike and Paul heard the noise and looked at one another in surprise.

"What's that noise, Mike?" asked Paul.

"A bird in the chimney perhaps," said Mike.

"Yes!" came Jack's voice. "It's a jack-daw, Mike! It's Jack!"

Paul got such a shock that he sat down suddenly on a chair that wasn't there. Mike got a shock too, but a very unpleasant one. He ran to the chimney and peered up —only to get a mass of soot in his face!

"Jack! Jack! How in the world did you get there?" asked Mike, in the greatest amazement and surprise. "Are the girls with you?"

"No. Only George," said Jack, jumping lightly down and stooping to get out of the hearth. "Come on, George."

Prince Paul picked himself up and stared in surprise at the two black-faced people coming from the chimney. Then he solemnly bowed to them and shook hands.

"We'll tell all there is to tell later on," said George. "There's no time to lose now. Dawn comes in a few hours and Mr. Diaz will be back to take Paul with him, so we have only that time to get you away safely. Come along back with us now—this hidden way that we have found leads back to Peep-Hole."

"The girls and Dimmy are waiting with lots of food in George's boat," Jack said excitedly to Mike. "We're going to the secret island, Mike. Think of it!"

Paul knew all about the secret island, for Mike had told him about it whilst the two had been prisoners together. His pale little face lighted up with joy. He took Mike's arm and squeezed it.

"Let's go quickly," he begged. So George took Paul, and Mike followed Jack, and they all disappeared up the chimney, leaving behind on the floor a great mass of soot.

Down the iron ladder they climbed, Paul a bit afraid for he was not used to adventures of this sort. Then along the hidden way they went in single file.

But suddenly George, who was leading, stopped in dismay. The others bumped into him.

"What's up, George?" asked Jack.

"Just what I feared!" groaned George. "The roof's fallen in again—and it's a bad fall this time. We'll never clear it! We're trapped!"

Jack pressed by George and looked at the fall of earth and stones in silence. It was true. It was a very bad fall — *now* what were they to do?

An Exciting Time

"Goodness, George! Whatever shall we do now?" said Jack anxiously. "We can never clear that fall—it looks as if the roof has fallen in for yards! We can't go back to the Old House—we'd just be walking into danger!"

George rubbed his chin and thought hard. They couldn't go forward—they couldn't go back—and certainly they couldn't stay in the middle!

"Seems as if we'd better go and have a look at that other blocked-up passage," said George at last. "You know — the one that branches off this one to join the secret way between the shore-cave and the cellars of the Old House."

"Right," said Jack. "The block there may not be so bad as it looks. It's our only chance anyway."

They all went to the place where the passage branched off. They squeezed down it till they came to the block. George pulled away some of the stones and tried to see how much of the passage was stopped up.

"I believe if the four of us could work at it we might clear it in time," said George at last. "And I've got a good idea too—the block is mostly of stones and bits of rock. If I pick them up, pass them to Jack, and he passes them to Paul and Paul to Mike, Mike could pile them up behind him and make them look as if there has been a good old roof-fall there! So if Mr. Diaz does come along he'll think it's impossible to come this way. And we'll be safely on the other side of the stones!"

"Good old George!" said Mike and Jack, who always loved a good idea. "Come on—we'll start."

"What do I do?" asked Paul, who was half-frightened, half-thrilled at being with the others. They told him what to do.

"You only just take hold of the stones I pass you," said Jack, "and pass them behind to Mike."

They set to work. George cleared away the stones, passing them to the others. Mike threw them behind him, and soon a great pile lay there, looking exactly as if they had fallen from the roof of the passage!

Soon George had cleared away quite a bit of the block. He shone his torch up and down it, and gave a cry of joy.

"I believe it'll be all right, boys! I can see the passage beyond already. We'll only need to clear a bit more, and we shall have a hole big enough to squeeze through."

They worked and worked. Paul became tired and they had to let him have a rest. Two hours went by. George felt rather anxious. He did not want Mr. Diaz to discover that Paul and Mike had escaped before they had all got safely away in the boat.

At last there was a hole big enough to squeeze through. One by one they got through it, and then George did a funny thing.

He glanced up at the roof near the block and then, taking a big stone, he struck the roof hard. A shower of earth fell at once.

"George! What are you doing?" cried Jack.

"I'm just making a small roof-fall," grinned George, his teeth flashing in the light of Jack's torch. "If I can fill up the hole we've made in the block, we'll be all right. We don't want our dear friend Mr. Diaz to squeeze through the hole too!"

"Good idea," said Jack. "Now hadn't we better go on, George? It's getting late."

"Sh!" said George suddenly. Everyone stood perfectly quiet in the passage. "Switch off your torches," whispered George. "I can hear something."

They all switched off their torches. Sounds were coming near—voices—angry voices!

"Oh, do let's go," whispered Mike. But George shook his head in the darkness and whispered "No."

"We don't want them to hear us," he said in a low tone. "They may guess where this leads to if they hear us, and go rushing off to the beach to find our boat. I think we're safe enough if we keep quiet. Put your arm round Paul, Jack—he's frightened, poor kid!"

They stood there in perfect silence. They heard Mr. Diaz and Luiz and someone else talking. They came to the roof-fall in the other passage and exclaimed about it.

"Look at that! They can't have gone down that way!"

"It might have fallen *after* they had gone," said the sleepy voice of Luiz. Then a sharper voice spoke loudly.

"This is disgraceful—to let the boy slip through your fingers like this! Are you sure there is no other way out of this passage?"

"There's a branch off it somewhere here," came Luiz's voice. Footsteps came up to the blockage through which George and the others had managed to squeeze.

"There's a great pile of stones here," said Mr. Diaz, peering over the stones that the boys had piled up. "And another roof-fall or something beyond. They couldn't possibly have got through that. No, it looks as if they escaped down that passage to Peep-Hole, and the roof fell after they had gone through. Well, our best course is to go back to the Old House and make a raid on Peep-Hole. The boys are sure to be there."

The voices and the footsteps grew fainter. At last they could no longer be heard. Everybody sighed with relief.

"Now we can get on," said George cheerfully. "I

thought somehow they wouldn't guess we'd gone this way —and anyway they don't know that it leads down to the passage to the shore-cave. Come on!"

They stumbled down the secret passage and at last came to an opening in the ground at their feet. Jack shone his torch down.

"This is where our passage joins the shore-passage," he cried in excitement. "We'll have to jump down into it. No wonder we didn't spot it when we used the shore- passage—we didn't dream of looking for holes in the roof, did we?"

They all jumped down into the passage below. Then they made their way quickly to the cave, sliding down into it, holding safely to the rope that swung there to help them.

"I wonder if the girls are there in the boat all right," said Mike.

The girls *were* there! They had been there for hours, anxiously waiting with Dimmy. They had not been able to imagine what could have happened to everyone!

They had talked at first, and then had watched and waited for the boys. But they hadn't come. Then Nora had begun to worry.

"Oh dear! They ought to be here now. Whatever can have happened?"

"Perhaps Mr. Diaz or someone was in the room for ages with Mike and Paul," said Peggy sensibly. "Jack and George couldn't possibly rescue them if anyone was with the others."

"That's true," said Dimmy. "Well, we must wait in patience. We can't do anything else! Are you two warm enough?"

"I'm glad of my coat," said Peggy. "It's a funny thing, but excitement makes me feel rather cold!"

They waited for another hour. Now all of them were

anxious and worried, though Dimmy tried not to show it. Then Nora gave a low cry.

"Look! I can see the light of a torch over there in the shore-cave! It must be them!"

It was! Jack, Mike, Paul, and George hurried across the sand in silence. They were tired and stiff now, but they knew that a long row awaited them! They were pleased that everything had at last gone well.

"Oh, Mike, dear Mike!" said Nora joyfully, so glad to have her brother back again that the tears fell down her cold cheeks. Mike hugged her and Peggy kissed kind old Dimmy, and got into the boat with the others. It was a good thing it was a big boat!

"I must say good-bye," said Dimmy hurriedly. "Don't push off yet, George—you've forgotten I'm not going with you!"

"Oh, Dimmy, I *wish* you were coming too," said Peggy, sad to say good-bye to her. "I hope you'll be all right. Anyway, George will be with you as soon as he rows the boat back from Longrigg."

"Good-bye, dears," whispered Dimmy. She got out of the boat. "Take care of yourselves. I'll let you know as soon as we have found out about Prince Paul, and what we must do with him. Good luck!"

"Good luck!" whispered the children. George pushed off from the little wooden jetty. The boat floated out on the water. George bent to the oars and began to row away. Soon nothing could be seen of Dimmy at all—she had vanished into the darkness.

The boat went on and on over the dark, restless sea. Jack had found the second pair of oars and was rowing too, to help George. The children spoke to one another in whispers, because George said voices carried so far over the water.

"Well, we've rescued you, Paul!" said Jack. "You're

safe with us now! And I don't somehow think that Mr. Diaz will be able to find you on our secret island! We'll have a nice little holiday there for a few days—and oh, won't it be *lovely* to be back there again, all by ourselves!"

"Lovely, lovely, lovely!" said the others, and began to dream about their island. Soon, soon, they would be there!

Off To The Secret Island

George rowed the boat silently over the calm sea towards the little fishing village of Longrigg. Jack helped him, and the children sat quietly in the boat until George said it was safe to talk.

"No one can hear you now," he said. "So talk away!"

And then what a noise there was as Mike told the others all that had happened when he was a prisoner with Paul. And Paul joined in excitedly, telling how he had been captured in his own father's palace and taken away to Cornwall over sea and land, in ships, aeroplanes, and cars. Poor Paul! He was really very glad to be with friends once more, for although he had not been very badly treated by Mr. Diaz and Luiz, he had been kept a close prisoner for some time.

Soon the moon came up and flooded the sea with its silvery light. The children could see one another's faces as they talked, and every time the oars were lifted from the water silvery drops fell off the blades.

"There's Longrigg!" said George, as they went round a cliff that jutted out into the sea. Everybody looked. The children had been to Longrigg before with George in his boat, but it looked different now in the moonlight—a huddle of silvery houses set in a cove between the cliffs.

"It's like an enchanted village," said Nora dreamily. "And I guess our secret island will look enchanted too, tonight, when we get there. Oh, I do feel so very excited when I think that we're really going there again!"

The children began to talk of their adventure on the

secret island the year before—how they had kept their own cow there and their own hens. How they had built their own house of willows, and had found caves in the hillside to live in during the winter. Paul listened, and longed to see the wonderful island!

They landed at Longrigg. George took them through the deserted village street to his brother's garage, a tiny place at the top of the street. A man was there waiting for them.

"Hallo, Jim," said George. "Here are the passengers for your trip. And mind, Jim, not a word to anyone about this. I'll explain everything to you when you come to see me tomorrow. Till then, say nothing to anybody.'

"Right, George," said Jim, who seemed very like his brother as he stood there, sturdy and straight in his dark overalls.

"Good-bye, George, and thanks for all your help," said Jack, getting into the car with the others. "Have we got the food? Oh yes—it's in the back. Good!"

"Good-bye," said George. "I'm going back to Peep-Hole now in case Miss Dimity wants a bit of help. Stay on your secret island till you hear from us. You'll all be quite safe there!"

The car started up and Jim set off up the cliff road. The children waved to George, and then the car turned a bend and was out of sight. They were on their way to Lake Wildwater—on their way to the island!

It was about forty miles away, and the car purred softly through the moonlit night. Paul was very sleepy and went sound asleep beside Peggy—but the others were too excited to sleep.

Jack watched the country flash by—five miles gone, ten, twenty, thirty, forty! They were almost there. Jim was to drive to where the children's aunt and uncle had once lived, and then leave them. They could find their way then to the lake, and get their boat, which was always ready.

"Here we are," said Jim. The car stopped. Jim got out. "I'll give you a hand with the food down to the boat," he said. So the six of them carried the food to where the boat was locked up in a small boat-house. Captain Arnold, the children's father, had built them a little house for their boat in case they wished to visit their secret island at any time. Mike had the key on his key-ring. He got it out and unlocked the boat-house. There lay the boat, dreaming of the water. The moon shone into the boat-house, and Jack was able to see quite well, as he undid the rope and pushed the boat from the house.

The food was put in. Everyone but Jim got into the boat. Jim said good-bye and good luck and strode back over the fields to his waiting car. The five children were alone!

Jack and Mike took the oars. Paul was wide awake now and was full of excitement, longing to see this wonderful secret island that he had heard so much about.

"It won't be long now," said Nora, her eyes shining happily in the moonlight. The oars made a pleasant splashing sound in the silvery waters, and the boat glided along smoothly.

On and on they went—and then, rounding a corner of the wooded bank of the lake, they came suddenly in sight of their island!

"Look! There it is, Paul!" cried Peggy. Paul looked. He saw a small island floating on the moonlit lake, with trees growing down to the water's edge. It had a hill in the middle of it, and it looked a most beautiful and enchanting place.

"Our secret island," said Nora softly, her eyes full of happy tears, for she had loved their island with all her heart, and had spent many, many happy days there along with the others the year before.

For a while the two boys leaned on their oars and

looked silently at their island, remembering their adventures there. Then they rowed quickly again, longing to land on the little beach they knew so well.

"There's our beach, with its silvery sand all glittering in the moonlight!" cried Nora. The boat slid towards it and grounded softly in the sand. Jack leapt out and pulled the boat in. One by one the children got out and stood on the little sloping beach.

"Welcome to our island, Paul," said Peggy, putting her arm round the excited boy. "This is our very own. Our father bought it for us after our adventures here last year—but we didn't think we'd visit it this summer! We left it last Christmas, when we were living in the hill-caves. They were *so* cosy!"

"Come along up the hill and find the caves," said Jack. "We are all awfully tired, and we ought to get some sleep. We'll get the rugs and things out of the cave, and heat some cocoa and have a meal. Then I vote we make our beds on the heather, as we used to do. It's very hot tonight, and we shall be quite warm enough."

"Hurrah!" said Mike in delight. "Give me a hand with this box of food. The girls can bring the other things, if Paul will help them."

"Of course I will," said Paul, who really felt as if he was living in a peculiar dream! They all made their way up the beach, through a thicket of bushes and trees, and up a hillside where the bracken was almost as tall as they were. The moon still shone down from a perfectly clear sky, and except that the colours were not there, everything was as clear as in daylight.

"Here's our cave!" said Jack in delight. "The heather and bracken are so thick in front of it that I could hardly see it. Mike, have you got your torch handy? We shall need to go into our inner store-cave to get a few things tonight."

Mike fished in his pocket for his torch. He gave it to Jack. "Thanks," said Jack. "Peggy, come with me into the store-cave, will you, and we'll get out the rugs. Mike, will you and Nora choose a place for a fire and make one? We'll have to have some cocoa or something. I'm so hungry and thirsty that I could eat grass!"

"Right, Captain!" said Nora, feeling very happy indeed. It was wonderful to be on the island like this—able to sleep in the heather and have a camp-fire. She and Mike and Paul hunted about for twigs and wood, and found a nice open place near the cave for the fire.

Peggy and Jack went to the back of the cave, found the passage that led into the inner cave, and crept through to the big store-cave beyond that lay in the heart of the hillside.

"Everything's here just as we left it!" said Peggy, pleased, as Jack shone his torch around. "Oh, there's the kettle, Jack—and I want a saucepan, too, for the soup tonight and eggs tomorrow morning. Dimmy put some into the box. Look, there's the rabbit-skin rug we made last year—and the old blankets and rugs too. Bring those, Jack, we'll need them tonight."

Jack piled the rugs in his arms. Peggy took the kettle and the saucepan. They went back to the outer cave, and then looked for the others outside. Mike had got a good fire going. Paul was sitting beside it in delight. He had never seen a camp-fire before.

"Nora, get the cocoa tin, a bag of sugar, and the tinned milk," said Peggy. "Mike, go to the spring and fill this kettle with water, will you? I'll boil water for the cocoa and we'll add milk and sugar afterwards."

Mike went off with the kettle to the cold spring that gushed out from the hillside and ran down it in a little stream. He soon filled it and came back. "What are we going to have to eat?" he asked hungrily.

283

"Soup out of a tin, bread, biscuits, and cocoa," said Peggy.

"Oooooh!" said everyone in delight. Mike opened the tin, glad that Dimmy had remembered to put in a tin-opener! He poured the rich tomato soup into the saucepan, and then set it on the fire firmly. "Shall I make another fire to boil the kettle?" he asked.

"Oh no," said Peggy. "The soup will soon be ready, and we've got to cut the bread, and get out the biscuits. You do that, Nora. Where's the biscuit tin, Mike?"

The soup cooked in the saucepan. Peggy sent Jack for cups and dishes and bowls and spoons from the inner cave. The kettle was put on to boil. Peggy cleverly poured the soup from the saucepan into the dishes and handed a plateful to everyone. Hunks of bread were given out too. The kettle sang on the fire, and the smoke rose in the moonlight and floated away in the clear air.

"This is simply perfect," said Mike, tasting his tomato soup and putting big pieces of bread into it. "I wish this meal could last for ever."

"You'd get pretty tired of tomato soup if it did!" said Jack. Everyone laughed. Peggy made the cocoa and handed round big cups of it, with tinned milk and sugar, and a handful of biscuits for everyone.

How they enjoyed that meal by the camp-fire! Mike said he wished they needn't go to sleep—but they were all so terribly sleepy that it was no good wishing that!

"I shall fall asleep sitting here soon," said Nora, rubbing her eyes. "What a nice supper that was! Come on, every-one, let's make our beds in the heather and wash the supper things tomorrow."

So they spread the rugs out in the soft heather and lay down just as they were in their clothes—and in two sec-onds they were all fast asleep on the secret island, lost in happy dreams of all they were going to do the next day!

Peace On The Island

All night long the five children slept soundly on their rugs in the heather. The three boys were in the shelter of a big gorse bush, and the two girls cuddled together beside a great blackberry bush. The heather was thick and soft and as springy as any bed.

The sun rose up and the sky became golden. The birds twittered and two yellow-hammers told everyone that they wanted a "litle bit of bread and *no* cheese!" The rabbits who had played about near the sleeping children shot off to their holes. A rambling hedgehog sniffed at Mike, and then went away too.

Jack awoke first. He was lying on his back, and he was very much astonished when he opened his eyes and looked straight up into the blue sky. He had expected to see the ceiling of his bedroom at Peep-Hole—and he saw sky and tiny white feathery clouds, very high up.

Then he remembered. Of course—they were on the dear old secret island! He lay there on his back looking up happily at the sky, waiting for the others to wake. Then he sat up. Far below him were the calm, blue waters of the lake. It was a perfect day—sunny, warm, and calm. Jack looked at his watch, and stared in surprise—for it was half-past nine!

"Half-past nine!" said Jack in amazement. "How we have slept! I wish the others would wake up—I'm jolly hungry."

He got up cautiously and slipped his few clothes off. He ran down to bathe in the lake. The water was delicious.

He dried himself in the hot sun and dressed again. He went to the spring and filled the kettle for breakfast. Then he busied himself in making a fire.

Mike awoke next, and then Peggy and Nora together. Paul still slept on. The girls were full of joy to find themselves on the secret island, and they flew down to bathe in the lake with Mike. When Paul awoke they asked him if he too would like to have a swim, but he shook his head.

"I can't swim," he said. "And I don't want to bathe in the lake. I just want to stay here with Jack."

They got breakfast. Nora ran down to the lake to wash the supper things. Jack fetched more wood for the fire, which was burning well. Peggy cut big slices of bread and butter, and popped some eggs into the saucepan to boil. "Two eggs for everyone," she said. "I know quite well you'll all be able to eat heaps and heaps! Nora, find the salt, will you? I'll boil the eggs hard, and we can nibble them and dip them in the salt."

"Let's have some of these ripe plums too," said Mike, uncovering the basket. "They won't last very long in this hot weather. And where are the biscuits, Peggy? Surely we didn't finish them all last night."

"Of course not," said Peggy, fishing them out from under a bush and taking off the lid. "I hid them there because I know what you boys are with biscuits!"

They sat round in the heather, eating their hard-boiled eggs, thick slices of bread and butter, ripe plums, and biscuits, and drinking cocoa that Peggy had made for them.

"I don't know why, but we always seem to have most delicious meals on our secret island," said Mike. "They always taste nicer here than they do anywhere else."

"Paul, don't you want your second egg?" asked Peggy, seeing that Paul had not eaten it. He shook his head.

"I am not used to your English breakfasts," he said. "At

home, in my own country, we simply have a roll of bread and some coffee. But I would like to eat my egg later in the morning, Peggy. It is so nice. I have never had a hard-boiled egg before."

Paul began to talk of his own land. He was a nice boy, with beautiful manners that struck the others as rather comic sometimes. He would keep bowing to Peggy and Nora whenever he spoke to them. He had learnt English from his governess, and spoke it just as well as the other children did.

He told them about his father and mother. He cried when he spoke of his mother, who did not know where he was. Peggy and Nora felt very sorry for the little prince. They comforted him, and told him that soon his troubles would be over.

"You are so lucky not to have to be princes or princesses," he told the children. "You can have a jolly time and do as you like—but I can't. You will never be kidnapped or taken prisoner—but maybe it will happen to me again sometime or other. There are many people who do not want me to be king when my father dies."

"Do you want to be?" asked Jack.

"Not at all," said Paul. "I would like best of all to live with you four children, and be an ordinary boy. But I am unlucky enough to have been born a prince and I must do my duty."

"Well, stop worrying about things for a little while," said Peggy. "Enjoy your few days here on our secret island. It will be a real holiday for you. Jack will teach you to swim, and Mike will teach you how to make a camp-fire. You never know when things like that will be useful to you."

The children all felt rather lazy after their late night. Peggy and Nora washed up the breakfast things, and Peggy planned the lunch. The children had eaten all the ripe plums and Peggy wondered if she should open a large tin of fruit. She would cook some potatoes and peas too, and they could have some of the meat off the cold joint they had brought.

"What about picking some wild raspberries, as we used to do last year?" asked Nora eagerly. "Don't you remember the raspberry canes on one part of the island, Peggy?—they were simply red with delicious raspberries!"

"We'll go and see if there are any still ripe," said Peggy. "But first let's see if Willow House is still in the little wood beyond the beach."

The children had built a fine little house of willow branches the summer before, which had sheltered them well on wet or cold days and nights. They all went running down the hill to see if Willow House was still standing.

They squeezed through the thick trees until they came to the spot where Willow House was—and it stood there, green and cool, inviting them to go inside.

"But the whole of Willow House is growing!" cried Peggy. "Every branch has put out leaves— and look at these twigs shooting up from the roof! It's a house that's alive!"

She was right. Every willow stick they had used to build their house had shot out buds and leaves and twigs—and the house was, as Peggy said, quite alive. Inside the house long twigs hung down like green curtains.

"Dear little Willow House," said Peggy softly. "What fun we had here! And how we loved making it—weaving the willow twigs in and out to make the walls—and you made the door, Jack. And do you remember how we stuffed up the cracks with heather and bracken?"

The others remembered quite well. They told Paul all about it and he at once wanted to stop and build another house.

"No, we don't need one," said Jack. "We can sleep

out-of-doors now—and if rain comes we'll just sleep in the cave."

Paul ran in and out of Willow House. He thought it was the nicest place in the world. "I wish I had a house of my own like this," he said. "Mike, Jack, will you come back to my country with me and teach me how to build a willow house?"

The boys laughed. "Come along and see if we can find some ripe raspberries," said Mike. "You'll like those, Paul."

They all went to the part of the island where the raspberries grew. There were still plenty on the canes, though they were getting over now.

Peggy and Nora had brought baskets. Soon they had the baskets half-full, and their mouths were stained with pink. As many went into their mouths as into the baskets!

"It's one o'clock," said Mike, looking at his watch. "Good gracious! How the morning has gone!"

"We'll go back and have dinner," said Peggy. So back they all went in the hot sun, feeling as hungry as hunters, although they had eaten so many raspberries!

They had a lovely dinner—cold mutton, peas, potatoes, raspberries, and tinned milk. Mike brought them icy-cold water from the spring, and they drank it thirstily, sending Paul for some more when it was finished. Paul wanted to do jobs too, and Peggy thought it was a good idea to let him. The sun had caught his pale little face that morning and he was quite brown.

"What shall we do this afternoon?" asked Paul.

"I feel sleepy," said Peggy, yawning. "Let's have a nice snooze on the heather—then we could have a bathe before tea, and a jolly good meal afterwards."

It was a lovely lazy day they had, and they thoroughly enjoyed it after all the alarms and adventures of the last week or two. Jack began to teach Paul to swim, but he was not very good at learning, though he tried hard enough!

They had tea, and then they went boating on the lake in the cool of the evening. "We might try a bit of fishing tomorrow," said Jack. "It would be fun to have fried fish again, Peggy, just as we did last year."

"Do you suppose we are quite, quite safe here?" asked Paul anxiously, looking over the waters of the lake as they rowed about.

"Of course!" said Jack. "You needn't worry, Paul. Nobody will come to look for you here."

"If Mr. Diaz knew about your secret island he might come here to seek me," said Paul. "Hadn't we better keep a watch in case he does?"

"Oh no," said Jack. "There's no need to do that, Paul. Nobody would ever find us here, I tell you."

"Where did you use to watch, when you were here last year and were afraid of people coming to look for you?" asked Paul.

"There's a stone up on the top of the hill where we used to sit, among the heather," said Jack. "You get a good view all up and down the lake from there."

"Then tomorrow I will sit and watch there," said Paul at once. "You do not know Mr. Diaz as well as I do, and I think he is clever enough to follow us, and to take me prisoner again. If I see him coming in a boat, there will be time to hide away in the caves, won't there?"

"Oh yes," said Jack. "But he won't come. Nobody will guess you are here with us."

But Paul was nervous—and when the next day came he ran off by himself. "Where's he gone?" asked Jack.

"Oh, up to the hill-top to watch for his enemies!" said Nora, with a laugh. "He won't see anything. I'm sure of that!"

But Prince Paul *did* see something that very afternoon!

The Enemy Find The Island

Prince Paul was sitting on top of the little hill that rose in the middle of the island. He was quite sure that his enemies would try to find him, and would think of coming to the children's secret island.

He sat there for two or three hours, watching the lake around the island. It was very calm and blue. Paul yawned. It was rather boring sitting there by himself—but the other children wouldn't come, for they said there was no fear of enemies coming so soon.

Paul saw Mike and Jack far below at the edge of the water. They were getting out the boat to go and fish. The girls came running down to join them. They had already asked Paul to come, but he wouldn't. He was really afraid of water, and it was all that the others could do to get him in to bathe.

Paul stood up and waved to the others. They waved back. They didn't like leaving him alone, but really they couldn't go and sit up there for hours. Besides, Peggy had said that if they caught some fish she would fry them for supper, and that really sounded rather delicious!

"We shan't be long, Paul!" shouted Mike. "We shall only be round the south end of the island, which is a good fishing-place. Yell to us if you want us."

"Right!" shouted back Paul, and he waved again. He really thought it was queer the way the four children seemed to like the water so much—they were always bathing and paddling and boating! But Paul liked them immensely, especially Mike, who had been a great help to him when he had been a prisoner in the tower.

He watched the boat leave the little beach and row round to the other side of the island. The boat looked very small from where he stood, and the children looked like dolls! But he could hear their voices very clearly. They were getting their fishing-lines ready.

Paul half wished he was with them, they all sounded so jolly. He watched them for some time, and then he turned round and gazed down the blue waters of the lake on the other side of the island.

And he saw a boat there! Yes—a boat that was being rowed by two men! Paul stood and watched, his heart beating fast. Who were the two men? Could they be Mr. Diaz and Luiz? He hated them both and was afraid of them. Had they come to find him again?

He turned to the opposite side of the lake and yelled to the four children in the boat there.

"Jack! Mike! There's a boat coming up the lake!"

"What?" shouted Jack.

Paul yelled again, even more loudly. "I said, *there's a boat coming up the lake*!"

The four children looked at one another in dismay and surprise. "Surely Mr. Diaz can't have found out where we are," said Mike. "Though he's quite clever enough to guess, if he knows we are the children who ran away to a secret island last year!"

"What shall we do, Jack?" asked Nora.

"We haven't time to do anything much," said Jack anxiously. "I think it wouldn't be safe to go and hide on the island—those men will search it thoroughly, caves and all. We'd better get Paul down here, and row off to the mainland in the boat. We could hide in the trees there for a bit."

"Good idea, Jack," said Mike. He stood up in the boat and yelled to Paul, who was anxiously waiting for his orders.

Paul had spotted their enemies

"Come on down here, Paul. We'll go off in the boat. Hurry up!"

Paul waved his hand and disappeared. When he appeared at the edge of the water, the others saw that he was carrying something. He had a loaf of bread, a packet of biscuits, and two tins of fruit!

"I say! You've got brains to think of those!" said Jack, pleased. "Good for you, Paul!"

Paul went red with pleasure. He thought the four children were wonderful, and he was very proud to be praised by Captain Jack!

"I just had time to push all our things into a bush," said Paul. "And I grabbed these to bring, because I guessed we might have to stop away for some hours."

"Good lad," said Jack. "Come on in. We haven't any time to lose. Tell us about the boat. How far away was it?"

As Jack and Mike rowed their boat away from the island, away to the mainland, Paul told them all he had seen, which wasn't very much. "I couldn't see who the men were, but they *looked* as if they might be Mr. Diaz and Luiz," he said. "Oh, Jack—I don't want to be caught and kept a prisoner again. It is so lovely being with you."

"Don't you worry," said Jack, pulling hard at the oars. "We'll look after you all right, if we have to stuff you down a rabbit-hole and pile bracken over it to hide you!"

That made them all laugh, and Paul felt better. The boys were pulling across to the mainland swiftly, hoping to reach it before the other boat could possibly catch any sight of them. The island was between them and the strange boat, but it might happen that the two men rowed round it and would then see the children's boat.

They reached the mainland safely. Jack chose a very wooded part, and rowed the boat in right under some overhanging trees, where it could not possibly be seen. Then he and the others got out.

"I'd better climb a high tree and see if I can possibly see what's going on on the island opposite us," said Jack.

"I'll climb one too," said Mike. "I'd like to watch as well. Come on, Paul, would you like to climb one too?"

"No, thank you," said Paul, who didn't like climbing trees any more than he liked bathing.

"Well, you stay behind and look after the girls," said Jack. Paul was pleased with that. It made him feel important.

But the girls didn't want looking after! They wanted to climb trees too! However, they busied themselves in looking for a clear space to picnic in.

Jack's tree was a very high one. He could see the island quite well from it. He suddenly saw the boat coming round one side of the island, and he knew who the two men were!

"Yes—it's our dear friend Mr. Diaz and his sleepy helper Luiz," thought Jack to himself. "They must have missed seeing the little beach where we usually land, and they've come round to the other side of the island. Well, that means we can keep a jolly good watch on them!"

Mike and Jack watched the boat from their perches up in the trees. The two men landed and pulled the boat on to the shore. They stood and talked for a while and then they separated and went off round the island.

"I'm afraid they won't find us!" Jack called softly to Mike, who was at the top of a tree nearby. "And unless they find the things we brought with us, that Paul so cleverly stuffed into a bush, they may not even think we've *been* to the island!"

"It was a good idea of yours to come across to the mainland, Jack," answered Mike. "We're safe enough here. We could even make our way through the woods and walk to the nearest town, if we had to!"

"Look! There's one of the men at the top of the hill,"

said Jack. Mike looked. The hill was not near enough to see if the man was Mr. Diaz or Luiz, but it was certainly one of them. He was shading his eyes and looking all down the waters of the lake.

"Good thing our boat's hidden!" said Mike. "I wonder how long they're going to hunt round the island! I don't want to spend the night in these woods—there's no heather here and the ground looks very damp."

The boys watched for two hours and then they began to feel very hungry. Mike left Jack on watch and climbed down to the girls, who had been picking a crop of wild strawberries, small and very sweet. Paul was with them, and he ran to Mike and rained questions on him about the men in the boat.

Mike told him all he had seen. "But what I really came down for was to say we'd better have something to eat," he said. "I'll clean the fish we've caught, Peggy, and light you a small fire. You can cook them, then, on some hot stones, and we'll have a meal."

He cleaned the fish they had caught, and made a fire. "I hope the men on the island don't think our smoke is anything to do with *us*!" he said.

They had a meal of cooked fish, bread, biscuits, and wild strawberries. Then Mike went up his tree again to watch, and Jack came down and had his share of the meal. It was really rather fun. The children enjoyed their dinner, and wished there was more of it!

"But we must keep the two tins of fruit, and the rest of the bread and biscuits for later on in the day," said Peggy, putting them safely aside under a bush. "Thank goodness Paul had the brains to bring what he could! We'd only have had the fish to eat if he hadn't!"

Jack and Mike took it in turns to watch from a tree the rest of the day. They saw no more signs of the two men on the island, but they knew that they had not left, because their boat was still there.

When it began to get dark, and the boys could no longer see clearly from their perches in the trees, Jack wondered what was the best thing to do.

He climbed down and talked to the others. "We'd better have another meal," he said, "and finish the rest of the food. I'm afraid we shall have to spend the night here."

"We could sleep in the boat," said Nora. "That would be more comfortable than the damp ground here. There are two old rugs in the boat too. And Peggy and I have explored a bit and found where a great mass of bracken grows. We could collect it before it's quite dark, and use that for bedding in the boat! It will be fairly soft for us."

"Good," said Jack. "Show us where the bracken is, Nora, and Paul, Mike, and I will carry armfuls to the boat. Peggy, will you get a meal?"

"Right," said Peggy. It was dark to get a meal under the trees, but the little girl did the best she could. She opened the tins of fruit—Paul even had been sensible enough to snatch up the tin-opener! She cut the rest of the bread into slices, and put two biscuits for every one. That was all there was.

The boys and Nora came back with armfuls of bracken. They set it in the boat. Then they went back to where Peggy was waiting. Jack had his torch in his pocket, so they were able to see what they were eating. They shared the fruit in the tins, ate their bread and biscuits, and drank the fruit juice, for they were very thirsty.

"And now to bed," said Jack. "Bed in a boat! What queer adventures we have! But all the same, it's great fun!"

Mike's Marvellous Idea

The children made their way to where the boat was tied to a tree. It was now piled with sweet-smelling bracken. Jack had taken up the seats, so that the whole of the boat was a bed. The two girls got in and cuddled down, and then the three boys settled themselves too. It was a bit of a squeeze, but nobody minded. They wrapped the two old rugs round them and talked quietly.

The lake-water lapped gently against the boat, saying "lip-lip-lip" all the time. It was a pleasant sound to hear. An owl hooted in a trembling voice not far off. "Ooooooooo! Oo-oo-oo-oo!"

Paul sat up in a fright. "Who's that?" he said.

Mike pulled him down,. "It's only a bird called an owl, silly!" he said. "Don't sit up suddenly like that, Paul, you pull the rug off us."

Paul lay down again and cuddled up to the other two boys. He was glad that the noise was only made by a bird.

The moon came up soon, and shone down through the black branches of the trees above. The water of the lake turned to silver. "Lip-lip-lip" it said all the time against the boat. Nora listened to it and fell asleep. Peggy lay on her back and looked at a star that shone through the trees, and suddenly fell asleep too. Paul was soon asleep, but Mike and Jack talked quietly for some time.

They couldn't imagine what Mr. Diaz and Luiz were going to do next. If they stayed long on the island the children couldn't go back there—and as they had no food, this was serious. On the other hand, if they tried to make their way through the thick woods nearby, they might get quite lost.

"If only we could make Mr. Diaz and Luiz prisoners, just as they made you and Paul, it would be grand," said Jack. "Then we could do what we liked."

Mike lay silent for a moment—then he made such a peculiar noise that he really frightened Jack.

"Mike! What's up?" said Jack in alarm. "Are you ill?"

"No," said Mike in a very excited voice. "It was only that I suddenly got such a marvellous idea I wanted to shout—and I only just stopped the shout in time. That was the funny noise you heard—me stopping the shout. But oh, Jack, I've really got the most *wonderful* idea!"

"What is it?" asked Jack in surprise.

"Well, it was you saying that you wished we could make Mr. Diaz and Luiz prisoners that really gave me the idea," said Mike. "I know how we could! If we could only get their boat away from the island tonight, they wouldn't be able to leave—and they'd be prisoners there!"

"Mike! That's a most *marvellous* idea!" said Jack. "It solves all our difficulties. You really are a clever chap! Once they are prisoners on the island, we can row to the village at the end of the lake, get a car, and go back to Peep-Hole in safety!"

"Yes," said Mike, trembling with excitement. "How shall we do it, Jack?"

"Wait a minute," said Jack, frowning in the moonlight. "I've just thought of something. Suppose Mr. Diaz and Luiz can swim? They could easily swim across to the mainland and escape that way."

"But they *can't* swim," said Mike. "I heard Luiz tell Mr. Diaz he couldn't, and Mr. Diaz said he couldn't either. It was when I was a prisoner up in the tower —they often used to come and sit with us there, and they talked to one another. So if neither of them can swim they really *would* be prisoners!"

Jack was so delighted that he wanted to sing and dance. He carefully took off his share of the rug and put it over the sleeping Paul.

"We needn't wake Paul or the girls," he said. "We will undress, Mike, then slip into the water over the edge of the boat, and swim to the island. You can swim as far as that, can't you?"

"Easily," said Mike. "Then we'll undo their boat get into it and row off! Oh, Jack, this is the most exciting thing we've ever done! I wonder if they'll see us!"

"I don't expect so," said Jack. "They'll be asleep in our cave, I expect!"

The boys undressed without waking the girls or Paul.

They slid into the water over the side of the boat and swam off in the moonlit lake, only their two dark heads showing on the calm, silvery surface.

It was rather farther to the island than they expected. Mike was tired when they reached the men's boat, but Jack, who was a marvellous swimmer, was quite fresh. He got in and pulled Mike in too. He undid the rope that tied the boat to a tree.

Then he pushed off, the oars making a splashing noise in the silence of the night. No sooner had they gone a little way out on the lake than a shout came from the island, and Luiz stood up. He had been asleep on some heather, and had awakened to hear the sound of oars.

"Hie! That's our boat you've got! Bring it back at once!"

"We'll bring it back some day!" yelled back Jack in delight.

"You just bring it back now, at once!" yelled Luiz, suddenly realising that he and Mr. Diaz would not be able to leave the island at all without a boat. "You wicked boys!"

"Good-bye, dear friends," shouted Jack, seeing Mr. Diaz suddenly appearing down the hill. He had been sleeping in the cave and had awakened at the noise of shouting. "See you some day soon!"

The two men were quite helpless. They could neither of them swim, they had no boat—they could do nothing but shout angrily, and that was no good at all! The boys simply laughed and waved to them.

When they reached their own boat, feeling rather cold and shivery, for they had no clothes on, they found the girls and Paul wide awake and rather scared. Peggy threw the boys their clothes, and called out to know where they had been and what all the noise was and where they had got the other boat.

"Can't you guess!" cried Nora. "They've taken the enemies' boat—and now they are prisoners on our secret island, hurrah! Oh, Jack, what a marvellous idea! We were so scared when we woke up and found you two gone—but we might have guessed you were off on some wonderful idea!"

"It's Mike's idea," said Jack, dressing quickly, "It's one of the best ideas he's ever had! It acted beautifully too—Mr. Diaz and Luiz are as angry as can be, but they can't do anything about it! As soon as it's light we'll row to the village at the end of the lake, get a car, and go off to Peep-Hole to see what Dimmy and George have done —and Mr. Diaz and Luiz can have a nice little holiday on the island!"

Everybody laughed. They felt sure they would *never* be able to go to sleep again that night, but after a while they began to yawn—and before the moon had begun to slide down the sky they were all fast asleep once more, with Mr. Diaz's boat tied safely alongside their own.

They woke when the stars had gone and the moon had slipped away. The sun was coming up in the east and the lake looked peaceful and blue. Not a cloud was in the sky.

"Goodness, I *am* hungry!" said Peggy. "And we haven't got a single thing to eat!"

Mike grinned. He put his hand into his pocket and brought out a large packet of chocolate!

"I kept this till this morning, thinking it would come in very useful!" he said. "We'll share it, and then we'll have to wait till we get to the village at the end of the lake for breakfast."

"Good old Mike!" said every one, delighted to see the chocolate. It had nuts in it and was most delicious. They sat in the early morning sunshine, munching it and giggling whenever they thought of Mr. Diaz and Luiz!

"There they are, at the edge of the lake, trying to see us!" said Peggy. "Well, they'll see us soon enough when we row out! What shall we do with their boat, Jack?"

"We'll leave it tied up here," said Jack. "It will be safe enough."

So they left the extra boat behind, untied theirs, and rowed out on to the lake. Mr. Diaz and Luiz saw them at once, and shouted, but the children took no notice at all. They rowed steadily away from the island down to the village at the end of the lake.

When they got there they tied up the boat and stepped out on to the sandy shore. They made their way to the village and soon came to a baker's shop. They bought warm new bread and some jam tarts. They went to the grocer's and bought half a pound of butter, some potted meat to spread on their bread, and some biscuits and chocolate. They also bought some ginger-beer, and then sat down by the roadside to eat a peculiar, but very delicious breakfast!

Jack and Mike lent their pocket-knives to every one to spread the potted meat and butter on thick slices cut from the new loaf. How lovely it tasted!

Then they ate the jam tarts and the biscuits, munched the chocolate, and drank the ginger-beer. They felt much better after their meal, and Jack looked about for a garage.

There wasn't one—but at that moment a bus rattled up and stopped nearby. The children went to ask if there was any bus that would take them near Spiggy Holes.

"My bus starts off again in ten minutes' time," said the driver. "I go as far as Cliftonside, and you can get a bus there to Spiggy Holes."

The children were pleased. They got into the bus and waited for it to start. It set off at last and rumbled down the country lanes for an hour until it arrived at Cliftonside. Out tumbled the children, and went to get the bus for Spiggy Holes. It didn't start for half an hour, so they went to buy some more ginger-beer, for it was a hot day and they felt very thirsty again.

They arrived at Spiggy Holes at half-past twelve. The bus stopped a mile away from Peep-Hole and the children took a short cut across the fields.

"We'd better just keep a watch-out in case anyone else is looking for Paul," said Jack. "You never know!"

So they kept a look-out, and walked beside the tall hedges to hide themselves till they got to Peep-Hole.

And what a surprise they had when they got to the field opposite Peep-Hole—for there on the grass was an aeroplane! It was painted a bright blue, and had silvery edges that shone in the sun!

The children stopped in the greatest surprise. Nobody was in the aeroplane. Nobody was about at all. They didn't know whether to go to Peep-Hole or not—did the aeroplane belong to the enemy? Or was it a friend's? It was all very mysterious indeed.

Alone At Peep-Hole

The five children stared and stared at the aeroplane. Paul went rather pale.

"It looks like an aeroplane from my own country," he said. "Do you think my enemies have flown over here to find me? If only I knew what had happened to my father —whether he got better or not! I am very unhappy."

"Cheer up, old son," said Jack. "We'll soon find out everything. I expect Dimmy has told the police to find out what's been going on in your country, and she'll tell us as soon as we find her."

"I want to see Dimmy," said Nora. "I feel safe when I'm with her."

"Well, let's go quietly to Peep-Hole without being seen, and find her," said Mike. So they crept along by the tall hedge, turned into the little lane where Peep-Hole stood, and ran into the small front garden.

The front door was shut. It usually stood wide open. They went round to the back door. That was shut and locked too! The children stared at one another in surprise.

"Has Dimmy locked herself in?" they wondered. "What's been happening?"

"All the ground-floor windows are shut too," said Jack, who had been round looking. "But there's one open up there—do you see it? I believe if I climb up that old pear tree there, I could wriggle along that branch and get on to the window-sill."

"Well, be careful then," said Peggy. "It doesn't look very safe to me!"

Jack climbed the tree, hoisted up by Mike. He wriggled carefully along the big branch that waved near the window. The other children stood below and watched him—but a shower of little hard pears fell on their heads and they went back a few steps, laughing.

Jack got safely to the window-sill. He opened the window and jumped inside. They heard his footsteps pattering down the stairs.

Then the bolts were shot back, the key was turned, and Jack opened the door. "Come on in," he said. "We'll just see if Dimmy is anywhere here—but there's not a sound in the house."

The children hunted everywhere for Dimmy. She was gone. The house was quiet and lonely, and the children didn't know what to do. When would Dimmy come back? Where had she gone? Where was George? Perhaps they could find *him*.

"Well, I vote we have something to eat," said Jack at last. "There's some ham in the larder—I've just looked—and some tomatoes too and stale bread. We can pick plums from the garden as well. Come on!"

Over the meal the children talked about what they should do. Should they stay at Peep-Hole till Dimmy came back? But suppose she didn't come back! They didn't feel very safe at Peep-Hole, so near the Old House, without Dimmy or George, because perhaps somebody might find out they were there and come to catch poor Paul again.

"Well, I don't think anyone has seen us come," said Jack. "And we won't light a fire, so nobody will see smoke from our chimney. We won't have any lights on tonight, either. We'll all sleep together in the top room of the tower, and lock the door and pile furniture against it. Then we'll be safe!"

"Things are getting a bit too exciting again," said Nora,

who was really beginning to long for a little peace. "I wish Mr. Diaz hadn't discovered our secret island—we should have been so happy and peaceful there. I don't like Peep-Hole without Dimmy."

"I'll slip out down to the beach and see if George is anywhere about," said Jack, thinking hard. "If he is he'll come back with me, I'm sure—and he could tell me what's happened to Dimmy—and *I* could tell *him* what has happened to Mr. Diaz and Luiz!"

The others laughed. They liked to think of Mr. Diaz and Luiz, prisoners on the secret island, not knowing when they were to be taken off!

Jack slipped out of the back door and the others bolted it after him. They decided to keep watch from the windows, to see if anyone came near. So Peggy and Paul kept a watch from the front windows, and Mike and Nora from the back. But nobody came near. Not even a dog barked anywhere. It was all very still and peaceful.

The children talked to one another. Peggy found her knitting, and knitted and chatted to Paul. Mike did a jig-saw puzzle with Nora, looking up every other minute to make sure that nobody was coming in through the back garden.

A loud thumping on the back door startled everybody dreadfully. Mike jumped and dropped the jig-saw on the floor. He had seen nobody come into the back garden. Paul and Peggy ran in from the front room, looking quite scared.

"Who do you suppose it is?" whispered Nora.

"Can't imagine," whispered back Mike. "Anyway, we'd better all keep as quiet as possible, then maybe they'll go away."

So they all kept very quiet. The thumping came again — somebody banging on the back door with his bare fists. "Bang all you like," said Mike in a low voice. "You won't get in!"

"Let me in!" cried a voice—and how they all jumped with

joy! For it was Jack's voice! It was he who was thumping on the door!

"What idiots we are!" cried Mike, leaping to his feet. "We might have guessed it was Jack—but I never thought he'd be back so soon!"

They all tore downstairs to open the door to Jack. He came in, quite cross with them:

"Whatever did you keep me waiting all that time for?" he asked indignantly. "I thought you must have gone to sleep!"

"Sorry, Jack," grinned Mike. "We didn't see you come, and we didn't expect you back so soon. We thought you might be the enemy. How did you get through the back garden without being seen?"

"Crawled under the currant bushes," said Jack, with a grin. "I thought I'd give you a surprise—but I seem to have given you a good fright instead."

"Did you see George?" asked Mike eagerly.

"Not a sign of him," answered Jack. "His boat was there all right—but I couldn't see him anwhere on the beach, or in the fields either. *He* seems to have disappeared into thin air just like Dimmy!"

"It's all very peculiar," said Mike. "Where in the world has everybody gone—and why is that aeroplane there —and what's been happening whilst we were on our island?"

"I wish I could tell you," said Jack. "What about some tea, Peggy? Are there any cakes in the tin?"

Peggy and Nora boiled a kettle for tea, and cut some bread and butter. There was honey on the larder shelf, and some gingerbread in the cake tin. They ate it all, and wished there was more.

"I vote we take something up to the tower bedroom for supper, and go up there now," said Mike, when they had finished. "We can lock ourselves in, and be safe till morning. The two girls can have my bed, and we three boys can share Jack's bed and that old sofa. We shall sleep till the morning!"

"I feel jolly tired now," said Nora. "It's all the excitement, I expect. Let's take the snap cards up with us and have a game. I shall go to sleep unless I do something!"

So after they had washed up the tea-things, Peggy collected some supper and Jack hunted for the snap cards. They saw that all the downstairs windows and doors were fastened, and then they went upstairs to the top bedroom of the tower. They locked the door and sat down to play snap.

Paul had never played snap before, and he was dreadfully bad at it. He simply could *not* see when two cards were alike, and the others made him jump when they yelled out "snap."

"I can see why you call it snap!" he said at last. "You snap at one another like dogs! It is a game for dogs, not children."

That made the others roar with laughter. And it was whilst they were laughing that they heard a strange noise. They all looked up.

"An aeroplane!" said Jack. "Is it that one in the field going away?"

They rushed to the window. No—the blue and silver plane was still there—but another plane was soaring round and round, on the point of landing. Mike caught up the field-glasses that lay on the window-sill, and looked at the aeroplane through them.

Then he gave such a tremendous yell that poor Paul fell off his chair and tumbled in a heap on the ground!

"Mike! What's up?" cried the others.

"It's Daddy's plane!" shouted Mike, dancing round in joy. "Can't you see the red on it? I bet Daddy and

Mummy have flown over from Ireland, because Dimmy is sure to have let them know about us and Prince Paul! Oh, if they're back everything's all right!"

The others screamed with delight, and hung out of the window to watch the plane. It circled down over the field, and came neatly to rest beside the blue and silver plane. The propellers stopped whizzing round. Two people climbed out of the cockpit, dressed in flying clothes.

"Come on! It's Dad and Mummy all right!" shouted Mike. He raced to the door and unlocked it. He tore down the stairs with all the others at his heels and unlocked and unbolted the front door. Then like a pack of dogs the children scampered over the lane, and across the big field to the aeroplanes.

"Children! We thought you were safely on the secret island!" cried their mother's voice. She took off her helmet and smiled at them all. They crowded round her and hugged her. Prince Paul held back shyly. But Mrs. Arnold drew him to her and gave him a hug like the rest.

"Where's Dimmy?" said Captain Arnold. But nobody knew!

The End Of The Adventures

"Come on back to Peep-Hole, Dad," said Mike. "We'll tell you everything there!"

So they all went back to Peep-Hole, and, sitting in the front room, they talked at the tops of their voices. All that Captain and Mrs. Arnold had heard was that the children had rescued somebody and taken him off to their secret island. Dimmy had sent them a long telegram because they had moved from place to place in Ireland, and she could not get hold of them to telephone the news.

Then they had tried to telephone Dimmy but had got no answer, so they had got into their aeroplane and flown straight over to Spiggy Holes to find out what was the matter.

"And here we are!" said Captain Arnold. "What about some food? I'm famished! We've got a hamper in the plane—go and get it, Jack and Mike."

The boys tore off to get it—but as they went across the lane to the field, they heard the sound of a big car coming down the road. They stopped and looked. Peep-Hole was at the end of the lane—the road stopped just there, so whoever came down the lane *must* go to Peep-Hole. Who was coming?

The car was full of men. There were at least five. Mike caught hold of Jack's arm and they fled back to Peep-Hole. "They might be coming to take Paul away!" he yelled. "Quick, come back and we'll lock the doors. Thank goodness Dad and Mummy are there!"

They shot back into the house and locked the front

door. The car stopped outside with a screech of brakes, and four men got out. They were all in some kind of uniform and looked rather grand. They walked up the path and thundered on the knocker.

"Who's that?" said Captain Arnold in astonishment.

"We don't know," said Mike. "But we've locked them out in case they've come for Paul."

"My dear boy, nobody can take Paul now I'm here," said Captain Arnold. "Open the door."

But somebody else opened the door. Paul had been looking out of the window—and he suddenly gave a most ear-piercing yell, shouted something in a foreign language, and tore to the front door. He struggled with the bolts, yelling all the time.

"He's gone mad!" said Jack in surprise. "Here, let me help you, Paul, since you're determined to open the door!"

The door opened. Paul flew through it, flung himself at the front man, and wept tears all down his chest! The man stroked him and patted him, whilst every one looked on in the greatest astonishment.

The man put down Paul and bowed most politely to Captain and Mrs. Arnold.

"I am Paul's father, the King of Baronia," he said.

"But we thought you were very ill, and nearly dying!" cried Mike, in surprise.

"Yes, I have been ill, but now I am better, much to the grief of my enemies," said the king, in a grim sort of voice. "Paul was made prisoner and taken away whilst I lay ill, and we did not know where he was. Then your Miss Dimity informed your good English police, and they sent the message to me that you children had rescued my boy, and had taken him to your secret island."

"Then is that blue and silver aeroplane yours?" cried Mike. "Paul said he thought it belonged to his country."

"Yes, we flew over in it, I and my four friends," said the king. "We came to see Miss Dimity, that brave and good woman, and she and your friend George told us all that had happened."

"But where *is* Dimmy?" asked Nora, almost in tears, for she really felt very anxious about Dimmy.

"Miss Dimity is coming in another car," said the king. "She and George and ourselves all had to go to the police to explain what had happened. She will soon be here."

And even as he spoke another car drew up outside, and out leapt George to help Miss Dimity. She got out, looking rather pale and tired, but just the same cheerful old Dimmy. She couldn't believe her eyes when the children rushed to greet her.

"I thought you were safely on your secret island!" she said. "What made you leave it?"

"Oh, Dimmy, it's a long story!" said Mike. "Come along in—look who's here!"

"Your father and mother!" said Dimmy, in amazement. "So the second aeroplane is theirs, I suppose. Captain Arnold, I *am* glad to see you! I couldn't seem to find out *where* you were in Ireland. What a meeting this is—Paul's father and friends, and you too, and the children!"

The little front room was too small to hold them all, so they went into the garden. George brought out seats for everybody, and it was a very gay, noisy party that sat out there and talked and talked.

"If only I could get my hands on Diaz and Luiz, the traitors!" said Paul's father angrily, as Paul told him how he had been kept prisoner.

"Well, you can if you want to," said Mike, with a grin. "We've made *them* prisoners now! You can catch them as soon as you please!"

"Where are they then?" cried Dimmy.

"On our secret island without a boat!" laughed Mike.

"And there they'll stay till somebody goes over and catches *them*!"

Everybody laughed in delight. It was very funny to think of the two bad men being caught like that.

"Tomorrow morning I and the policemen will go over in a boat," said the king grimly. "Diaz and Luiz will be *most* surprised to see us! They meant to prevent my son Paul from being king after me if I died—and now that I am very much alive, they will be sorry they ever thought of such a plan!"

"Will you take Paul back with you?" said Mike, feeling sorry that they were to lose a boy he liked very much.

"Yes," said the king. "But next term he is to come to school in your good, safe country of England, and maybe he could go to your school, Jack and Mike?"

"Oh, good!" said the two boys, pleased. "We'll look after him!"

"I'm sure you will!" said Paul's father, clapping both boys on the back. "You've looked after him marvellously so far!"

"Well, what are we all going to do tonight?" said Dimmy. "I'd like to ask you all to stay with me, but Peep-Hole is too small! I could put Captain and Mrs. Arnold into my spare room, but there's no other room, I'm afraid."

"We shall go to the nearest town and stay at the hotel there," said the king. "Paul must go with us, for I feel I cannot let him out of my sight! Tomorrow we will come again, Miss Dimity. Thank you a thousand times for all you have done!"

The king and Prince Paul, and the four men in uniform said good-bye and went to their big car. It started up, and, with a terrific noise, shot up the lane.

"We've forgotten all about the hamper of food," said Jack suddenly. "Let's go and get it now, Mike. I feel as if I could eat my hat!"

"I'd like to see you!" said Mike. The two of them set off to the aeroplane. They climbed into the cock-pit and found a large hamper there. They carried it between them to Peep-Hole.

They all had a picnic in the garden—George too. How they enjoyed it! They told their stories again and again.

"Mr. Diaz, Mrs. Diaz, and Luiz all came to Peep-Hole in a furious rage the night you went to the secret island," said Dimmy. "Luckily by the time they got here, George was back, so between the two of us we sent them off. They were quite sure that the prince was here with you."

"They must have found out somehow about our island, and where it was," said Mike. "Well, it's a story that everybody knows, so that wouldn't have been very difficult. Oh, wouldn't I like to see the faces of those two on the island tomorrow, when the king and the police go to fetch them!"

And, indeed, Mr. Diaz and Luiz did get a dreadful shock when a boat, full of English policemen, arrived at the secret island the next day! The two men were busy working at making a rough raft to paddle across to the mainland and they did not hear the boat arriving. They looked up from their work to see the King of Baronia walking towards them, with five men behind him!

The children heard all about it the next day. "That finishes Mr. Diaz and his plots," said Jack, pleased. "What a good thing we came to Spiggy Holes for our holidays! Young Paul would still have been a prisoner, and we wouldn't have had all these adventures."

That evening George came running in, in a state of great excitement. "Come and see," he cried. "Come and see!"

The children and Dimmy ran out into the road—and there, coming down the lane, drawn on an enormous trailer, was the finest little motor-boat that anybody could wish for!

"It's coming to Peep-Hole!" cried Jack.

So it was! It was a present to the four children from the King of Baronia for all their help to his son. The children could hardly believe their eyes!

"What a wonderful present!" they cried. "Oh, George, let's launch it this evening!"

It was impossible to get the motor-boat down to the beach. It had to be taken to Longrigg and unshipped there. George's brother helped. It was launched on the calm, evening waters, and everyone got in, Dimmy too. It was so easy to drive that the children could take it in turns.

The motor started up with a lovely whirring sound. The little boat leapt forward. Mike swung her out to sea, feeling as proud as could be. A motor-boat of their own! How lucky they were!

Now they're off, all the way back to Peep-Hole. Good-bye, Mike—good-bye, Jack! Good-bye, Nora and Peggy! You deserve your good luck, and we loved all your adventures. Maybe we'll hear more of them another day. Good-bye, good-bye!

THE END